CW01501939

12 NOV 2021

Renata Šerelytė

The Music Teacher

Translated from Lithuanian
by Marija Marcinkute

Noir

First published in Lithuanian as Vardas tamsoje
Text copyright © Renata Šerelytė
English translation copyright © Marija Marcinkute
The moral rights of the author and translators have been asserted.

Published by Noir Press Ltd
www.noirpress.co.uk
noirpress@hotmail.com

Cover design by Le Dinh Han
Cover photo by Svaiga Seliokaite
Noir Press is deeply grateful for the generous support of the
Lithuanian Culture Institute in bringing this book to publication.

978-0995560031

I

WE SERVE THE PUBLIC, WITHOUT PREJUDICE
Sign above the door of the police station

Atali, the Chief's secretary, with a long plait of tow coloured hair and the red eyes of an albino, popped her head through the door and froze, mouth open, attempting to work out what she needed in my office.

I have the suspicion that she rummages through my papers in her spare time.

'I'm still here, Atali,' I said pleasantly. 'I'll be here for another ten minutes,' I added, casting a glance at the stack of complaints. 'Anyway, there's nothing much interesting today. An anonymous complaint about R.B.'s moral dissoluteness; the author must be from the intelligentsia as I couldn't spot any grammatical mistakes. Does a writer live in our area, do you know?'

Atali blushed to her hair line.

'There's a meeting scheduled for Monday,' she mumbled and closed the door and in her haste, half of her long plait caught in the door.

'I know.'

Atali pulled out the plait and slammed the door.

*   *   *

Darkness is never caught, though it is careless and leaves a trail of untidy evidence and silent witnesses. True criminal motives are never uncovered; darkness is like a maniac with no parents or childhood, so court psychiatrists and attorneys have nothing to pore over. Darkness is the soft velvet covers of the case files; the cold touch lingers until you close the final page.

If only darkness would help the investigation! If it at least corroborated one version of events. It leaves us, however, only with a wistful bitterness, which is so characteristic of artists, and not the slightest bit of use to a logical person. Art will not save the world; it will be the death of it. You are completely right, my dear reader, to think that Stalin's gulags couldn't have been dreamed up without the inspiration of an artist. Even more so Hitler's excesses. And Brezhnev's love of the baroque was malignant and helped neither the economy nor society. Art is no better than spirituality; they're both ambiguous and compromised.

I always take a great deal of pleasure in noting that the brain is the human's best asset. We serve the brain, not humanity; humanity without a brain isn't up to much, though as a phenomenon it is quite wide-spread. And it can be exciting.

With the door closed the voices, the whispers and the distant clinking of the cleaner's bucket faded away. I noticed what seemed like cobwebs floating across the pale sky, or perhaps it would be more accurate to say they looked like Atali's hair pulled from between the teeth of a plastic comb (those two sided combs with their different length teeth, which one unpleasant, well-known writer, who had suffered from them as a child, called 'nit combs').

I'm neither nostalgic for the old times nor for double sided combs. My hairstyle is about as perfect as that of an inmate at the Pravieniskes Prison. Which is why I'm no favourite with the hairdresser or understood by women; men don't seem to have an opinion on the subject. Which is strange. Usually they comment on everything. Especially anything to do with mechanics. They would dismantle my work pistol if I placed it on the bar. I carry it in my handbag like a well-known Lithuanian poet used to do. I wonder if she killed any critics? Historians don't divulge. Which, again, is a shame. If there was a corpse, even a historical one, a connection could be drawn, joining art and the masses; it would testify that poets are not monsters but people.

What is more dreadful than glorifying the living dead and even citing their words? It's not even as if their words are special – they can't bring anybody back from the dead or offer any comfort.

I leave the bullets at home, in a spice box. From time to time I check they haven't turned into cinnamon. Having said that, shooting a person because he's a poet is wrong, no matter if the bullets are real or just pepper corns. Life is sacred unconditionally. Especially at the weekends, when I'm off duty. If some idiot turned up and decided to break the long-held tradition that you don't shoot or strangle anybody at the weekend, he would be condemned by every-body. Don't kill on Saturdays, my dear reader, no matter how bad the situation, even if you're hounded by depression, by rodents or by the very devil himself. Nobody will come to your funeral and a generation of dogs will piss on your grave; for all I know you'll be cursed down to the fourth generation. I'm not sure if that is dog or human generations.

A shape similar to that of a wardrobe appeared indistinctly. The cool autumn dusk was reminiscent of a soft flannel handkerchief smelling faintly of chloroform – probably already used for that purpose. The shape moved at the speed of a wardrobe too.

Only one person had such shelf-like shoulders.

'Good evening, Chief,' I greeted him, and just about managed to refrain from dropping a curtsey.

The shelves swayed. There was an indistinct growl and his green eyes sparkled unhealthily.

As the chief moved off, a bad feeling came over me – as if it was Monday when something bad always happens.

I was breathless when I reached home and unlocked the door. Everything was in the right place. The furniture hadn't been chopped up; there were no quotations from the book of Revelations scrawled in blood across the walls. My cat was sat calmly next to an overturned aloe plant.

'Yin Yang!' I said severely. 'Aloe is excellent for healing wounds. Now how will I heal myself if I'm attacked by some maniac?'

The cat watched in silence, probably hypothesising on the accuracy of this statement.

'Well, fine, aloe probably wouldn't be enough on its own, I'd need some vodka too. A compress and all that . . . You know.'

Yin Yang understood. She meowed.

I'm fascinated by the simplicity of animals. They don't change with time; while people deteriorate but continue to believe they're brilliant, animals stay the same – perfect. Perhaps it wouldn't be like that if people stopped talking about how wonderful they were all the time.

Opening the cupboard, I decided to put on a hat; it was cold outside.

A plaster cast head with a scraped nose stared at me from the shelf. It reminded me a little of Pushkin or Klepavicius, the bachelor vet who had gone crazy with age. He had decided to start treating people, but prescribed them pet medication out of habit. His patients were so loyal they would take the medicine and some of them even got better. Having recovered miraculously, they would go as far as to lick Klepavicius' hand, gazing with big wet eyes into the doctor's dry and watchful face. It wasn't in search of a cure that I went to Klepavicius' clinic, but to buy tulips. The aged Asclepius was much better at growing plants than he was at healing.

Every March Atali celebrated her birthday. She celebrated at the station, of course, which was her home and sanctuary. For the occasion she would coil her tow plait into a knot on the top of her head; it looked as if somebody had put a wicker basket on her head. Still, you could put a basket or a tyre on your head, but you couldn't hide from anybody in this little town. However, it was better not to surprise people if possible; better to be bald or have no head at all.

On the way I bought a bottle of Merlot and, with that, the slapping of my bag against my hip ceased being so irritating. Suddenly it was as precious and important as a stone to a drowning man.

I passed the Soviet military cemetery and climbed the hill. The bench was awaiting me; lonely, slightly rotten. The distant lights of the town reflected on it like spilt oil. I touched the surface – no, it wasn't sticky.

Beneath my feet the lake rustled – the station paperwork curling up to sleep.

Behind me something crackled. I jumped.

It was just the wind – a warm flannel handkerchief that lulled and glued the mouth – and October leaves, furrowed with narrow, dead veins, the sap slowly turning the aluminium white of death – that was why the leaves made so much noise when they were thrown against the tombstones which had once boasted red stars. The stars were faded now, coloured by the leisurely flow of time.

Fifteen years had passed. He wasn't going to come and stroke my long hair.

On the bench I had only the leaves embroidered by death and a bottle of Merlot.

It was getting cold. The wine was gone. My watch told me it was eleven-thirty. I needed to move. You never knew, at midnight a Soviet soldier might rise from his tomb and offer to take me home. Yin Yang wasn't used to guests and definitely wouldn't appreciate one like that, scattering soil and sawdust and worms, and, bending down to stroke her, he would leave slimy green finger marks on her soft fur.

I so wish that you would take me home. Alive, not rotten. As clean and careful as a stray cat, owned by nobody and attached to nobody. Your eyes are light, almost yellow. You have golden hair on your wrists and your chest. Even your trousers are like the skin of an animal, covered with shiny velvet needles. You used to wrap yourself around me like a playful predator, entering me painfully, your damp tongue and your teeth coming to meet my childish kiss.

'I'll be late for school.'

Dawn streamed through the thin curtains like molten lead.

'You have algebra class first thing?' His dark face leant over me like an Orthodox icon in the darkness.

'Yes. And I haven't done my homework.'

'But you don't want to get a fail?'

'I will anyway. I'm no good at maths.'

He leant back, sat up in a lotus position and looked down at me – a golden Buddha, completely at peace.

'I'll never give you a fail.'

'But you could choose a better repertoire for me. I'm so fed up with all those patriotic war songs. Nobody ever asks for an *encore* . . .'

He leant over me again and I noticed the sensual wrinkles at the corners of his lips, but also I saw the animal hunger that gleamed, hidden, deep in his eyes.

'You want an *encore*?' His breath on my face smelled strange, a mixture of sandal wood and undigested prey.

I wrapped my legs around him and bit hard on his pillow; I wasn't allowed to scream as the dentist downstairs wasn't open. When they began drilling teeth and the tortured sinner screamed, then I could scream too, not from pain but with the kind of infinite bliss which could only be given by an angel, and not just any angel – a four winged seraphim.

'I'll see you this evening,' he said, seeing me off. 'Make sure nobody notices you.'

'They won't,' I murmured, intoxicated, nearly falling down the squeaky stairs.

On the way out I heard the voice of the dentist. 'Well, open wide, Kitty.' Through the small window flashed a thick neck and a small snake-like head and, then, the next moment there was a mewing full of horror and dismay.

I ran along the path out of the garden, hidden away behind the tall nettles, the burrs and the blooming apple trees.

I know now that nobody buys up empty wine bottles so they can float them on water like love boats, purple flags flying. Sophia, Monastyrskaya Izba, Alaverdi, Cabernet Sauvignon . . . Would you sell this siren-song for a miserable 15 cents? Kiosks are like prisons, the cold hand of a murderer cuts your throat there and love is replaced by perversion.

If late one night, a stray wave washes a bottle to your feet, it will be my message to you.

You could kiss me now – passionately – there is no one back stage except for the year one girl wearing a ribbon bigger than her head, mouth open with fear and oblivious to everything. She'll probably have to be pushed out on to the stage to recite her poem about the Leader of the Proletariat.

No. She won't.

It's our turn.

'Imagine you're not here, my love,' he says. 'Learn to put up a facade. Don't let them get to you. It's you that must get to them. And now – let's have you on the stage.'

Supressing a shiver, I realised suddenly that I had forgotten to fasten my Komsomol badge to my blouse. An empty space gaped on the space where my heart pounded. My Gracious God – they had told me that the Communist Party General Secretary was in the hall. I scanned the first row but only managed to see the accountant, Theresa, a few recently appointed teachers and the chairman's secretary. They all gazed at the music teacher infatuated. I felt like killing them.

'The Cruiser Aurora,' the presenter for the evening announced.

The music teacher's fingers stroked the keyboard as gently as they had my breasts. I shuddered. I am not here. I am not guilty. You are guilty.

'And like before, in black navy jackets
March their fearsome night patrols'

Scorching chords rained down upon the heads of the teachers and secretaries. They deserved it; it was a punishment for their sinful passion. Anyway, how wonderful that patriotic repertoire was; you couldn't punish anybody with Santa Lucia, could you?

And there we go; Theresa had begun to weep. I smiled, content, and was about to sing more but the teacher pushed me from the stage, followed from the hall by the pitiful sound of sobbing rather than applause.

'Not bad,' he said. 'That was good. You could be a prosecutor; you're so cold blooded.'

'Really? No cock ups?'

He laughed, took me by my chin, but let go immediately; coming after me from the stage, having fulfilled her civic duty, the arrogant year one girl glanced at us suspiciously, her interest in the world recovered.

'See you at rehearsal.'

'See you, Sir.'

What would we rehearse? What sheets of music were we going to open? What tempo would you play? Allegro? Andante? Largo? Vivace? Like a bud, my pink nipples would swell beneath your touch; the air would be filled with a dreamy music, never before recorded; lips would open, emitting the strange, hypnotic sound of sea creatures and a round spore of life would slip in and spin amongst the stars.

The bench stood melancholy in the large gravel square.

Chinese Lanterns, with their bright tetrahedron calyxes, used to grow there. It was the red-light district. But in those innocent, ideological times, they signified not shame, but rather the embodiment of the holy flame of the revolution.

Now, there are no more graceful lanterns; there is nothing to illuminate our dreadful immorality.

Nothing. Only the gravel into which high heels sink. Repenting debauchees will have a lot of it to swallow.

Gravel mixed with sand, pebbles, rough pieces of lava, tasteless crumbs of clay; enough to make you thirsty. Yin Yang sat on the table like a blue glazed statue; my hands stretched out involuntarily to check that she was real.

Those glowing eyes of Bubastes, with their stubborn wildness trying to teach me that I was subordinate to their moonlit faience, Egyptian blue. Why did I keep such a terrible creature at home?

I drank some mineral water to calm myself down.

I like blue faience.

02.08.2001

A fourteen year-old was walking home towards the suburbs, when, by a field of maize, a black Lada drew up beside her. A man, about thirty, asked her where a certain man lived. The girl happened to know the man. She got into the car; she would show him the way. The stranger took her into the maize field and raped her. During the interrogation the girl grew hysterical, gabbling so incoherently that we considered having her examined by a psychiatrist. She neither remembered the man, nor the car registration, only how very yellow the maize had been into which the man had pushed her; she recalled too that a twig had kept stabbing into her side, and, well, obscenely, and not really suitable for the report – the large, hairy organ of the offender. She laughed shrilly and added that it might have been pleasant if the circumstances were different. Enraged, her mother stopped the interrogation and took her daughter home.

The medical expert established that ... Actually the expert was disciplined for having lost the test tube containing the sperm. When he started the test, he said, he had discovered an anomaly – the sperm seemed to be that of an animal. Whether wild or domesticated he couldn't say exactly. Under the girl's fingernails he had found hair of unclear origin; the girl assured him she had pulled them from that monstrous ... organ. Its structure was reminiscent of a dog's hair. It was compared with the victim's dog hair, but they did not match. Perhaps she had stroked another dog. The victim didn't remember having done so.

The only witness was the endless maize field. And it was unreasonable to expect much from that.

The owners of black Ladas were checked. It had been a decade since they had stopped producing black Ladas. The girl insisted that the car looked new; it shone beautifully, flashing in the sunlight. What can you do? Village girls were not as demanding as those in towns who had seen everything.

The victim's mother was suspicious of the neighbour who ran some kind of dubious business and, according to rumours, smuggled. He was thirty-four and drove an old Audi. Her suspicions were raised, she explained, by his salacious gaze and the fact that he loitered outside their fence. A quick check ascertained that at the time of the rape he was under arrest for fighting with a prostitute at the station after he had tried to avoid paying for her services. The prostitute not only confirmed his alibi, but also stated that the man was quite potent and didn't have particularly hairy testicles as far as she had noticed.

The victim's mother placed a complaint with the regional public prosecutor about our failure to pay attention to a valuable witness' testimony (she meant herself). The Chief grew annoyed and accused the girl of being a victim of perverted fantasy.

What strange passions the case aroused! Unnaturally large organs, obscure substances, the odd behaviour of the victim – it seemed that she had begun to enjoy the incident! Only her mother demanded justice and revenge (*I'll tear that pervert to pieces!*), while the victim herself seemed to be in an odd trance.

How small we are in the eye of the Universe.

When I looked into my teacher's eyes, a feeling as hard and bitter as gravel gripped my stomach. In their depths, I saw a drowned waxy figure.

It was Sunday morning, the clinic was closed. Outside, sleet was falling like thin porridge.

His warm hand calmly stroked the inside of my thigh, ruffled my sad Venus' bush.

'Don't worry, I'll look after you. Everything will be over by the time of final examinations.'

I leant against his shining Buddha body. Somewhere, in the depths of the wild garden, a heart was beating, unable to drop the golden apple. My lips divided soft body hairs, rowed across the dark horsetails of the underbelly, until I found the sandalwood snake in hiding, ready to fall; I caught it with my lips.

There . . .

Would you heal me or kill me?

Through the window, I could see two maple trees; they looked autumnal, sad and red, victims of a vicious murder. The evidence had been swept away by the wind and winter would soon hide the criminal too.

And what could the witnesses tell us? Those dry little seeds, looking like one-winged insects chasing around in the wind?

'Double espresso and double brandy.'

I settled on a high stool at the bar. Sarkiene, the bar owner, pulled out some hair spray from under the counter and sprayed the crest of hair which was already sticking up from her head like a mammoth's tusk. She turned to me and smiled absentmindedly.

I repeated the order.

She came to herself.

'A . . .' she bustled. 'Just a moment, dear prosecutor.'

'I'm not a prosecutor,' I reminded her.

Sarkiene, though, had the habit of not listening to wise words.

'Not at work today? So, you can have some brandy. Excellent, Madame Prosecutor. You need something to wash away the . . . eh . . . the nastiness of all those murders.'

I sighed. 'Yes, but not with hair spray. Please, if you don't mind, don't spray any into my glass.'

Sarkiene pulled out the can of spray again and examined it carefully.

'It's very good hair spray, Madame Prosecutor.'

After a pause she added, 'Three fifty.'

'Really? Brandy got so cheap?' That cheered me up.

Sarkiene gazed at me for a moment.

'Madame Prosecutor, the brandy costs ten *litas*. I was talking about the hair spray.'

'I don't drink hair spray.'

Sarkiene blushed. She counted the money in silence, pushed the change towards me and made a show of hiding behind the fridge with the Coca Cola.

She had probably retreated there for another beauty procedure; to varnish her nails or something she didn't want me to see. I really did not understand the pleasures of cheap cosmetics, you see.

Later I dropped into the local ethnographical museum to see an exhibition of summer landscapes by a group of local painters. I had been soberer the first time I went, so the artistic secrets of the subconscious failed to move me. I hadn't noticed, that first time, how the painters had captured the horrors of existence or the bright surrealist features in the smoky landscapes. Now, I swear, the painting next to the door was the image of Salvador Dali's Burning Giraffe and not a forest look-out tower.

On the way out, I nodded to the cashier and she returned the nod, then quickly lowered her eyes. She probably had something she felt guilty about; perhaps she had stolen something from her elderly neighbour's garden. It's difficult to find a purely innocent person in a small town. It's even more difficult to find one among law enforcement agents; everybody knows it's much more fun to uncover the crime and corruption of a law enforcement agent than an ordinary citizen. At least on Sundays.

Passing the cemetery, I noticed a lonely poster stuck badly to the concrete wall. It was fluttering in the wind. It whipped suddenly loose, the half-hidden eye flashing, and stuck against my chest.

A surreal feeling, having been refreshed by brandy, stirred in the substrata of my subconscious.

I peeled the poster from my chest. It featured the face of an electoral candidate, his slogan and list number. Nothing interesting, as unfortunately is usually the case. The most interesting features of the poster were the lips and teeth of the future deputy mayor. The mouth told you something not only about a candidate's lifestyle, but also about the tangibility of his promises. If the candidate was grinning widely and his teeth were impeccable he wouldn't care about the ordinary voter. He would be more concerned about finding a good dentist rather than dealing with the problems of the nation. That's why it's so important to maintain a modest smile. Or even better, no smile at all. Sometimes the most sullen people win, because the voters think that a forehead creased by a frown is the sign of a good brain.

I rolled the poster up and put it under my arm. I liked his moderately slanting lips. I would bet a bottle of vodka he would win the election.

My surrealist mood was begging for another brandy; I could hear its fragile melodious voice, so similar to that of a whales' love song.

Should I go to Sarkiene, put my head on the bar and feebly ask to be sprayed with her favourite hair spray and to have something beautiful formed out of my hair? A mammoth fang stiffened for all eternity? Maybe it would help. Sarkiene would probably refuse; I didn't have enough hair to form anything.

Also, Madam Prosecutor shouldn't let herself go like that. You never know if it could come back to bite you one day. It's not just suspects that have their weak points.

But who will judge me, who will condemn me? You, shining soul, which hasn't yet ripped free of the slippery amphibian shell or opened your eyes?

*   *   *

The train was racing through the darkness into nowhere.

When it stopped, I would swiftly tear open my sleepy eyes; through the window, in a square of dead light, the Cyrillic names of the stops flashed, flickered and mingled – Malinovka, Zemlianycnaja, Bolsaja Cernikovaja. Raspberry, Strawberry, Blueberry. None of them tasted of summer, or of the forest hot in the sun. At times I would notice an elderly woman with gooseberries in an aluminium can, a mother with lacquered high heels, both calm and in no hurry. But in Malinovka a father clambered onto the train, all sweaty, dragging a young woman behind him, drunk and swearing, waving with a beaded handbag that had hairs stuck to it. The living are always in a rush, but the dead overtake them.

Whose child is that, there on the platform, his shirt red from raspberries?

'Are we nearly home? Why did you take me so far?'

'Because it's better,' he replied without opening his eyes. 'Nobody knows you there. I have some reliable friends there.'

'The doctor . . . is he your friend?'

He didn't reply.

I remembered the man we had visited – his happy smile, bursting into a laugh, though neither the teacher nor I had said anything funny. '*Nesoversennoletniaja?* She's under age? Well, you've got a sweet-tooth . . . How old is she? Seventeen? Well, in Ukraine she'd be married with two kids.'

The teacher instructed me to wait and disappeared behind the leather padded door. I put my ear to the door, but could hear nothing, not even laughter.

A narcotic winter ruled in the operation theatre, filling even the tiniest cracks with its heavy yellow light. My nails stuck into the teacher's hand, but he eased them free and stroked my cheek.

'Don't worry. Everything will be fine. I'll wait outside.'

'*Nebojsia, devuska, necego tut bojatsia,*' the doctor said, pulling his gloves on. 'Don't be afraid, little girl, there's nothing to be afraid of.' The instruments clanked.

'You aren't a child anymore, sweetheart, you're a woman and should be proud of it.'

I closed my eyes.

Yes, I'm proud that it was the touch of the cold steel that made me a woman.

'Would you like a drink?' He stroked my cheek again.

'No. I need the toilet.'

Silently, he handed me some cotton wool, wrapped in paper.

'Shall I go with you?'

'No, don't.'

A station with a Lithuanian name flashed by. I held tight to the toilet door waiting as the black blood pool ran into the toilet bowl.

The small, badly-lit station with the small boy holding raspberries disappeared for ever in dark woods that hid the flicker of Cyrillic writing.

II

From a distance, I saw a red hat by the office door.

God Almighty! The writer who said – he was terrible and only became famous after death – that Monday was a hard day was right.

'Good morning, Miss Koko!' I shouted loudly, almost in her ear. 'Why so early? It's not yet nine!'

Miss Koko's sly withered lips grimaced.

'I don't want to talk in the corridor,' she whispered. 'They might hear.'

'Who?'

Miss Koko looked at me, surprised.

'You should know.'

She entered the office first, looked round, and then produced a jar filled with grey barley porridge from her old handbag.

'They poisoned my porridge,' she muttered vehemently. 'I spat it out right away. It was bitter as hell. I rinsed my mouth with vinegar and drank some chamomile tea.'

She shoved the jar in my face.

'See? You see the strange spots? Incredible.'

'You probably didn't rinse the jar properly.'

The old woman stopped talking and cast an evil glance in

my direction. She probably thought her neighbours had bribed me.

'Send it to the laboratory.' She put the jar on the desk. 'Let them check it. You'll see. They'll definitely find some poison. I'll bet they'll find a huge concentration.'

'Last time we sent your cutlets to be checked we didn't find anything.'

Miss Koko flared.

'They probably replaced them!' She screamed. Her hat trembled. 'You left the cutlets unattended, so they just replaced them! They're clever, those smugglers!'

'Then you told us your neighbours were reselling counterfeit alcoholic drinks.'

The old woman frowned. Her dry face shrank completely.

'They're capable of anything,' she said, dispirited.

'But, Miss Koko, nothing was proven. Your neighbours are normal, decent people.'

The old woman raised her faded eyes. Even the irises seemed bleached.

'Ah . . . decent! Of course they're decent! They're decent villains! They've even caught the police in their nets!' She put the jar into her bag. 'Well . . .'

She turned towards the door, pausing halfway hopefully. Possibly she expected me to stop her and attempt to dispel her doubts about the police. As I had no intention of doing so, she turned to face me and declared solemnly, 'I'm so scared that hair has started growing on my face, and you do nothing!' She pulled at a hair on her chin. 'So far scissors are enough, but what next? I won't let them torture me like this. I will go to the President!'

She slammed the door and left.

I needed Atali to make me some coffee. Miss Koko was the very picture of death and sad imbecility. The physiatrist had diagnosed her without hesitation: age related dementia. Is that what it all comes to? She was a teacher, and not just any old teacher, a French teacher. She used to recite Verlaine and Apollinaire to her pupils. They, the dunces, hadn't understood a thing; nobody speaks French in the provinces. They don't all even speak Russian (though they love Yesenin!). She had her hair cut à *la garcon*, painted her lips red. Men would take fright and run away, while the school staff complained that the way she looked wasn't suitable for a Soviet woman. And then – age related dementia. Poisoned porridge. Plots. Why? All those Russian teachers, who used to declaim Yesenin by heart (*Sagane, ty moja, Sagane!*) stayed enviably healthy and even changed their qualifications, started teaching RE and aesthetics. One of them, whose husband had left her, started raising pigs, no matter that she lived in the town centre. Who said town isn't good for pigs?

The psychiatrist explained that the damage to the patient had been caused by intellectual loneliness. There might have been some hope if the loneliness had been unintentional, but French? Verlaine? Rimbaud? What hope was there?

I stuck my head out of the office.

A senior police officer was talking on the phone near the outside door, and, next to the office, on the edge of a chair, the jar of porridge was sitting, grey like a prick of conscience.

The officer finished his conversation.

'Arnold, do me a favour, take it to the lab.' I pointed at the jar.

'That nutty woman again?' Arnold looked unhappy. 'You'd be better off throwing that porridge in the bin. It's a waste of time.'

'What language did you study at school?'

'English. Why?' Arnold looked surprised.

'You won't understand then . . .'

Atali flashed by with her untidy plait. She cast a nervous glance in my direction and disappeared behind the Chief's door.

Disgusted, Arnold took the jar.

'I wouldn't be surprised if that mad woman put the arsenic in her grains herself,' he muttered.

'Why arsenic? It's much more convenient to poison yourself with alkaloids; they're more difficult to find in the body.'

Arnold blushed.

'Well.' He coughed, adjusting the walkie-talkie that dangled against his muscly thigh. 'I just read some, as you say, Flaubert . . .'

'Madam Bovary?'

'Well, yes.'

'Not a bad choice. A criminologist should be familiar with literary crimes.'

Atali appeared in the corridor with a tray and a coffee pot, ignoring Arnold, who immediately forgot poor Emma Bovary and fixed his gaze on the secretary as she glided to my office.

'Thank you, Atali,' I said closing the door.

'You're welcome,' whispered the albino and, with her eyes lowered, dashed from the office. In the corridor there was a bang and a shout, followed by the sound of breaking glass.

Arnold was bent down collecting the broken jar and, visibly disgusted, attempting to shovel the spilt porridge into a heap.

'She just burst out,' he exclaimed, seeing me. 'She doesn't look where she's going. She bumped into me and I broke the evidence.'

'Never mind,' I said. 'Just throw it in the bin. She'll bring some more in. Just hurry up before the Chief appears.'

Arnold sighed.

Why should he sigh? He was young and full of life. Certainly not because of the broken jar. Because of Atali? Atali, that alien creature? He couldn't catch her, not with her speed and acceleration. And he wouldn't know what language to use even if he did. Or what words to address her with.

A wild apple tree knocked against the window with its arthritic fingers. A red leaf stuck to the glass.

17.09.2000

A ground floor resident of a two-storey building in the suburbs, a round, red-headed woman, called the police. She complained that Agripina Z. in the flat above wouldn't open the door in order to take some brochures about the movements of astral bodies. 'I'm a big specialist in this area,' the woman confessed, 'and take a small charge for introducing people to the spirit world. Perhaps one of you would be interested?' she sang, gazing adoringly at Arnold. He didn't want any, but asked with a frown where the stink in her flat came from. The woman was offended. It seemed she had some kind of olfactory impediment and couldn't smell anything. 'What idiocy!' Arnold mumbled. 'One day you'll get poisoned by the gas and will have no idea about it.' The woman, whose poor sense of smell was compensated for by good hearing, snapped back that the spirits were on guard and would never let that happen.

The stink was coming from upstairs.

Having forced the door, we had to hold our breath. Arnold called in the forensics. Agripina lay on her bed and above her a rusty butterfly of death quivered in the dusty ray of sunlight.

The woman, having no issue with the smell, was about to push into the flat, but Arnold stopped her and threatened her with a fine for interfering with police work. Reluctantly, she left; she had been hoping to see some traces of the other world. There was no chance, however, just the evidence of human, bodily weakness blooming like evil flowers. In the corners, on spread newspapers, stood stiffened piles of excrements. A bucket next to the bed was overflowing with urine. The bed linen was damp too. A bottle of medicine stood on the bedside table, the tablets spilt across it, covered with unknown liquid, looking like a ghostly colony of mould. Woman, leave! This is the kingdom of rot and decomposition; there is nothing here for you and the spirits. You might wipe away a fingerprint. There was an abundance of fingerprints, as if death, the main suspect, in a sick desire for fame, wanted to appear in court. And, perhaps it could even get legal aid. The walls and furniture were smeared with dirty fingerprints, as were the prints hung at the level of a basketball hoop, and the mouldy barbiturates on the table. There were patches of blood on the under sheet, on the bread, which was hard as an axe, and on the butterfly, poisonous, pungent, flapping its paper-dry wings.

The experts found that the woman had died of suffocation. A piece of bread was found in her breathing channel. The teeth marks matched with the teeth moulds of the deceased. As Agripina had difficulty in walking because of her dislocated hip, she died in the place she had been eating – her bed. Some crumbs were found in the folds of the sheets and under the bed. All the fingerprints were of the deceased. The blood, urine and excrement were hers too. The barbiturates had been prescribed by the doctor a good ten years or more before, though not yet consumed. No traces of them were found in her blood.

They failed to catch the butterfly. Never mind. It might have just been a moth. And anyway, our laboratory didn't perform biological experiments; it wouldn't be right to send the moth to the regional lab. Particularly as it was more or less irrelevant to the cause of death.

'Atali!' The chief's voice thundered in the corridor. 'Discipline the cleaner – the floor is filthy!'

My door opened with a bang.

'Your clothes, now!' he ordered, lightning flashing in his eyes.

I jumped and nearly dropped my cup of coffee. The Chief's orders frequently sounded indecent.

'A corpse in The Copper Foot Inn.' He immediately dispelled my erotic illusions. 'A girl, probably under age. In the bath. A service lady found her. The forensics expert is on the way.'

While locking the door I noticed that the red leaf was gone from the glass; it had fluttered away leaving the ghostly shape of its capillaries etched upon the window.

The police station's Audi was already waiting outside, the exhaust roaring like a siren of a disaster, the pipe billowing threatening bluish-black smoke.

The owner of The Copper Foot Inn met us, distressed.

'What a disaster,' she said, wringing her arthritic fingers. 'Just as the first foreign guests arrive, and here you go . . . '

'Stop panicking.' A youngster with a shaved head, who was hanging around the reception desk, calmed her down. 'If you know how to use this properly, it'll be a good advertisement!'

'Don't be so callous, son!' The woman shushed the youngster, though his words seemed to have given her some ideas.

A middle-aged man, who was reading a newspaper in the lounge, stood up from the armchair, glanced at his watch, mumbled something like 'God damn it!' in English, and quietly walked out.

'You see!' moaned the owner of The Copper Foot. 'Already running away . . . All the clients will leave!'

'The man's gone to the café,' her son said, demonstrating once again an enviable level-headedness. 'He's got a date. He's snared a local bird. Stop stressing, Ma, think logically. You see, the police have arrived, get them upstairs quickly if you don't want all the clients to see them.'

'A clever kid,' the Chief said, walking upstairs.

The girl, about sixteen or seventeen years old, had her head on the side of the bath and smiled at us with an open deathly grin, decorated with foam.

'She died about five hours ago or so.' The forensics expert looked at his watch. 'In the early hours, at about seven. I haven't noticed any traces of violence. But still, the pose of the corpse is somehow unnatural. Theatrical.'

'No water splashed around the bath,' I interrupted. 'It doesn't seem like there was a fight.'

The forensics expert looked at me dubiously.

'These days you can drown somebody from a distance,' he said in full seriousness. 'With telepathic forces, for example. You suggest to the person that they need to go under – and done! Easy as that! Making somebody do what you want isn't as difficult as it might seem.'

He bent towards the bathtub.

'The sides of the bath are uneven and the bottom is coarse. Behind the rim I found some spots of dried blood. Be so kind as to hand me a bag and I'll take a sample.'

While the forensics expert was scraping at the blood particles, the Chief seemed to have come up with the basic scenario.

'Poor girl overdosed,' he said gloomily. 'See, the irises are widened.'

'My intuition tells me she hasn't overdosed,' I contradicted him.

The Chief fixed his brilliant green eyes on me.

'Overdosed,' he said slowly and emphatically.

'No, Chief.'

'I rely on logic here.'

'And I rely on my intuition.'

'Intuition can't be checked!'

'But logic should not be absolute!'

Silence descended. The forensics expert, a dry, grey man, looked at us, embarrassed.

The Chief growled huskily and waved his paw-like hand.

'Never mind. Let's inspect the room, have lunch and question the witnesses.'

The girl's head lay on the side of the bath, her dead eyes still inquisitive and clear. Her hair seemed a little different, as if it had started growing whiter.

Which was nothing unusual; after death a man's hair still grows and breathes. It can even change colour.

It was just strange that it should happen so fast.

'My lovely, dearest, most sinful one! Don't worry – I have a schedule of my risky days. I circled them in red pencil. My body will never betray us again. Soon the final exams will be over, and there'll be nobody to care about singing, or dance, or even how it's become somehow indecent to sing. It's so sad! Lithuanian grammar is so non-musical and there's no infectious vivace in the laws of physics.

In the garden, the apple trees were once more covered in mad pink blossom and the nettles had grown so tall you couldn't see my head or hear my steps as I ran along the secret path. The indescribable physical pain and the dizzy longing had led me to trample random paths through the nettles and now I was lost among them, and freeing myself from this labyrinth – I couldn't find you. Where are you, oh Spring, so full of torturous desire, when blossom, damaged by oak leaves and strawberries, falls like snow onto my hair?

'The political situation being what it is now,' you said as I sobbed on your chest, having unexpectedly found you at home, 'I need to go to Vilnius more often.'

'But why? You're just a music teacher!'

He smiled and said nothing.

He tried to beat some common sense into me, having calmed my immature, agitated body, stroking my wild Venus' grove.

'The most important thing now is for you to pass your exams, get your diploma. It'll be easier this year because you won't have to memorise the history and social sciences of the Soviet Union. Have you chosen what you're going to study at university?'

'Law.'

'Good idea. I'll help you to put your entry in, and make sure you get a place in a hostel, and everything.'

'I won't be able to survive on the grant alone. My dad's an alcoholic and won't support me.'

The teacher bit his lip.

'Don't worry. I'll give you some money.'

'Where from? How?'

'Times are changing, I'll probably move to Vilnius as well. But remember, you'll only get money for three years. I'm not God.'

I hugged the golden body of my Buddha.

He was God. He was. He was just not aware of this himself.

He smiled and ran his finger down my belly.

'Largo,' I whispered, eager to meet his approaching lips in the darkness. But you shouldn't make love to God in the darkness, his different shapes penetrating your body, to the accompaniment of twilight whispers.

'Would you like some wine? I brought some from Vilnius. Merlot. My wine glasses got dusty while I was away.'

'I like dust,' I said enthusiastically. 'It's like a veil of soft innocence.'

He lifted his eyebrow; slightly surprised perhaps.

We toasted each other.

The evening coolness crept in, jungle-shadowed, mottled python's pattern, paranoid yellow candlelight revealing the secret rotting core of things.

'Who is the girl in the picture?'

'Where?' He rose, slightly troubled.

'There on the bookcase.'

He stood up, went to the bookcase and pushed the photo in between the books.

'It's my cousin. She died when she was 17.'

A silly laugh caught in my throat.

'So then I won't die! I'm eighteen!'

'Don't,' he said drily and went into the kitchen with the glasses in his hands. He opened the tap and let the water run. Longer than was needed.

The jungle-shadows carried the ghostly sparks further into the night; its sickly light touched the windowsill where there seemed to be a military cap lying.

I fell asleep and forgot about it.

The witnesses were gathered in the hall by the reception. The main witness seemed to be the owner's son. He seemed to have already organised who was going to talk and what they would say.

The girl who worked there poured forth a lava-like eruption of personal impressions and emotion. How horrible, how terrible it must have been for the girl! Immediately she thought of her own daughter who came home late at night. And on and on she went; in short, she was of no use.

The owner described the girl as a quiet and calm guest. She hadn't noticed anything suspicious during the week that the girl stayed at The Copper Foot.

'But I noticed something.' The surly boy cut her short.

The owner went quiet.

'So,' I encouraged him. 'Go on then, young Sherlock.'

'A man used to visit her,' the boy blurted out.

'What man?' The owner was nonplussed. 'I didn't see anybody.'

'How could you?' the boy said pitifully. 'You're always watching your soaps, while I was on the reception.'

'Oh God!' The owner exhaled.

'What age? What did he look like?' I asked.

'About forty-five. He looked smart. Lovely coat, real leather,' the boy said. 'What else? Reddish hair, shoulder length. Not sure the style suited a guy his age.'

'May be her father?' the landlady suddenly interjected.

The boy cast a slightly mocking glance at his mother.

'Not likely, Ma, not likely. He dropped a condom on the way up the stairs. He didn't notice it, so I took it.'

The landlady turned puce.

'Where did you put it? Where? You hopeless reprobate!' She hissed.

'Where? Where?' the boy mumbled, perhaps regretting having blurted it out. 'I traded it in . . . for a Crazy Zoo.'

'For a what?'

'What do you mean, *what*? A chocolate egg with a toy inside.'

'Did the man tell you his name?' I asked the boy.

'No. He just used to leave a five *litas* note, that's all.'

The owner ground her teeth.

'Ah ha! So that's where the champagne and girls come from.' She dragged it out.

'They're girlfriends,' the boy corrected her. 'One from my class, the other from another . . .'

'Another?' the owner screamed. 'I'll show you another!'

They didn't seem to hear me thank them. I turned towards the door.

'Good evening.' An unfamiliar man greeted me in English as I passed through the door.

I stopped. Brown hair, about fifty, grey jacket, a checked hat and grey moustache. Unusual. What was he doing in the town centre? Was someone interested in buying the sawmill?

On my way back to the station, I couldn't get the thought of the mysterious man who had visited the girl out of my head. He followed me silently, and when I turned, he would vanish into the air among the dry leaves, turning, for a fraction of a second into the image of the hangman, whose soft tissue and hair peeled away painfully and silently, disintegrating. That was the effect of the warm October air, the tepid sun and the plaintive cry of migrating ducks.

If the girl hadn't killed herself, but was murdered, he would be the main suspect. I would wait for the conclusion of the forensic report.

What if the boy had made it all up? Teenagers have vivid imaginations and feel the need to show off.

The evidence found in the room corroborated the boy's story; a condom, the butts of a strong cigarette, the kind women don't usually smoke, glasses with one still containing wine.

In the girl's passport, on the visa page, I found a strand of fair hair. A reminder, perhaps, of a first love. The passport raised some suspicions: age – twenty one, she had visited Germany twice, there were no return stamps. The stamp covering the side of her photo was blurred and worn away. The Chief thought the passport was a counterfeit. He said he would contact the relevant institutions and regional unit right away. After lunch.

Girl with the ice-clear eyes, where were you going to travel with that strand of fair hair in place of a visa?

My *Allegro* died, my *Andante* sank deep into the water. On the night of the prom, suspicious classmates glanced over at me and began to whisper quietly, the ruder ones not holding back an occasional loud laugh. The fake apple blossom in my hair must have given them a clue, that and the dry, synthetic rustling of the pink flounces of my dress. Even the adults must have understood the language of those dry leaves. My tutor gazed at me pitifully, and the PE teacher, letting me through the narrow classroom doors, perhaps attempting to pat me on the shoulder, instead, having such disproportionately long arms, grabbed at my breast.

I didn't go with the others to watch the sun rise. I dived into the blooming nettles, the pollen specks penetrating my skin like potassium nitrate.

Short of breath, I raced up the stairs and knocked quietly. Nobody answered. I pushed the door and it opened silently.

Dust motes swam in the light of the rising sun, rising from the bare floorboards, responding to the distant siren call of the sea. In the corner lay some bundles of books and old newspapers. There was a note on pink paper pinned to the wall – not for me, but for the cleaner from the clinic.

'Dear Antanina, would you kindly burn all these old papers.'

He had not even signed it.

The sun light changed slowly, from red to golden. It was no longer the victim's fingers that stroked my dress, but him, the sinner, who had transformed into a distant music. But not the heavenly melody I wanted to hear – I longed for the hum of the dentist's drill.

I untangled the knots binding the magazines and books and they scattered on the floor. There were leading articles from the daily *Komjaunimo Tiesa*, articles about agents and traitors. A music textbook for year 11. Beethoven's biography. Music manuscripts. His cousin's picture, on the back of which was written, 'To my lovely and gentle animal, Eliza, 1975.' She had a seductive smile and nervous, fearful eyes, as if she had been hypnotized by a predator.

Downstairs somebody cleared their throat and spat loudly. I pushed the papers into a heap, rushed down the stairs and bumped into Antanina who was wiping her lips. I dived into the weeds so fast that I failed to hear her shout, 'thief', or the second clearing of her mouth, not to mention the spitting that followed it.

Having recovered, a terrible feeling of sadness descended upon me. I imagined Antanina's face, red with anger, accusing me in the staff room of breaking and entering; so we, Odete and I, hid in a quiet corner of the hostel park and got drunk under the blooming jasmine bushes.

'Will you keep my things safe while I'm taking my exams? I can't leave them with dad. Magde will soil them . . .'

'Of course.' Odete had no intention of taking any exams; she was in the process of negotiating a dish washing job in the school canteen and getting ready to marry.

I leant on her bony shoulder and cried.

In the empty wine bottle a wasp droned – the sad song of the captive was barely audible under the heavy June blooms that threatened to tumble upon us.

I called the lab and learnt that the forensics expert had left for the village to dig potatoes. He would be back the next day. 'Don't worry,' the lab assistant assured me, 'the corpse is nice and safe, tucked up comfily in the fridge.'

I slammed down the receiver. I had nothing substantial so far to work on, just a vague pattern, the figure of a stranger fluttering in the air. The Chief had disappeared too, without having solved the puzzle of the passport.

'Atali, be a darling and bring me some coffee.'

Atali lifted her head from the computer.

'Won't be a minute.'

I sat at my desk, reached out for the pile of files and nearly screamed in horror; my fingers dug into wet, soft silk rather than the rough material of the expert's report. Red fought fiercely with purple and the last cold drops of dew clung to the rims of the flower cups, ready to drop.

What kind of flower was that? I had never seen one like it before. My secret admirer (I hoped that it was he who had sent me the flower) had strange taste.

A bitter, disgusting taste, accompanied by tiny shudders, bristled up and down my oesophagus, causing terrible stomach spasms.

And, yet, how nice – the electoral candidate would now have a competitor and each night when I touched his electoral forehead with my unfaithful lips, he would feel the sourness.

The phone rang.

'Listen.' The Chief sounded upset. 'I won't be in the office today; I need to take my cat to the vet.'

'God! What happened?'

'The neighbour caught a mouse in a trap and gave it to him to eat.'

'How thoughtless!'

'Not thoughtless, it was a conscious criminal act!' said the Chief, his voice steely, and put down the phone.

Poor Omar Khayyam! I hoped the mouse hadn't eaten any of those pink, appetite-increasing little balls which dutiful housewives sprinkle all over their store rooms. The Chief wouldn't survive his cat suffering a long and torturous agony; he lived all by himself with no next of kin, not even a TV.

When it was dark, nocturnal, oily waves rippled in off the cold water of the lake. Colder still was the chattering of tiny teeth beneath the ground (which thankfully only those who suffer from claustrophobia can hear). And with them came a sense of dread and anxiety which stole into the police station over the unsolved and as yet uncommitted crimes. At times it threw up some poor beaten woman on an oily wave, who sat in front of me, looking at the forms and refusing to make a complaint.

'Dear citizen, I am not a psychoanalyst or a priest!' I lost my patience. 'I need evidence. You will have to go to the doctor. You need to be examined. I need medical evidence written down . . .'

'Written down? Why written down?' The victim kept her bruises hidden beneath the table.

She didn't understand the importance of evidence and expert witnesses. She just wanted me to go and see her husband, dressed up in my uniform, and pin him to the wall. Actually, to be more exact, she wanted me to go to the gravel pit where he worked. She had seen that in a film. After that, men are usually a little gentler.

Having not come to any kind of agreement, we both left; I headed towards the lake, she towards the cemetery. And the creaks and squeaks of the rotting floor boards greedily devoured her tangled, peroxide curls.

Yin Yang greeted me at the door, her back arched like a bow. I opened a tin of Play Cat.

The phone rang. They had been able to save Omar Khayyam; he would have to stay on a special diet for a couple of days. The neighbour was lectured on the difference between normal cats and Persians and was threatened with a fine for cruelty to animals.

'By the way . . .' The Chief's voice sounded bright and young again, his happiness restored. 'The girl's passport doesn't, in fact, belong to her. The passport belongs to a prostitute who left for Germany a year ago. We'll have to establish the girl's identity . . . What? I'm coming, darling. I'll give you some water right away!'

The beeping of a disconnected phone followed.

Oh damask rose, how beautiful your petals are in the early morning when the sun touches them with its finger tips, I mumbled putting down the receiver.

It had started to rain.

Rain washes away the traces. It softens the bruises, and sings a lullaby to the unsleeping animals tethered underground.

III

In the very depths of consciousness, where the gates to super-human cognition open, I pictured my childhood home in the suede-grey twilight. I could even touch the ominous soft fluff of the silence. On the north side, shaded by the house, nothing grew except moss and Calvatia, puffball mushrooms that remind me of reptile eggs. There, on the seabed, a white clown jumped, its long, tattered sleeves shaking. His jumps were reminiscent of dance moves. He tottered all by himself with no spectators, not even the gentle stream of time running its course.

Attempting to untangle the tango loops that had turned to salsa, I rose from my bed, still in my dream. The cat slid from the quilt and bumped on the floor.

Through the gap in the curtains the street lamp's blue light shone, the patter of the rain had been replaced by the roar of the trees on the seabed, and, deep in my subconscious, the conviction was maturing that I had seen the Antichrist. It was written on the suede surface of the darkness, in intricate writing, the letters of which was reminiscent of beasts and monsters' plaits.

From the bottom of my bed the candidate gazed at me with a dignified expression; the night before I had drawn a

Clark Gable moustache on him. Now, to be perfect, he needed only a uniform, and – more importantly – a cap.

I would leave that art work for the evening, when I would bring home some old posters made for celebrating National Police Day from the station.

I poured some cream for Yin Yang and fished out some cat treats that stank of wet cardboard.

'Look! Make sure it lasts the whole day,' I warned the yawning cat. 'If you overeat, I won't take you to the vet; you'll have to sort yourself out.'

Yin Yang observed me crossly. 'I am not like that stupid Omar,' her eloquent eyes seemed to say.

Seven fifteen. Don't forget the important things. Lipstick, the colour of dark chocolate. So fitting for the bridge between September and October.

The phone rang.

I froze.

Picking it up, I thought – only in films does a provincial investigator receive a call at seven in the morning. A witness, the killer or the victim, if it isn't a murder case.

The Chief doesn't care what hour he calls, though. And it doesn't even have to be about a case.

'Let's talk about something you wouldn't dare to tell even your friend . . .' The trembling voice broke and exhaled loudly; possibly indicating passion.

'And what can you tell me that I don't know already?' I enquired, interested. 'And at seven in the morning at that?'

The receiver roared silently, failing to find the words.

I decided to play *vabanque*.

'Is that Pocius from class 7a?' I said sternly.

The silence broke and the receiver gurgled, as the caller choked, perhaps on passionate confessions of love.

'Call me in the evening, Pocius. Then we can talk about what you don't dare tell your friend. Now, unfortunately, I need to go to work.' I sighed. 'Routine is the enemy of love.'

The receiver clicked and the sound of pips followed.

'Maybe I was right,' I thought, putting on my jacket.

A couple of weeks before, Mrs Pociene, the mother of Pocius in 7a, a decent woman who traded Turkish sandals in the market, had come in to the station to make a complaint against her telephone provider for sending her terrible, fabricated statements. It turned out that somebody had been secretly using her telephone to access a sex line. As she had no husband and even the best investigator couldn't pin it on her ninety-year-old mother, who could hear only with a hearing aid, we questioned her son, a tall, spotty teenager. He was so scared of the police that he admitted to it straight away.

The poor soul, he was probably only trying to call his teacher; in the provinces telephone numbers differ from one another so little.

I blew a kiss to the candidate and slammed the door. A light fog, a grey satin veil, was drifting slowly back towards the lake, to glide across the water with its decorative folds and pleats and drown quietly, leaving no sign of violence.

If the forensics expert hadn't returned from his blasted potato digging, there was no chance of even dreaming about getting any results. The girl would remain unidentified until the next day, or even longer. Which was no big deal; nobody worried too much about identity in this town. And anyway, every day an endless number of nameless and unnoticed people died. If a person dies unexpectedly, it seems like a strange exception.

I chased the fog over leaves that were like wet bandages. But the fog could not advise me, or give me answers, or divulge the secrets of the dead that were wrapped in its watery shroud.

By the end of July, a cool breeze wafted in from the other world, with wings made of chrysanthemums, white and soft, leaving petals in your hair, melting and soaking in like arsenic.

A small dose of poison can often act as medicine and is used to treat people faced with certain death.

I sat down on a bench under the statues of Lenin and Kapsukas, who didn't surrender an inch to each other, either in height or in the swing of their arms. Dumbly, I gazed at the door of the music faculty.

The last exam was over. I got a 'Four', not the top 'Five'. 'Don't worry,' a boy with a large head, born to work in the court office, comforted me. 'That lecturer is really mean. He never gives a 'Five'. If he did, it would probably kill him.'

I turned my head up, towards Kapsukas, but he took no notice of me – he was too busy indicating to Lenin a broken pine tree with its trunks besmeared with white lines.

I caught a whiff of sulphur as somebody sat down next to me, pushing aside my plastic bag full of notes and textbooks.

'Congratulations.'

If it had been Lenin speaking in Lithuanian, I couldn't have been more surprised.

On the bench, his legs crossed and a cigarette in his hand, was my beloved music teacher. He wore white trousers and his face was scraped blue. A thin golden chain dangled on his chest. Not a teacher but rather some kind of peacock. He looked so strange and unexciting, I could have almost cried.

'You're congratulating me?' I mumbled. 'What for?'

'You just passed your entry exams.' He exhaled a small cloud of smoke and stroked my knee with his cool sandal wood hand.

'Well, it's not . . . clear yet . . .'

He looked into my eyes sternly, reproving me for my lack of faith.

'You passed. I know.'

He threw the cigarette butt into the lilac bush, took out a small key from his pocket and handed it to me.

'The key to locker 307 at the central Post Office. At the start of each month you'll find an envelope with money. On top of your grant, this should allow you to live comfortably. As an orphan from the provinces and as somebody needing social support, you'll get a place in the hostel without any question.'

His characterisation of me sounded like expletives. I cowered.

'Thank you,' I mumbled, looking at the lilacs. A grey smoke wriggled up from the bush, rising convulsively from the cigarette butt.

The last time we met, as if to negate the despair, I screamed wildly, sinking my nails into his back, my teeth biting into his shoulder and shuddering in horror that somebody had stolen the soul of my golden Buddha and I was making love to a statue. The trains which passed noisily behind the small hotel carried my screams far off into the steppes and the forests; the eyes of the dead followed the express as it passed through their remote stops.

I know where those reddish-purple flowers with their frost-frozen calyxes grow – in the damp forest fields. If you get lost out gathering berries, and, having lost hope, lift the heavy branch of a fir tree, you will see there a bunch of these shining, tiny heads. They grow from the eye sockets of the dead, and their gaze binds you to them for ever.

''Morning, Atali. Has the forensics expert called yet?'

Atali shook her head, making the early morning coffee.

'I hope the potato digging hasn't done him in. I recall cases when people have ended up getting ploughed over and only the horse was able to testify, as it was the only one who was sober there.'

Atali turned her eyes on me; to my surprise, I saw not indignation, but quiet admiration.

I was confused.

'Where's Arnold?' I asked quickly.

'He left with his team to deal with a domestic conflict,' Atali said, stretching towards me with a cup of coffee. 'The wife was hysterical; she started smashing plates and grabbed a knife. The husband got scared and called the police. By the way . . .' She lowered her eyes. 'The Chief seemed greatly agitated, so, on my own initiative, I sent out the victim's photo and fingerprints . . . Hers and her secret visitor's.'

'That's good, Atali. But I think they're hardly likely to have their prints in their files. The girl looks as though she was decent; I doubt she would have had any business with the police. And the visitor . . .'

'Drug addicts get involved in crime very young,' Atali said wisely.

'It's not clear yet if she was a drug addict. We don't have the forensics' conclusions. Damn that potato digging! Potato digging should be forbidden. Intellect is going to hell.'

Atali's eyes darted towards me again. Fascination had been replaced by horror. I stopped talking, swallowed the last of the coffee together with the coffee grounds and placed the cup on the desk. I never would have thought that Atali could be so concerned about the loss of intellect.

'Thank you, Atali. I'm going to get down to work now.'

'You're welcome. Let me know any time you need more coffee.'

'No . . .Yes. Okay. If there's any important news, let me know.'

This time I found a yellow water lily on my desk. I sighed, imagining my poor admirer wading through the swamps at night with his trousers rolled up, with the cold faces of *kikimoras* and the carcases of drowned deer poking at his calves.

But why a water lily? I had brought from home a large botanical guide. There must have been some connection between these plants; that's usually the case with evidence left deliberately. Neither modern psychoanalysis, nor Hollywood detective films attempt to disabuse me of this theory. Especially the latter.

I glanced at my watch. At nine, Sarkiene and the owner of the shop *Viola and Niola* were due to arrive: Sarkiene claimed to have seen the man with the girl at her bar, and at *Viola and Niola* the poor girl had bought some tights.

As it turned out, she had bought the best quality tights, Italian, Filodoro, size three, black. Seventeen *litas* and eighty cents plus VAT. She had even stretched them with her hand, to check that they were not too flimsy. She had paid, thanked her and then left. She had come in to the shop sad, and left even sadder, though you would have expected the opposite; Italian tights could cheer anybody up. How had she been dressed? Brown coat with a fur collar and ugly, crude, modern boots. There was no man with her.

Sarkiene bit her lip. Her eyes, thickly lined with black pencil, almost popped out – that meant she was trying to concentrate. She quietly listed all the dishes that the couple had ordered. When I cut her short, saying that it wasn't important, Sarkiene was upset.

'They drank a whole bottle of Merlot!' she grumbled unhappily. 'Isn't that important?'

'No,' I snapped back. 'If you didn't put poison in the wine, then it's not important! Wait . . . Did you say Merlot?'

'Merlot.' Sarkiene brightened up.

'Hmm . . . Don't you have any other wine?'

Mrs Sarkiene looked at me as if I was an alien.

'Madam Judge . . . You talk as if you don't know what wines I serve.'

'Well, yes, true,' I agreed. 'But that's not important. It's not proof.'

Sarkiene shrugged her round shoulders.

As well as the Merlot, she remembered the man's cufflinks; they were so shiny, probably gold.

'Wait. Could they be like these?' I showed her the photo of the cufflink found in the bathroom.

Sarkiene nodded. Yes, they were the same, but they didn't look as attractive in the photo, as it was a black and white shot.

'Did you notice any other particular traits? A scar? A phrase he used? Any speech impediment?'

Sarkiene looked at me and blushed. Perhaps she considered the last inappropriate.

'No,' she mumbled. 'He had nice hair, chestnut. But when he bent down to pick up the lighter, it slipped forward over his eyes.'

I leant back in the chair.

'Do you think it was a wig?'

Sarkiene sighed.

That could be considered a *yes*.

After seeing off the witnesses, I left the door half open in order to allow the stink of cheap perfume to dissipate – it was worse than chloroform.

Outside, a silent gust of wind disturbed the tops of the distant trees, as if some bald demon had let out a ghastly cackle.

Though, not necessarily bald. The length and the colour of the hair of the wig could have been (theoretically) the opposite of his real hair, which could have been short and, let's say, light. In other words, identical to the strand in the passport.

If the forensics expert didn't give me any results soon, I would poison his potato cellar.

What about the blood on the side of the bath? If the sample was the same as the victim's and there were lines of the corpse's fingers similar to those that would be made if she had gripped the sides of the bath as her lover suddenly grabbed her extended feet and pulled them sharply . . . Yes, then her head would have immediately submerged beneath the water. A classic case of drowning, without any sign of violence.

Could the forensics' assistant examine the corpse's fingers? Should I call the laboratory? Or should I go there?

No, I didn't trust that old widow. Her child had recently been plagued with boils, so she tortured him, taking a blood sample and then staring day-and-night through a microscope, hoping to discover some kind of treasure – a golden Staphylococcus.

I hoped she didn't accidently switch the victim's blood sample with her son's. What would happen if she found some, let's say, heroin?

It was half past twelve, but there had still been no sound of the Chief's voice in the corridor. Strange.

'Good afternoon.' The cheap chloroform was swamped by the sweet fragrance of forget-me-nots; it felt like the entire riverbank had marched into the room.

I turned round.

In the doorway I saw a burning bush. It was the redhead from the outskirts of town – the mediator between the two worlds.

'Hello. And what would you like to inform us about now? Something more to do with the upper floor?'

'I . . .' the lady murmured and looked round. 'Could I sit down?'

'Please do.'

'I can barely stand on my feet, you see.' She sank into the seat with difficulty.

'May be you should be going to the doctors, not the police?'

The lady wafted her ring-covered fingers helplessly.

'You see . . .' She blushed heavily and lifted her pleading eyes to mine. 'The GP . . . The GP won't understand me. And you are a woman. That's the most important thing. You see . . .'

She seemed on the verge of tears.

'Please, calm down. What has happened? Is it the upper floor terrorising you again? As far as I understand the flat hasn't been sold to private owners and the council have let some builder move in.'

The lady waved her hand, irritated.

'I don't care about builders! I'm possessed by a demon.'

There followed a moment's silence. On the pavement outside a woman's lonely heels clicked.

'He undoes the hook and creeps in. You see, I take *Noctal* at night and don't hear a thing.' The lady grabbed at her full chest. 'Its body is as huge as a bull's. It presses down on me heavily and tortures me. It bites me and . . .' She lowered her eyes. 'And all the rest.'

'You mean . . .?'

The woman nodded.

'Here, the teeth marks – see.' She rolled up her sleeve and showed the bruise.

I examined it.

'Interesting. Looks like regular teeth marks. Not a demon's.'

'Whose then?' The woman grew angry.

'These marks are too human.'

She gasped.

'Human?' she repeated, disappointed. 'Could it be a man's? An ordinary man's?'

'Unfortunately, yes, ordinary,' I said with regret. 'Possibly, the builder's. We've received some complaints about him; he's accused of sexual harassment and hooliganism. He beat up his wife having found her with a lover. That's probably his only demonic trait. Did you happen to touch his horn in the darkness?'

The woman rose slowly from her seat, like a convict released from the gallows, and turned towards the corridor without a word.

'If he comes again,' I shouted, 'try to tear some physical proof off him . . . Some evidence.'

The reply was the wintry slam of the outside door.

I doubted she would be back. She definitely wouldn't try to get any proof. In the paranormal world you can't prove much with physical evidence.

I spent August on my father's run-down farm, though I would have preferred to have stayed at the school hostel. Unfortunately, it was closed for the summer, turned into a warehouse for drying herbs and storing gardening tools.

Odete went to the seaside with her husband-to-be. She was lucky to be getting married to a man who had no need of womanly charm, and, what's more, someone who wasn't poverty-stricken either. I wasn't even able to collect my little pile of books, or my few clothes; so I had to make do with what I had taken to town for my exams.

I slept in the attic, among old apple boxes. I put down a mattress and gathered bed linen from the old laundry. Magde, my father's girlfriend, was too lazy to do the washing so she would throw up old clothes or sheets into the attic when they were too dirty to use.

She hated and soiled all of my mother's belongings – I couldn't understand how my father could stand that. It must have been worse than tooth-ache! But not only could he stand her – he even slept with the slut, I could hear the animal sounds, the huffing and puffing, as if he were emptying his bowels rather than making love.

Ripe cherries, sharp and black with juice, dripped through the rotten roof of the outside toilet onto the blackened floor, soaking into the steaming soil, staining the dirty sheets of the mathematics textbook and my mother's drawings and sketches. The era of toilet paper would never arrive for that toilet.

I read Latin books that I had stolen from the village library. I gathered overripe gooseberries in the garden and as I had no photo of my teacher incarcerated in a golden locket, I stroked the fake-leather bag holding the money he had given me. I pressed it to me chest like a second heart.

My father and Magde had little interest in my plans, though they remembered to ask if I had enough money for the start of my studies.

'I don't,' I lied, faking a sad expression. 'I'll try to borrow some. Could you give me something?'

My father leant backwards and Magde laughed, patting my shoulder with her square hand, fit to strangle bears. If she knew what I wore on my chest, she would have pulled it off, together with my head.

September came and both my hearts began to beat harder.

I left at dawn, while the bear pit nestled in its bedding of white fog. And when the heat dispersed the damp, milky wisps, there was no trace of me left at the crime scene.

In the afternoon the wind rose. The caretaker had swept the red leaves into the corners of the courtyard, as if to the four points of the compass, leaving them as homes for the ants, and they swirled in the air, whispering: *the devil loves hasty work, the devil loves hasty work*. They were only ordinary provincial leaves and see how they whispered; if that was what the leaves were whispering then what about the stray dogs and the jackdaws? When you talk about natural phenomena, you're not generally referring to ordinary people – they're too high for that. But how much higher exactly, nobody knows.

You shouldn't be overzealous in trying to solve a crime, because you never know what it might lead to.

That was the Chief's opinion. Having discovered that Atali had disseminated the victim's photo, he was unhappy.

'How will it help? We need to wait.'

The telephone rang.

It was the forensics expert; he had returned from the village. He invited us to supper. He would be making *cepelinai* – potato zeppelins.

'Where, for heaven's sake, are the results of the tests?' I asked, attempting, as far as was possible, to be polite.

The Chief waved his hand.

The forensics expert, at the other end of the line, most probably did the same. He explained that his fingers had got rough; you see, he had scraped the mud from the potatoes without wearing his gloves.

'You're not going to play the violin!' I screamed, losing my composure.

'A scalpel is an equally sensitive instrument,' he said and put down the receiver.

I bit my lip.

I thought of the dead girl lying in the freezer, listening to the first sounds of decomposition in the depths of her deep and heavy body, quiet as the flutter of eyelashes.

Well, she would probably build to a crescendo, to *forte* or, God forbid, *fortissimo*. That worthless forensics expert needed to be sent to the capital's Concert Hall.

'Don't worry.' Atali handed me a glass of water.

The Chief agreed.

'No need to get over-excited. Everything is under control. All will become clear in time.'

It would be better, I thought, if there was no time, just space, then you could excuse yourself not by saying you didn't have enough time, or you had too much of it, but rather by appealing to the appalling distance between thought and action. I locked myself in my office.

At my desk a woman was waiting with a bag on her knee. She had a large knot of hair on the top her head, as if she had wrapped it around a jar.

It was the mother of the fourteen-year-old, violated in the maize field.

'Good afternoon.' She pushed her bag forward, as if it was a shield.

'Good afternoon. You're here about your daughter's case? As you know, it's closed. It's buried. You know that. I'm sorry, there's nothing I can do about it.'

'No, dear prosecutor. I . . .' She stuttered.

Here we go, in addition to being a judge, I had now acquired a prosecutor's title. Not too long until I became the General Commissar.

'Do you have some new information, or do you want us to re-open the case?'

'There's no point . . . All the information is underground.'

'How – underground?'

The woman shrugged.

'You said it – the case is buried.'

Outside the wind howled, tossing handfuls of leaves and fine gravel against the glass, so that it rattled like the thin bones of a skeleton.

'Well, it was just, let's say, a vivid phrase,' I said attempting to back-track a little.

The woman gazed at me for a long time. I could see from the expression on her face that she didn't believe me. Scratching at the rusted buckle of her bag, she managed to conquer her distrust of me and force herself to speak.

'You see, my daughter . . . I suspect . . . She's pregnant.'

My arms dropped.

'For goodness sake! This is definitely not a matter for the police.'

'How is it not?' The woman jumped up. 'All this started when you did your interrogation. Before that, she was a nice pure girl.'

'Until what? The rape?'

'No. Until the questioning!'

'I think that's enough.'

'You allowed the badness into her!' the woman screamed, enraged, waving her bag, its metal corners sparkling like lightning. 'You defiled my child, my pure and decent child, to be given to God!'

'Arnold!'

'Inviting the chief devil won't help! I just sprinkled myself with holy water! Besides, I studied how to be an exorcist in Vilnius, in Kalvariju Street, next to the market!'

When the dull footsteps of the policeman were heard in the corridor, the woman grew scared. She turned pale and cowered in her seat. When Arnold and his assistant burst into the room, it was pitiful to see the shrunken knot of her.

I sniffed. Was I just imagining the smell of sulphur?

The depths of evil are dark and mysterious, we will never overcome it using traditional methods. But have you ever seen a policeman who was an exorcist? Perhaps in some ridiculous B movie. Every decent policeman has a very limited knowledge of exorcism and the best he can do to abstract evil is to arrest it for a couple of days. One famous, but rather unhealthy writer, said that, though instead of three days he talked of all eternity, casting himself in the role of the policeman.

There were heavy steps in the corridor again; my insides tensed. But it was not Evil that entered, just Arnold returning with a frown.

'We've just had a report from the Mars district. A pensioner has buried her old cat in the yard of a block of flats and lit some candles. The neighbours are accusing her of unsanitary behaviour and a breach of their children's rights.

'How are children related to this story?'

'The pensioner buried her cat in the sand pit and won't allow the children to play there.'

In the corridor a gust of wind blew hail past the door – it looked like Atali. Cups clinked. The smell of coffee. Aha, so it was Atali.

'You need to go and tell the pensioner to bury her beloved cat somewhere else. She won't be able to sit by the sand pit all night; the children will manage to dig the cat up and drag it somewhere to rot. Has she got relatives buried somewhere? I'm sure they won't mind the company of her cat. Who doesn't like cats?'

'And if she doesn't agree?'

'If she doesn't, then fine her. Fill in a report. And the remains will have to be confiscated and destroyed. You can borrow a toy spade from the local children. So why are you still here? Go!'

'It's that it's such a minor case,' mumbled Arnold, shifting from one leg to the other.

'Minor? Cat exhumation? That's not serious enough for you? My good man, you're not some kind of Rambo. Thank God. Listen, it's so much more important to bury a cat than to blow up a petrol station or shatter the supermarket windows with a machine gun. When you wake up all sweaty one dark night having dreamt of death stretching its bony fingers towards you, an invisible grateful paw will stroke your cheek and death will step back a couple of paces.'

Arnold shrugged. Obviously I hadn't persuaded him. He left reluctantly.

It was getting dark. The wind had quietened down and no longer tossed the leaves, though somewhere close there was a gentle, incessant whisper – in Atali's room the fax machine rustled like autumn leaves, pouring out messages from other police departments around the country: the girl was not identified . . . Not identified . . . Not identified . . .

29.09.2001

A woman reported to the police that her three-year-old daughter had disappeared. She had been walking in the park – and then she disappeared. As if into deep water. The mother had been drinking wine on a bench with her friend; they were telling each other about their unhappy lives, and when the story had reached its culmination, the child (the result of the unsuccessful life) had gone. She had curly, fair hair, a puffy face and wore a pink jacket. Her face had been all smeared with chocolate.

The friend stated that she believed that some members of a sect dressed in white had taken the girl. Then she immediately started talking about a huge monkey that had escaped from the Ignalina nuclear power plant which might have taken her. The mother seemed to be more sensible – the fact that she came to police rather than to the *Higher Intelligence* her friend had suggested, proved that.

Having searched the park where the child had been left, we found some sweet wrappers, scattered around like in the fairy tale about Hansel and Gretel. We also discovered prints in the soil, where it wasn't covered by leaves, of a child's shoes and larger ones. The larger prints belonged to a female foot, size thirty-nine, with a heavy ridged heel. Further on they had probably walked on the asphalt path. The heath, the wild blackberry bushes and the gravel pits threw up neither witnesses nor evidence.

The soldiers of battalion number five searched the surrounding woods, poked in all the lakes, but couldn't find the girl – dead or alive. When, two days later, we began to lose hope, the girl reappeared unexpectedly. She was sitting in the sand pit of the nursery school, eating a chocolate. She looked neither scared nor hungry, and when her mother grabbed her and spanked her on her bottom, she screamed like a healthy child who had been punished unjustly.

'You, little toad!' her mother shouted. 'If you vanish again, you'll see what I'll do to you! How do you think we'll survive if I don't get your maintenance benefit?'

We questioned the girl to no avail. She mumbled that some woman had given her a sweet, and that they had then both gone to play. At that age, children aren't capable of recognising people and places.

But, despite that, a couple of days later the child's mother burst into the police station and put in a complaint against the bar owner, Sarkiene.

'It's her who stole my little child! That poser, sprayed up with hair spray and perfume!'

Her evidence? The girl, seeing Sarkiene, had cried out, 'Auntie, give me a sweetie!' And then she had asked Sarkiene when they would play the chu-chu train game again and if she would be the engine.

A search of Sarkiene's house uncovered no clues. We did find size thirty-nine shoes with ridged heels, but there was no soil on them. ('Half of the town has such shoes,' Sarkiene shouted. 'Even some men.') The sweets she had on sale in the bar were of a common type, any café sold them. Besides, there was no clear motive why she might have had the urge to take the child. She was a divorced, lonely woman (her husband lived with another woman and her children in the neighbourhood). She looked decent; though divorced, lonely women often did. The rooms in her flat were full of glittering trifles, art bought at the market, fluffy toys and dolls. One of them was the size of a child, with fair curly hair, a pink dress and a nose smeared with chocolate. It was brand new, bought the day before, with the price tag still on it.

Did it mean anything?

Perhaps. A real child isn't as lovely as you might think, with its wild screams and demanding its rights, pushing away from your loving arms, biting and kicking. You can't tell it your most painful and saddest secrets. It has enough of its own. It wants fairy tales about bears, about dragons and the struggle with death in the shapes of archetypes; they die, come alive again, marry and live happily ever after. Who, what and with whom isn't important – a child is a person of action not sentiments.

'It's not nice to be suspicious of a poor woman,' Sarkiene said, taking an offended tone. 'So what if I have no family and have to watch how my former husband takes the children of another woman for a walk every day? Is that a crime

for which you'll put me in jail? You can't judge someone for
their secret wishes, otherwise there would be no free people
left on earth.'

The purple flower that was pictured in my large botanical
guide looked considerably paler, more like a toadstool: the
quality of Soviet print was to blame for that.

'Autumnal crocus,' I read in it. '*Colchicum autumnale.*
Very poisonous.'

I shook my head. My admirer really was mad; dizzy with
love, so eager to poison me.

Was he hoping that I might gobble his present up?

It upset me to discover, too, that despite its positive traits
(it was suitable for treating gonorrhoea and skin diseases), it
had a considerable number of negative traits. It was a powerful sedative; you might not wake up after consuming it, and
if you did the sensation wouldn't be pleasant as your sleep
would have been accompanied by diarrhoea and vomiting.

Good gracious – what a terrible pattern between these
clues! I wasn't at all happy to have discovered them. I would
have to warn the guard not to let anybody suspicious into
the station.

I thrust the guide into the cupboard and fixed my gaze
upon the wall.

What wet and cold swamps they are, the icy swamps of
death. Chilling you right to the heart.

IV

This time the Antichrist didn't move – the wooden pole was dug deeply into the soil and only the red shawl shone sullenly in the eternal twilight.

What was its rotten frame supposed to be protecting the well from? The well had been dry for a long time anyway.

I wanted to step out into the yard, just for a moment, but time's invisible wall stopped me. I could see my home in the distance; recognise it by the warmth that filled me – a fragile glow like that from a large, friendly animal.

Nothing had a concrete name – no category, no state, no quantity.

My alarm clock, affected perhaps by these oppressive dreams, broke.

I was woken up by the loud sound of the television; Yin Yang had sat on the remote and was watching the brawling crowds in Pamplona's street being chased by bulls.

I took the remote from under her and flicked over to the state channel.

A voice-over was talking about the suspicious past of some secret service agents; caps with stars flashed across the screen. Stierlitz from 'Seventeen Moments of Spring' came and went, as charming and as indifferent as ice, his *Sturmbannführer* uniform not interfering with his accentless Russian accent. Which was not surprising; all Russians act like they're foreigners or aliens from Alpha Centauri.

I was about to switch it off, when the voice stopped suddenly and on the screen, for a fleeting moment – a fraction of a second that stretched into an eternity – my beloved music teacher appeared. He was wearing a serious suit and an even more sober tie that resembled a noose. With an indifferent gesture, he shooed away the reporters that were trying to get into his office. The image disappeared, but not before I had noticed the curve of his eyebrow and the cufflinks that flashed like golden bullets at the camera.

And then, slowly, like a rewound tape, the presenter's voice returned. 'Information concerning the past of current agents has either been destroyed or is in the secret archives in Moscow where no one can get their hands on it.'

I glanced at the mirror. My God, my face was green from the plaque left by the dream. I looked like a mature cheese.

It was only when I was drinking my coffee that I came to my senses. The dream I had seen of the television programme had seemed so realistic even though it was ridiculous, that it might even have been believable. Who could say that the unbelievable was not possible? The head of the Criminal Department, Professor Axe, would have given me a 'fail' for entertaining such thoughts; thank God, he could only do so in his dreams now.

It turned out that my beloved teacher, with his elegant, passionate fingers, had not only learned to play Tchaikovsky's Waltz of the Flowers or the wedding song of whales – it seemed there was sheet music that existed that required not just some tone-deaf pianist, but someone who could play on any manner of instrument, a real virtuoso.

It was eight already.

I had managed to convince myself that there was no need to hurry – everything would become clear given time – so I made another cup of coffee. Then Atali called.

'You've received the forensic results.'

I choked on my coffee.

Could it be true? According to my conservative estimate, the expert, exhausted by all that potato digging, would have brought the results in the next morning. How was it possible to trust people? If he had done the work with numb hands, the tests would probably have to be done again.

As I slammed the door, I remembered my friend from university. He had big teeth. He was a square, short boy; we used to call him Nutcracker. He couldn't boast of any great intellect, but was incredibly pedantic. He used to love rummaging through old files and cold cases, as if he was searching out the evidence of his noble origin, or a secret poison to defeat the King of Mice.

He had settled in the archives when he graduated.

I would send him an e-mail, I thought. He might have some secret information about my teacher. He wouldn't dare ignore my email, that tiny, little, ugly nutcracker! The industrious runt would be feeling guilty about his poor behaviour – he had once tried to stick his hand up my skirt. I would subtly and wittily remind him of the incident – gently – so as not to alienate him, enticing him with almond spiced erotic possibilities.

The warm wind stroked my ankles and slid up my thighs like an incorrigible harasser. I pulled my coat tight around me and ran up the steps into the station, my sharp heels stabbing through the leaves – scraps of clothing, material, fibres with micro particles that had been soaked with pungent bodily perspiration, the poisonous saliva of an alcoholic, the green foam of an epileptic, and the urine of the incontinent.

The policeman on duty was cursing into the telephone. 'Ugly bitch.' I nearly fell back through the doors, onto the slimy clothes of the exhumed corpse, crawling with microbes. He blushed slightly when he saw me. I remembered, then, that he had married recently and sighed, relieved.

People cursed like that either to a prostitute moaning that there is nobody to protect her, or to their wife. And they're both unlikely to put in a complaint.

There was a plant stood on top of the forensic report. The leaves, which were like those of a Lily of the valley, leant forlornly to one side, beneath which were little white buds hanging like short strands of Italian pasta. With a wry smile, I opened the guide and discovered that the root of this specimen was used in traditional medicine. Its folk name was whore's grass. There was no need to wonder if it was poisonous – the name said it all. In addition, the guide informed me, women used to rub it into their cheeks to make them pink. A prelude, presumably, of sin.

One detail though was curious: whore's grass bloomed from May to June, so now it should have been bearing berries, not petals. Where, I wondered, had my admirer managed to find a blooming whore's grass?

But, hold on, perhaps the forensics expert had brought it in with the report? But hardly. He was a bachelor; to him women were a subspecies, not a gender. And he didn't like flowers. If he had a crush on somebody, he would have brought them the most beautiful parts of a corpse – a curled eyelash with skin attached; a finger with a varnished nail; an ear with a brass or silver ear ring.

I threw the poisonous macaroni into a drawer and opened the report.

The corpse was female, about sixteen or seventeen. Her height was 168 cm. She had light skin, chestnut hair, blue eyes. No injection punctures noticed. On the finger pad and palm of the right hand there was some light bruising present; a slight bruise had been identified on the elbow. No other marks of violence had been noticed.

Reading, I sensed the dim figure, formed first in dreams, taking its first steps into reality. I could hear quiet footsteps, softer than those of a cautious lover.

Death was caused by sudden drowning, the forensics expert wrote. The drowning had been recent, the corpse was blue and there were blood spots in the eyes. The maceration of the skin was slight. The irises were widened, but it was unlikely that the cause of death was drugs, though even a specialist toxicological expert might fail to identify this . . .

'Why?' I asked the report.

. . .because irises can widen from great horror as well. The thymus gland of the corpse was abnormally large; the victim might have had a scare and drowned after fainting. However, an unconscious person does not necessarily drown, so violent drowning was also a possibility . . .

'Jesus Christ, how many hypotheses,' I commented, annoyed. 'Who is doing the investigation – the forensics expert or me?'

The blood on the side of the bath coincided with the victim's blood type. Her finger prints were there too. The prints on the wine glass belonged to the victim as well. The other prints belonged to the mysterious guest.

'I'll send the finger prints to Nutcracker.' The idea leapt into my head. 'Well, what else was of interest?'

While completing the examination, I discovered the girl was pregnant. She was in the third month of the pregnancy.

Just what we need! I thought, annoyed. I didn't like this development. It was too banal. A cheap detective trick. This wasn't a novel, for God's sake! This was real life!

I shook my head, chasing away the thoughts that fluttered towards me with their dry, paranoid, tiny, little wings. I typed in Nutcracker's email address.

I sent a note that mingled eroticism with neurosis (oh how I like the brotherly sound of these two words!), and then stared dumbly at the screen until Atali appeared.

'Coffee.' She put a steaming cup down.

'Thank you, Atali.'

'Something wrong?' Atali's pink eyes skimmed my drawn face attentively. 'What have you been dreaming about?'

'The Antichrist, as always.'

Atali's lips twisted.

'Don't worry,' she said gently. 'He doesn't belong to the criminal class, so you don't need to be concerned about him.'

'Doesn't belong to the criminal class? I think . . .' I sighed, but Atali was already through the door, running towards the thunderous voice of the Chief and an insistent moaning, probably that of an arrested offender.

'He has depression,' the Chief shouted. 'That's why he'll stay here for a while, in my office! There's no rule that he can't live in the office . . . and not just because it hasn't been considered – the bureaucrats aren't capable of foreseeing anything, they're all too short-sighted!'

Atali tried to say something, but the Chief wouldn't let her finish.

'I'll feed him and will clean his shit myself!' He shouted, his voice brooking no contradiction.

I ran out into the corridor.

The Chief was standing outside his office, ruffled, his eyes flashing. In his arms there lay an idle bag of Persian fur – Omar Khayyam.

'Let me at least take out the *aloe vera* plant from your office then,' Atali said. 'Cats like to chew them.'

'Let him chew it,' the Chief muttered. He glanced around sullenly at the gathering in the corridor and then slammed his door.

'Cats need to relax as well!' His voice came through the office door.

'Who has depression?' the policeman on duty asked. His question was interrupted by the phone ringing in his booth. He rushed to answer it, the black thread of depression trailing behind him.

'Go back to work. Disperse,' Atali ordered.

Atali did not direct the command at me; she smiled at me pleasantly as if I was mentally deficient.

I had no idea how I had managed to get into Atali's good books; she was renowned for being cold and for being diffi-cult to understand. It was probably better not to know, as the fruit of the tree of knowledge has the bitter taste of quinine, and if you use it treat mental illness, you need to be careful not to overdose, as not only will you not learn anything, but it might well kill you.

You could also die from the fragrance of the fruit of the wild apple tree that wafted in through the open window of the clinic, fanned in perhaps from the stirred memory, rather than from the street outside. The window pane and the sills were no longer covered with the warm May dust, but instead with pattern of pink spots left on your skin by blooming nettles, which resembled the multiple spots of blood lesions that appear when the chest or stomach is fatally compressed.

You, blossom of the wild apple tree, tool of violence, my hair is full of your alkaline poison.

The boring, doddering Professor Axe was delivering a lecture on Cesare Lombroso's theory of atavism.

'A crime, my dear friends, is a natural and unavoidable phenomenon, like birth, death or mental illness. A criminal can't be fixed, they must either be destroyed or isolated from society. A born criminal's atavistic features manifest themselves not only in their behaviour, but also in their bodily characteris-tics: the shape of the skull, the length of their arms, their hairi-ness. By these traits it is possible even to tell what crime they are going to commit – whether they will kill or rape or steal . . .'

The shape of the skull of the boy sitting in front of me definitely wasn't perfect and his ears stuck out, further accentuating this fact. Might he be a spy in the future? Or a traitor to his country? He bent forward, zealously noting down the professor's speech and the theories that promised his imperfect skull some future misfortunes.

And should I go for a date with the man who had approached me in the park the day before? His watch strap shone like new hand cuffs on his hairy arm, he wore a golden necklace on his chest – I was tempted to take him for a walk, together with a barrel organ and a hat for collecting money.

He was of such an atavistic type, that it was better not to take the risk; if I was the victim of an orangutan, like in the famous Edgar Allan Poe short story, nobody would go looking for that killer animal. Even Professor Axe was elegantly crushing Lombroso's theory with the latest social and criminal data and finally he slammed his lecture note-book onto the stand so that the whole audience froze. It's only possible to generate that kind of silence when the severed head rolls.

I leant on my arms and nearly started crying. It was pouring outside; grey streams ran into the pavement cracks, channelling them deeper – as pitiless and inevitable as tooth plaque.

'Well, what are you so sad about?' Atali said. 'What's torturing you?'

It must be premenstrual syndrome, Atali. Or possibly just existential horror. Anyone can suffer from the latter, while only women suffer the former. And women, as you know, are not people.

Anyway, I was not entirely sure my symptoms weren't accompanied by aural hallucinations: a barely audible Arabic melody was seeping in from the corridor, a reed instrument was loudest, the singer's voice was so high my ears rang.

My patience snapping, I opened the door into the Chief's office.

It was empty apart from Omar Khayyam, who was stretched out across the desk, gazing at me with a 'Lion of the harem' eyes – as if I was one of his cats. From the tape player on the shelf, eastern melodies warbled pitifully, complaining about something.

I closed the door and tiptoed away.

The station felt almost like Istanbul.

By the end of the second year some secret societies began to appear in the faculty. Their members would wink mysteriously when passing each other, or exchange pioneer salutes (some reminiscent of the *Heil Hitler!* salutes still fresh in the memory). At times they even greeted each other with slogans: *'Long live God!'* I attempted to identify which one of them was this secret God of theirs, but was not able to.

Instead, the conspirators soon focused their attention on me. A determined dark-haired girl, who kept adjusting her glasses, approached me in an empty classroom, pressed me against the wall and shouted so loudly, that her voice echoed from the empty dome, 'Do you love Jesus?'

I grew confused. This was exactly what my grandmother had used to ask me early in my childhood; I would snap back to her, 'No, there is no God, only Lenin.'

What should I say now, when Lenin had proven to be so short lived?

The girl had possibly expected a prompt answer, so she was slightly disappointed. She gave me a leaflet, told me that the *seraphim* would save me from evil, and stamped down the stairs, like a true soldier of God.

The leaflet invited me to a 'God's Friends' meeting. Obviously, I decided to attend as I really was looking for a friend, and if not God, then at least some moderately good-looking boy.

The members of the secret society gathered in the palace of the Ministry of Internal Affairs. You could hear their hymns from a distance; only a deaf person could resist their allure, or somebody with ears glued with wax, like the sailors in The Odyssey.

A pleasant man, microphone pressed in his hand, was stirring the audiences' brains, drowned for so long in the depths of atheism. He criticised the Catholic Church, psychoanalysis and infertility treatments. When he reached a particularly intense note of criticism, the choir behind him shouted, 'Amen!'

'We are not afraid of the works of evil, we reject false science!' the preacher shouted.

'Amen!' moaned the choir.

'We need neither Jung nor Freud – they both served the Devil!' The crowd hummed with delight.

'We don't need it, away with it! Let's break their yoke!' an old woman sitting next to me screamed, her chin wobbling like jelly. 'We've had enough of suffering!'

One of the choir, having reached a state of ecstasy, slammed cymbals together. The terrible noise swallowed up the words of the preacher. My eyes fogged over. I recovered only when the worried-looking old woman prodded me.

'Listen, child,' she screamed in my ear, stinking of raw onion. 'I know what *jung* is, I can still remember! But can you tell me what this *freud* is?'

As I didn't answer, struck dumb by the deafening noise (a laying on of the hands for healing had started, they fell down as if they were being cut off at the knees!), the woman continued, 'Is it something that you shove between a horse's teeth?'

I grew dizzy.

In order to stay on my feet and not join the heaps of unconscious bodies on the floor, I crept out, holding on to the wall.

A young man stopped me by the entrance, offering a bible printed in Denmark, for a hundred roubles; it was in Russian, printed on transparent paper.

'So why here, on the front page, is it written *Not for sale*?' I asked pointing at the text. 'You can't trade God's word. You need to give it as a gift. Not that I would thank you for it anyway.'

'So what are you saying? That God's word is not dear to you?' The young man ruffled like a rooster, offended.

'It's dear, my friend, very dear,' I mumbled, reaching for the door handle. 'But I won't have any food for a week.'

The young man shouted something (probably, 'Infidel! You should be burnt!') but his voice was swallowed by the heavy door, and early spring twilight descended upon me as gently and carefully as the handkerchief of a sexual pervert.

When they graduated, the members of these secret societies would only be able to find work that suited them in the prosecutor's office – nowhere else would they be able to condemn the devil and his deeds with such fierceness and ferocity. They would even condemn the judges to hell fire if they dared doubt that their holy righteousness corresponded to the spirit of objectivity.

The most important thing is to condemn the worst and most wicked shortcomings and weaknesses of man, while the person, who is but the tool of his shortcomings, can get on as he wishes.

Some writer must have said that!

'Listen, Atali, is there anything new in those labyrinths of yours?' I pointed at the ruffled ribbons of fax paper.

Atali shook her head silently.

'And have you disseminated the victim's photo to the public? It's impossible that such a young girl was totally anonymous; she seems to be from a decent home. We should also try boarding schools, special schools . . .'

Atali shook her head again.

'I'm very sorry,' she said, looking at me forlornly. 'Very sorry. By the way, will you request an additional forensic report?'

I considered.

The forensics expert seemed to have done everything; he had added so many hypotheses with his conclusions that it read more like a novel than an official report.

'Won't you order a toxicology report?' asked Atali.

'Probably not . . .' I murmured.

'You should,' she objected gently.

Our eyes met. Mine, surprised. Atali's, severe, with gleaming, boiling steel lights glimmering in their depths.

'Well, as you wish.' Atali lowered her eyes and nervously pushed her papers together. 'If there should be the need you can always exhume the corpse. And so, if all the reports are concluded . . . Will you give the instructions to allow the burial of the corpse?'

'I can, but who will cover the funeral expenses?'

'A local businessman has offered; the owner of the furniture salon.'

'Really?' I was surprised.

'The story reminded him so much of a soap opera that he just had watched. He paid for a mass to be said, though the priest was initially sniffy about the idea – he wouldn't pray for suicides. Why he thought it was a suicide, I don't understand. He was presented with several different versions of what could have happened.'

'Society chooses the most pleasant.' I sighed. 'By the way, I suppose they didn't dare order a gravestone?'

'They ordered it,' said Atali, pleased. 'It's not expensive, but it's stylish. They showed the drawings. An angel, wings pressed tightly together, on a dark stone. Its shape slightly resembles that of a wardrobe – well it's all a question of taste. The white text says, 'Stay in the light of the seraphim.'

'And the name?'

'They will engrave the name and the surname found in the passport on it.'

Silently, I closed the door.

The prostitute would be better off continuing to ply her trade in Germany until the end of her days, because if she decided to return home how horrible it would be to see her own grave standing there! And the owner of the furniture salon weeding it. Perhaps he had been one of her first clients?

03.12.2000

A couple, Pavel and Anastasia Burdiugin, approached the police. Pavel's father, Ephraim Burdiugin, called Grandad by everybody, had disappeared. It was very strange because Ephraim, who was ill with Alzheimer's, had never gone far from the house, fearful that if he left it empty, thieves might break in and steal his stamp collection. On the day he disappeared he had been wearing a brown fur coat fastened with a belt, felt slippers with rubber overshoes on his feet, and, because it was snowing lightly, he had taken his daughter-in-law's umbrella as well as his cap with ear tabs. Harry, a local tramp, had been the last to see him when he stopped to rummage in a container behind a shop: Old Burdiugin, Harry said, had clearly forgotten where his *chata* – his hut – was. 'But it didn't occur to him to ask me; nothing occurred to him anymore, poor fellow. Them like him should be shot to stop the suffering: theirs and others.'

The Burdiugins' nearest neighbour was an unmarried French teacher, well over seventy. They didn't get on well. Miss Koko was suspicious that the Burdiugins had poisoned her water and food: how they did it she couldn't explain. She had suggested the possibility of telepathic waves.

When questioned, she admitted she had seen old Ephraim on the day he had disappeared. Somebody had been scratching at the door; she thought it was a cat. She opened the door and nearly died of fright – in front of her an old man stood with his mouth open, a tooth sticking out; at first she thought he was going to bite her. Without even saying, 'Good afternoon', or anything (behaved just like a peasant!), he merely mumbled in Russian, 'Does Pashka live around here?' Miss Koko snapped back at him in French. Then the old man pressed his lips together, hiding his tooth away and furrowed his eyebrows, and then Miss Koko realised she was in danger. She grabbed a plank from a corner of the porch and hit him on his head.

What had happened next, Miss Koko had no interest in. The most important thing was that she had protected her honour and dignity. She admitted that later she couldn't find the plank anywhere.

It was a hopeless case; nobody else had seen or heard about *Grandad* after that. Sometime later, a decayed corpse was found in a drainage ditch close by. The osteological expert identified it as the body of a significantly younger man, most probably that of some homeless person. Before the experts had even started their examination of the corpse, the Burdiugins protested that they weren't inter-ested in the unidentifiable mincemeat that had been found. 'Give us our Grandad.' He would have to be freshly dead and well preserved in order for them to be fully certain. 'God forbid, we should end up burying a stranger's bones! Have you got any idea how much funerals cost these days? To say nothing of dinner and a mass? And what if, then, after the funeral, right during the dinner, when we're no longer mourning, Grandad should ring the doorbell alive and in one piece?'

Where are you wandering, *Grandad*? Have you been struck dead by a blow from a birch plank? Are you alive? Or are you already a spirit, which your kin will repudiate, beating their chests?

The rain didn't stop and neither did the Oriental music. I felt so depressed that I told Atali I was going home. I wasn't feeling good, I said, she should call me if anything came up.

Atali nodded sympathetically and advised me to take some aspirin.

I fed Yin Yang, covered myself with a quilt feeling like a withered damask rose, and, suffocated by my own poisonous smell, fell asleep.

Professor Axe coiled a 'fail' in my study book with relish; he took so long I managed to turn grey with horror.

When I asked why, the professor snapped that my ears were like those of a lynx, and he couldn't give a good mark to a student with atavistic features.

I realised, then, that an erroneous theory had established itself in the world and I had no other choice than to place my head upon the block, bare my neck and wait obediently for the professor's heavy register with its metal bound corners, shiny as the blade of a guillotine, to descend upon me.

V

The teacher was smoking a cigarette, his back towards me. The wind, sounding like the wheeze of unhealthy lungs, flung grey cinnamon-scented ash into my face. Perhaps it was not cigarette ash, but that from a rather large burning banknote blowing in the wind! How silly. You could have bought me a present; some jewellery. You never gave me any.

'Okay.' The teacher turned towards me. In his hand he was holding a large stone with soil on the bottom, roots of couch grass dangling from it. 'Take it.' He placed it on my chest. It was the biggest diamond in the world.

I jumped up in a sweat. With a soft bump, Yin Yang fell from my chest. She mewed, offended.

I was disgusted. Next time she would sleep on my face. No wonder they used to hang them in the Middle Ages. They are truly animals of the night; stone statues at the entrance to the cemetery, your escort to the Kingdom of Death. I remembered an old, long forgotten case of the death of a solitary artist in mysterious circumstances; when he was found he already smelled, surrounded by hungry, screaming cats. The old man's face had been chewed – by rats or cats it was never ascertained.

Yin Yang sometimes bit my nose – only its tiny head knows whether it was affectionate or not.

I imagined myself without a nose – the remains of my sleepiness vanished.

I glanced at the clock – it was one-thirty. The hour of ghosts, as Remarque wrote. The curtains were tightly drawn; if somebody knocked at the window I wouldn't look, as I was sure it would be the old man with his chewed nose, come to unravel his secrets *post mortem*.

But nobody cares who chewed his nose – not whether it was the rats, the cats or the town's female pensioners.

I made some chamomile tea and found some dried up marzipan cake in the drawer. One fat tabloid writer said once that nothing chases away ghosts better than eating.

I had just managed to take a bite when somebody knocked on the window.

Here we go! Would it be the old man then? Hopefully he wouldn't be able to squeeze himself through the air vent?

I opened the curtain a fraction. On the street, in the shadow of the switched off street lamp, lit only by a grey fissure in the night sky, a postman stood, wearing his uniform hat and carrying a bulging bag, his black eye sockets staring at me. Without a word, he pulled out five grey envelopes, and placed them on the windowsill. I noticed his dry, withered hand, which looked like a map coloured by uneven spots. Then, possibly seeing the curtain move, he disappeared suddenly, before I could open my mouth.

I ran outside in my pyjamas and took those five grey missives from the other world.

'Dear Eliza! You are already seventeen but still so naïve. Don't you think that your childhood has dragged on for too long? But I like it. I wish you could stay like this for ever.'

'Eliza, your nipples look like small blue glaciers. When they melt in my mouth, Spring will enter your body and horror will mingle with happiness.'

'Eliza, just listen to how I improvise on Beethoven's sonata! Isn't it a miracle? How quickly my fingers run along the black and white keys of the grand piano and how lustfully it sighs when touched so gently . . .'

'Eliza, Eliza, don't fret and shout that it's better to die. It's never better to die, it's always better to live.'

'Eliza? Do you hear me? You clothed yourself in wreaths and fake marigolds to stop me from touching your body, a fresh instrument of spring flowers and fresh wood? But I so yearn to play you! This desire is stronger than anything else – I will recreate you.'

I stood with the teacher before a dark mirror. I saw my pure, scared eyes and my hair scattered across my shoulders and his hands, holding me from behind and his elegant fingers, the nails of which shone in the blue moonlight like sharp diamonds perfect for cutting glass. The teacher exhaled onto the back of my neck, his breath like light wind stirring my hair, it fluttered in the space of the mirror, grey and soft foggy strands that prevented me from seeing anything behind me, just his hands and a soft girlish face which didn't belong to me . . . What was my name? The name would explain everything. Tell me my name.

But the hands just squeezed my stomach. I felt the sharp blue nails digging in. I screamed wildly and woke up.

The cat, scared by the scream, rolled off the bed.

'Was it you scratching me, you son of a whore?' I said, breathless.

The cat mewed.

The alarm clock buzzed in agreement.

I would have to forgo the morning coffee, my heart was so jumpy, it felt like it was going to jump out of my throat.

I would drink cold chamomile tea instead, and that bone-hard marzipan cake will go back in the drawer. Some writers have no idea about ghosts.

I pulled a red synthetic jumper over my pyjamas, glanced sleepily at the lipstick, waved my hand and left.

Atali, who wore flared trousers and a jumper which dangled down to her knees, looked tidy and pale, as if washed in acid rain. She smiled and said, 'Good morning. That jumper suits you very nicely.'

'Really?' I said dubiously. I glanced in the glass of the duty-policeman's booth but could only see the rotas stuck to it. Well, if I looked all up and down like those graphs . . .

'Coffee?' Atali said, knowingly.

I pressed my hand to my head. It had stopped beating wildly.

Instead, a nervous tick in my eye had started twitching. On my chair stood an ugly, leafy plant, in full, dirty blossom, the colour of wax. It stank unpleasantly. Black henbane, the guide informed me. Otherwise called stinking nightshade. It had strong alkaloids – hyoscyamine, scopolamine, tropane. The raw materials have to be collected wearing gloves and protective glasses.

I took out a glove from my work case, took the henbane with two fingers and was about to throw it out, but for some reason and against my will, I stuffed it into the drawer. Perhaps the steaming stink had already affected my psyche. I hoped I wouldn't start seeing UFOs and little green men! It would offend the Americans – you see, only big nations are allowed to communicate with other civilisations. The small ones have to make do with their own little devils.

I slumped onto the chair and wiped the sweat from my face.

Atali had better be quick with that coffee.

Only somebody with a distorted imagination could think of spending their summer holidays at the school hostel. And that was me. I didn't wish to return either to my father's farm or back to the town where I had finished my secondary school. 'Haven't you got some cosy and peaceful Arcadia to go back to?' My roommate, a plump, posh girl, was surprised. 'Why ever not?'

I told her that before leaving, I had experienced an unhappy love affair in that blessed Arcadia. If I returned there for a holiday, it would remind me of Him and my suffering would be renewed.

My roommate's eyes widened; I had obviously convinced her.

The next summer I didn't want to go back either. Irma, the placid dove, found me a farm near Vilnius where I could stay in return for some work; I would have to pick gooseberries, to weed rows of fruit and so on. For that I was allowed to stay the whole summer and even use the food supplies there.

That's where Arcadia is, my dear Irma – where the sun rise is met by the lively, unobtrusive noise of nature, not the dead silence which strangles any kind of life as late as midday, when Magde gets up to cure her hangover and pulls my father moaning from his bed. His stomach pains have probably returned again. Bent double he plods outside, squats on the stone among high weeds, the yellow top of his head shining with the greenish patina of *Artemisia absinthium* and his teeth grinding. He quietens down only when Magde rides through the uncultivated wilderness like some kind of Trojan horse, covered with burs, her breasts full of seeds, thorns finding their way into the reed-like thicket beneath her large belly, which looks like it has been trampled by wild boars, and the just cooled trace of semen slithers down her thick thighs like new-born tiny snakes, drying there, failing to reach her cracked heels.

The owners of the farm were an arty type. I found an easel in the attic, paint and an unfinished canvas. In the living room there was a reproduction of Van Gogh's self-portrait. Even the kitchen utensils were artily scattered around. But while I was there, art would have to give place to discipline – even Van Gogh. I wouldn't stand anybody looking at me through twisted, uneven eyes. And if the sullen yellow face started to annoy me, I would pick some dill and hang it to dry right in front of the self-portrait.

The feeling of having a home was akin to religious ecstasy. Home is a god which listens to you loyally and never leaves you, even if you swear and blaspheme and renounce it three times.

For some reason I felt that the farm, surrounded by its silent zone, might suddenly disappear and leave me on my own. So, in order not to be left with nothing, I erected a shed at the bottom of the garden using old planks. I would sit there in the evenings, listening to the way the dark garden rustled above the holed roof. If I stayed there for too long, the black humming would turn into the powerful rush of a waterfall; the shed wouldn't survive it. I would crawl out on all fours and go running towards the house which waited for me, its door open, my salvation.

One midday in July, while I was lying in the garden, stuffing myself with cherries and reading Flaubert, I heard the hum of a distant car engine. The sound was so unusual to the ear that my mouth hung open for a moment. When the car stopped by the fence, with a choke, and died with a sneeze, I was already on my feet, my cherries and the Flaubert in the nettles.

The gates clanged.

'Hi!' The shout in English bumped awkwardly against the heavy, sleepy silence of the garden.

I would have to explain to the silly foreigner that he had lost his way.

'Hello,' I said in Lithuanian. The foreigner looked at me, surprised. He was tall and slim, with hair down to his shoulders and hands in his pockets. Only a green frockcoat and yellow gloves were missing – he would have been the spitting image of Rodolphe Boulanger, Madame Bovary's lover.

'The owners won't be back until the 20th of August,' I said, in a rather hostile mood. I wanted to get back to the cherries and Flaubert and Emma, who was in the process of poisoning herself with arsenic. 'They've gone to the sea side.'

'And who are you, nature-child?' He measured me with his eyes and smiled. Perhaps my proportions were not right.

'I am not a nature child.'

Mister Boulanger guffawed, ran his fingers through his hair, pushing it back, then said, in a relaxed manner, 'Well I travelled so far and all for nothing. You could at least give me some water, because if I die of thirst . . .' He fixed his gaze on me. 'If I die you'll be eaten alive by your conscience.'

'I will not,' I snapped back. The nineteenth century toff had grown annoying. 'My conscience won't eat me up. The police will take you to the morgue and pop you in a fridge where you will lie pleasantly until the post-mortem is performed and the non-violent cause of your death is identified. And then you will be able to fully enjoy the multitudinous tears of your relatives.'

The toff was lost for words. He cleared his throat, ran his hand through his hair again, this time brushing it down onto his jutting collar bones, and said, his tone serious now, 'Hmm . . . Aren't you Themis' servant?'

'No,' I snapped. 'The servant of nation, honour and conscience.'

'Good gracious,' Madame Bovary's lover sighed sadly. 'Doesn't it amount to the same thing?'

I didn't reply. Then the toff apologised and introduced himself, scotching my notion of him being the ghost from Flaubert's novel. No, he was an old friend of the owners, a reliable person, a poet. 'Please, forgive me for disturbing you. I'm going back to town.'

'Wait!' For some reason the cherries did not seem so attractive now. And besides, wouldn't the owners be angry about the manner in which I had greeted their old and reliable friend? 'I'll get you some water. Also, I'll put the kettle on and make some green tea, with big leaves.'

The poet, who was about to turn back through the gates, stopped.

'It's very useful if in your blood there's too much . . .' I stopped, confused, but the poet wasn't embarrassed and completed my sentence.

'Too much cholesterol? Oh yes, I have a terrible amount of cholesterol. More than blood.'

The tea drinking lasted a long while. When the bow-legged, tipsy shadows crept in from the depths of the garden, the jokes were not so funny and the soaked tea leaves had acquired the chill of a deep ditch.

'I made a bed for you in the living room, under Van Gogh. If he bothers you . . .'

'Who?' the poet interrupted. 'Van Gogh?'

I didn't answer.

'He won't bother me, he won't,' he assured me and stroked my shoulder. The hand lingered there a fraction longer than appropriate. 'I'm used to lunatics. I'm probably one myself.'

The green tea leaves, divided into trapezoids by their dark veins, faded slowly, losing their rich colour, sinking slowly to the bottom.

Instinct's bright lantern defined the edges of confusing shapes. The full moon was like a blue x-ray shining through the visitor as he crept across the creaking floor boards, his ribs sparkling with the electricity of the other world. Nameless bones. Elbows. The fifth vertebrae of the spine and ribs. Cool finger bones descended to close my eyes and bright eye sockets bent so close I could see through my closed lids the seams in the artificial skull sparkling with an artificial fire.

The yellow enamel of teeth crumbled on my lips, dry splints of bones stuck into my heart. I curled into a ball but the visitor didn't like the pose; he might break a bone not secured by cartilage or muscle. Angrily, sockets flashing, he told me to stretch out like a Prussian soldier in the line and slowly, in the light of blue x-ray, he counted my ribs, starting from the top.

In the morning my guest was gone. Under the teacup there lay a note with a poem. We were two leaves from the same tea bush, with dark veins and irregular, fading faces . . .

When I returned to the hostel in the autumn, I hung a picture of a human skeleton on the wall, having coloured it in bright blue. Irma, above whose head board Harrison Ford was pinned, turned her nose up, but she had no idea that the skeleton, with its chilling, bright, immortal flame was probably the best way to define what we call art, imagination, inspiration and also helplessness. Thank God that the violent art had left only a poem as evidence of forced entry. So broken, not flowering, it would never ever enter the history of literature – the irregularity of tea leaves is really nothing in the course of history when compared to the breakdown of the government and the destruction of the homeland. Though they all have the same ontological value.

Stinking nightshade, henbane, how blue the moon that shines above the heath where you grow! And how terrible is the scream of a creeping admirer when he pierces his bare foot on a rusty nail sticking out from a rotten picture frame.

*   *   *

Oh merciful God! Nutcracker replied!

'Dear colleague,' Nutcracker wrote, in a dry official tone, possibly attempting to tame his reinvigorated feelings. 'Your message was quite unexpected. Remembering your zealousness . . .' (What did he have in mind? Time must have warped my image in his memory!) ' . . .and promising work . . .' (He must have remembered that I failed the history of law exam.) 'I am sending confidential information which I managed to acquire. I don't fully understand why you might need it. Could you please delete and destroy it. Good luck in your job. I am attaching my wife's picture.'

A polite request not to approach him with an erotic subtext.

I examined the photo. Nutcracker's bespectacled wife seemed like a pleasant looking rabbit.

'I won't approach you, I won't.' I sighed looking through Nutcracker's information. 'I wish you happiness, Sir Bertillon, and your dark wife, Miss Amelia; God save you from drowning among the cards of the database.'

Aha . . . What did we have here?

'Strictly confidential. Agent Allegro. 1985.'

God!

Fingers suspended above the computer keyboard touched other keys, unevenly placed, and a ghostly whale song swam through the air, ruptured, trembling with pauses and mistakes.

That's what he lacked – a uniform. And I had thought it was human warmth!

Biographical facts . . . Place of birth . . . Year . . . Attended music school, piano class . . . I knew this. He was very close to his cousin, though there was no information confirming inappropriate relations. He was not under suspicion following the strange and premature death of his cousin. His studies at the conservatory – had not been completed. He had special training in Moscow. He lived for some time in Belorussia SSR, Vitebsk region, the town of Novolopock. Not married. Dutiful, intelligent, good self-control. Good physical shape. Took part in operations . . .'

I ran my eyes across the coded titles, stopping at the last few lines.

'We hold no information regarding his current activities. P.S. Dactyloscopic prints match. That's all.'

Before deleting the information I glanced once more at the stern eyes below the military cap. How could he have put up with the 'pranks' during rehearsals? The smudged ink on the manuscript sheets, the horns drawn on Mozart. Such a gaze would forgive nothing.

I went out into the corridor.

All was quiet and empty. Even the policeman on duty looked unreal, though he was reading a newspaper.

I paused at the Chief's door not daring to knock. The scenario which I now considered the most plausible, seemed more suitable for a psychoanalysis session or a screen play rather than the case, though it was as true as sharp glass cutting through the soft pads of the fingers, eyeballs stretched, irises wide with terror, penetrating deeply, down to the blue bone – only the bone could halt the glass blade. Such truth should not be revealed to anybody. Particularly to the justice system; it was not the business of the justice system. It was mine! And I would be guided by my memory.

The Chief, stroking Omar Khayyam, agreed that the case had hit a wall. The girl had not been identified, the suspect was no more than a ghost, and anyway, was there one at all? The conclusions of the forensics expert allowed us to conclude that the girl had died from heart failure. He called the other small discrepancies merely literary and made the decision that the girl should be buried.

I waded through wet foliage to the lake, sat on the bench and for five minutes observed how the spherical-shaped mist lifted from the surface of the water and swam to suffocate its victims. Though in official protocols it was written that M. died by poisoning himself with oil diluent, and R. had suffered paralysis of the nervous system, there would always be things that couldn't be made to fit, because they didn't belong either in the arena of common sense, or to anybody or anything at all.

The August night engulfed the farm, a shadowy nutshell among the stars, the velvet threads of darkness connecting all, like ocean waves. The wide eyes of the deer see the glistening. The soft noses of roe-deer sniff at it carefully and God's world fades out along with the nine tines of the deer's antlers, a sparkling wreath – deep into a time-free abyss.

The shadow of the drying dill which hung from the ceiling fell, like Morpheus' deformed fingers, across the eyes of Van Gogh who never slept. When the candle gutted and scaly midnight rustled through the darkness, there came from the thicket of cherry trees down by the side of the river, a sad, dying scream.

I plucked up the courage to go outside only at dawn. The heavy tops of the apple trees swam in the fog. An apple bumped somewhere in the depths. In the place where the painful scream had sounded, a red sun was now rising.

I wrapped my shirt more tightly around my chest and ran back inside, shaking with cold. The previous night's scream reminded me that I shouldn't grow too close to this home; it might sink into the depths my memory for ever and only my hands would remember the nice things about it.

Between the second and third cup of coffee, when the sleepiness had started to retreat, the last snatch of my dream flashed by; a three-year-old child stuck its fair head through the gap in the door and with otherworldly, dream-like eyes, pierced my soul, its gaze-blade severing the physical layers, even those fragile ties which connected my non-bodily desires and my dreams. It penetrated deep, searching for the clear, shining and unbreakable blue diamond-like core.

I ran out of the office and bumped into Arnold. He was carrying a heavy plastic bag double-knotted at the top.

'What have you got?' I asked, a strange feeling coming over me; it looked like the senior policeman had double-tied my dream and was going to dump it into the container, where the homeless, black as birds of doom, would attack it and tear it to pieces.

Arnold looked embarrassed. He hid the bag behind his back.

'Nothing,' he muttered.

I sniffed.

'It stinks!'

Arnold, hypnotized by the poisonous-green suspicion streaming from my eyes, had to admit that he was carrying the contents of Omar's litter box. The Chief had asked him to dispose of it as he was busy; he had to go to the furniture store to discuss the new sofa for his office.

'I wouldn't be surprised if the sofa will be calculated into the cost of the funeral,' I mumbled and in a sour mood turned back into my office.

Atali's stern voice came through the open door. 'Please, don't bother us with such trifles . . . If you wish, you can fill out a complaint form, but, in my opinion, you would be better off going to the priest with this instead. A few years ago I would have sent you to the communist party committee; that was the highest spiritual institution then. Now, regrettably, that position has been filled by God. No, not the president, Madam, please don't mix them up.'

That Atali was clever. I would have said the same.

10.06.2000

Two kids, one eighteen, the other nineteen-and-a-half, legally of age, though – by their mental development – Neanderthals (not being be able to read by the age of ten), had axed an old couple for two hundred *litas*. They acted like they were gangsters from the nineteenth century, like the Stratton brothers in London – rough and unskilled. They showed no criminal knowledge or sense, as if they had never watched police films, or they had watched so many that all intuition or sign of boundaries had been erased by the one stupid and undeniable fact – that the essential element of a crime is a victim. It's the most obvious fact, everything centres on it, sound and process and time which doesn't disappear after death. The criminal and the circumstances – they are only peripheral parts of the case. That's how the newspapers portray it; and those who don't believe the newspapers – they don't believe anything.

An empty can of sardines lay on the ground next to the well. Nobody would pour milk for the tabby cat any more and the jasmine, blooming crazily, weighed down by the curd of white blossom, didn't change colour even after the tragedy. Nature is the most impartial judge; it will place the criminal's bones next to the victim's, the rotting conscience and scattered memory will mix with the dreams of the roots swelling in the earth, with the rain and the clouds, not singling out anything and not granting too much priority to anything.

Roman law had decided that the most important thing is the cause of the crime – spoil, money. Everything seems clear, except that the money for which the killings occurred becomes immaterial and drops into the devil's purse. How rich the Devil's kingdom is and how poor God's!

Perhaps that's why the woman left, having announced that she would go to the president, not God.

'We respect your decision,' Atali said, seeing her off, 'Do as your conscience suggests.' But the conscience is not always the best advisor either. Atali forgot to add that. Never mind. When a person listens to the voice of the heart it's even worse.

A paedophile once asserted that he had been directed by a voice in his heart. Perhaps it's not just the brain that gets located in places unsuitable for them. Old Darwin failed to notice that and put Homo sapiens at the top of the evolution ladder; personally, I prefer amoebas, paramecium, infusoria – they don't even have a heart.

'I put some brandy in your coffee.' Atali placed the cup on top of the petal that had fallen from the sweet brier. For some reason she blushed and adjusted her hair that was neatly plaited into a ship's rope.

'Excellent. That's exactly what I needed.' I cheered up immediately.

'Remember, tomorrow is the funeral of our victim,' Atali reminded me and left.

Our victim? I nearly choked on the coffee. It sounded as if the whole station had made a novitiate of the poor drowned creature. The pathologist was particularly guilty, having enthusiastically shown off his use of the scalpels, pincers and saws. He should get the harshest punishment – he should be forced to marry his half-brained lab assistant, so that rather than murmured endearments he would have to listen to hymns of praise to the golden staphylococcus which does such terrible deeds in the human body. Acne is nothing compared to the infection you get squeezing it, that is a whole different story – you'll end up in a wheelchair and curse the day and hour you plucked up the courage to get married.

A child's cry came from the corridor.

In the evening twilight, a fair-haired boy stood in the corner leaning against the fire extinguisher on the dirty green wall, lonely and wraithlike. He seemed to be wiping away a

tear. I couldn't make much out as the light from the policeman's booth didn't reach him, in the same way that the tiny
bathyscaphe cannot illuminate the ocean's deepest secrets,
which avoid its bright beam in the deep darkness.

How could I communicate with the apparition? Maybe I,
too, should break down in tears? Would my tears explain
everything and plead for his forgiveness?

The Chief's door slammed. A woman with short, untidy,
peroxide curls ran out, slapped the crying boy on the cheek,
grabbed him by the hand and dragged him out, cursing. On
the way, so as not to fail rousing the policeman on duty who
was sat peacefully and comfortable, she shouted, 'You sit here
like some prosecutor! You should be out chasing killers!'

It took five minutes for the policeman to think of an
answer, but by then the woman was long gone.

'Well . . . And then who then would answer the phone?'

The Chief, holding the cat's woven basket and locking the
door with his other hand, muttered angrily to himself.

'They should sort out their insolent kids themselves . . .
They spoil them and then they do whatever they want!'

'What did he do?'

'Stole a bag of sweets!' The Chief looked at me sullenly. In
the basket, Omar Khayyam hissed like a disturbed cobra.

'So the shop assistant dragged the poor child here?'

The Chief snorted.

'The shop assistant? Of course not. His mother! She has
the principles of the devil. When she discovered that the
child couldn't be locked up, she told me – no – she ordered
me, to charge her child. Crazy woman! She would be better
off spanking him with a belt at home. She can write out a

charge sheet on his bum. Whatever she likes! You see, the police even have to spank her children.'

He slammed the outside door.

It suddenly seemed so dark and silent – Atali's room was already empty – that I sensed that beneath the brown lino-leum four huge tortoises were pushing the whole station with their wrinkled, thousand-year-old noses through the ocean depths.

I leapt through the door, but instead of being plunged into the mysteries of the deep, the phosphorous eye of the returning submersible blinded me; I tore myself away from the white-hot stream and, nearly falling over, went head first into the darkness.

In order to understand the crime, you need to get into the criminal's shoes. Am I a criminal? Or perhaps I was once? The passing of time blunts the teeth of the crime, but the breath of an animal is terrifying even if it comes from a toothless mouth.

An empty nutshell sailed on waves of wine.

The knob on the gate squealed, touched by an impatient finger, but nobody came out from the cemetery. Only a gust of wind blew like a sigh, but a sigh that had been unrecog-nisably altered by the uneven layers of the soil, by the choco-late coloured turf, the grey silt and the lime-coloured sand, the sedge planted on the graves, reminiscent of narrow bladed knives. The sigh escaped not from yellowing teeth and crumbling neck vertebrae, it was the soul, the death robe of the rotting bones that sighed.

It wasn't just hopeless, but also senseless to attempt to find Eliza's grave there. She hadn't fought for the Soviet homeland

and had not been buried under a five-cornered star accompanied by a parade. But anything can be moved through time and space. And so that green knoll by the gate did not belong to anybody any more. Memory will supply the names.

Memory is my home.

My whole life I have been a guest here with not enough time to get close to things. To acquire a home, you need infinite, endless time, when every detail opens out as a separate universe. My grandmother, who died soon after my mother, had a large grandfather clock; behind the yellow glass its wheels turned calmly and undisturbed. Time was kept safe, surrounded by airless space. It seemed impossible that it should stop working. But everything that seemed impossible began when my father threw the broken clock into the chicken-den-turned-rubbish-heap. It seemed too expensive to fix and the idea that it might be a memento of grandma never occurred to him. As an old Marxist, he probably felt that a person should be remembered by their deeds, not their possessions. And as everything was back-to-front in his life, he forgot Marxism as well. The same fate awaits any ideology not present in every step of life, even when urinating (which is, in fact, a very important moment for remembering).

Nobody touched me in the dark corridor, or sniffed at my feet. She was probably asleep, inside the box of bed linen.

'Kitty, kitty! Come here, I'll give you some cat food.'

The cat didn't reply.

And again, the same distorted sigh filled the room, causing goose bumps to rise on my skin, and ruffling my hair and the curtains.

She had probably gone out through the window. What for? Why? She wasn't in heat, and, anyway, Yin Yang had been neutered.

I ran outside.

There was not a soul to be seen, only a late jackdaw by the hedge. No, not a jackdaw, it was silver haired Atali, eyes full of longing, gazing up at my windows. I was about to invite her in for a cup of tea, but she avoided me awkwardly and ran away.

And so the street was completely empty. On the roof two infatuated leaves fluttered, clinging to each other, rustling gently, singing about the horror of approaching death, comparing it to soft white bedding where they would sleep happily.

VI

All around, as far as you could see, was a wide expanse of water. The softly glistening sludge on the surface hid the dark frightening depths, like the fur of an exotic animal. If I fell in, I wouldn't know what to do; I'm not a water bird!

I closed my eyes and allowed myself to be carried by the anti-gravitational force of the dream.

When I opened my eyes, the antigravitational field was no longer there, but the dream was still present. I sat at the desk with the pungent taste of sludge in my mouth, bent into a hunch like a wounded Neanderthal child. I saw, as if from a distance, the child crawling towards the bed, leaving behind wet fish-amphibian traces. Climbing onto the bed, the child grabbed the dangling under-sheet with claw-like hands and feet, screeching like a buzzard; and only then, when the weariness of the dream had penetrated muscles and tendons and bones did it start to breathe like a normal human being – or to be more exact, like a woman.

The alarm clock began to ring. I pressed the button angrily and lay there for a long time unhappy about the shapes that came to life only in lost dreams. Reality is dull and linear, with the possibility of reincarnation removed; if only I could become a conscious Jasmine blossom, then I wouldn't need to search for evidence or witnesses, to say nothing of criminals.

Feeling under the bed for my slippers, I glanced at the wall and shuddered. The candidate's gaze had grown severe, bristling with the cruelty of prehistoric times, the time of the sabre-toothed tiger, fangs sticking from his mouth which just a moment before had smiled at me innocently. The somnolent state is prone to such changes. Unfortunately it's not contagious. A somnolent MP is, in any case, more pleasant than a Social Democrat, as he is governed more by instinct rather than party interest.

In a vague hope that Yin Yang had returned and would be sitting outside the front door, I stuck my nose outside.

Nothing. Not even dirty foot marks on the steps. There was nobody but a man in jodhpurs, pedalling a bike onto which a tin container was fastened by a rope. He didn't even turn his head towards me. Women in knickers obviously no longer surprised him, and surprise is the driving force of life and philosophy.

As we were going to bury our victim that afternoon, it seemed sensible to dress modestly, while at the same time in an unusual way; funeral fashion is a kind of cultural event, especially in the provinces. A black leather skirt would do, with boots and a military-styled jacket. It's a pity a gun isn't counted as an accessory or jewellery; it would have looked good tucked in my belt.

Having locked the door, I unlocked it again, stuck my head inside and quickly scanned the corridor. The cat hadn't turned up. The furniture regarded me in speechless surprise and the bright yellow autumnal sun slid softly towards me across the slippery kitchen floor.

I closed the door and strode along the pavement, cursing and trying not to think what the sun would do when it reached the thick black door.

In the detention cell, which was usually a harmonious and quiet place, passions were boiling and meaty curses flew in all directions.

'Two drunk prostitutes,' the policeman on duty reported. 'They were brought in in the early hours from a farm on the outskirts. They bit the client. Both of them.'

'Hey, mummy,' a voice called through the bars. 'You look good! Let's go to the bus station!'

'Shut up, you maggots!' the policeman on duty shouted. 'You watch; I'll fine you for insulting the officer!'

'Listen to him!' the prostitute sneered. 'It's a compliment, not an insult!'

'You go fine yourself!' shouted a well smoked bass. 'You ain't no eagle, and we ain't no maggots!'

The duty policeman blushed and raised his magazine to hide his face.

No longer listening to the prostitutes' complaints, I hurried along the corridor, called, 'Hello,' to Atali, asked for a coffee and closed myself in my office.

On the desk, instead of Yin Yang, who I had vaguely hoped to see there, stood a plant, somewhat similar to dog-fennel, with bright yellow petals, gathered into a whisk.

'Aha!' I shouted victoriously. 'This one I know! Common tansy!'

I smelled it. It smelled peculiar; its odour was of both preserved innocence and stiffened death robes. A very suitable flower for a spinster biology teacher.

Atali brought in some coffee. She looked slightly embarrassed.

'What's the matter, Atali?'

Atali bit her dry lips.

'One of the prostitutes is going crazy. She wants to talk to you . . . But you're within your rights not to agree. The girl is drunk and mad.'

'What does she want? To give away the pimp? To list her clients? We don't punish the clients and there aren't so many pimps; local girls are pretty self-motivated.'

Atali fixed her eyes on me. In the dim grey surface I saw the inhuman reflection of my image.

'She said she needed to lighten her conscience,' she whispered.

While I was thinking how to answer, Atali, having taken the pause as the sign of agreement, disappeared. I had just finished drinking the coffee, when the witless prostitute entered, having cracked the lino in the corridor with her high heels. She sat in front of me, all pale, a stain on her jumper – vomit and perfume from the market to judge by the stink. She looked like a captive bird; each of her fingers was girdled by a ring of unclear metal, two of them studded with large empty eyes.

'So what do you have to tell the justice?' I ask coldly.

The prostitute's jaw dropped.

'Name? Surname? Age? Education? Profession?'

The questions, it seemed, failed to reach the prostitute's

brain. Her eyes, circled with black makeup, gazed dumbly at the common tansy.

I grew annoyed.

'Can you stop staring?' I said, unkindly, putting the tansy into a drawer. 'It looks like you're going to eat it. I wouldn't advise you to. Unless you have worms. Ascarids.'

'Not yet,' the girl replied, her voice gentle. 'But if I have to eat shit, as one old man threatened, anything might happen.'

'And how old are you?'

'Sixteen.'

I looked at her more closely. Familiar features flashed through a layer of powder like a peeling mural, further damaged by vodka fumes.

'You're the girl from the maize field?'

The prostitute smiled like a child that had been caught out. She didn't reply. Perhaps she thought it was some police in-joke. She looked around, heavy with premature soberness.

Oh God! This was what it meant to not solve a crime. Violence, with no big effort, had forced her to surrender to it fully.

Or, possibly she had recognised among her clients the man with the huge . . . the huge . . .

'I . . .' The maize field victim opened her mouth. 'I . . .'

A noise came from the corridor. The prostitute in the detention cell howled. The door was thrown wide open and the severe, top-knotted mother flew in like a ball of lightning. The girl, upon seeing her, grew so frightened she turned paper pale. Only the makeup under her eyes stayed black.

'You devil's spawn!' The mother grabbed the child by her chest and pulled. The jumper gave with a nasty ripping sound.

'Hold on, hold on, Citizen!' I jumped from the chair 'You can't just break in on an interrogation!'

The mother's eyes widened.

'Interrogation? What interrogation? She didn't do anything!'

I sat down. It was true, she had done nothing.

The other prostitute flew in through the door. She looked like she had escaped from hell; her tights were ripped, her hair ruffled, blueish veiny breasts stuck out of an unbuttoned blouse and on one of her full cheeks was a deep red patch.

'And what have you done?' She roared grabbing the mother by her knot. 'You, old maggot, you spat on me with acid.'

When the policeman came in with some support, it was too late. The whore had untangled the mother's head knot with her long green nails and an empty mayonnaise jar fell out. It rang sadly as it rolled beneath my desk.

It all happened so fast that the coffee grounds were still hot.

When Atali took the cup and brought back some freshly brewed coffee, the hot summer sun cast shadows in other parts of the office transforming the recent events and turning the dusty artificial sea shell on the windowsill into a large yellow ear.

And for a short time my office became a make-shift confessional. And the station itself, flooded with the sulphurous yellow of the sun, became a temple, drawing in devils and angels, where sin and forgiveness were dispensed in the form of protocol.

The colours of September were rich and cool, with a hidden sting. I would take up extra-curricular activities in the autumn in addition to my studies, so that it would not penetrate too deeply, so that the dry crackle of the morning ice would not to remind me of the puddles beneath the dark windows of the clinic, which looked like lagoons silted with leaves, so that a perilous potato-digging-sadness would not draw me down.

The previous year I had joined a choir, but I soon dropped out, as communal arts are boring. That year I developed an interest in theatre. For the audition I was told to act being a fly stuck in shit (what a perverse imagination the members of those panels have!). Surprisingly, I was accepted. Irma, who improvised being a tea pot, failed to enter into Melpomene's select circle; the audition panel members probably lost their patience waiting for Irma, puffing insipidly, to finally came to the boil.

All this was but the prelude to the same hard, painful end – the final show. It differed from the audition in that we took the part of people, not teapots. I got the role of a woman who had wandered from the path of decency. When the lover slapped me hard across the face, skilfully using the palm of his other hand so as not to hurt me, I was so ashamed that I slumped onto the stage and nearly started crying.

The ridges and gaps in the stage floor, so patient and distant, informed me more clearly than the silence in the hall, that it was not my fate to become an actress. Only a pulsing vein connected me to the stage, but no blood ran in that vein.

'Good afternoon!' the Chief said. He had put on a deep red tie especially for the funeral.

'My cat disappeared,' I told him gloomily.

The Chief flinched. 'What?' He adjusted the knot of his tie. 'How long ago?'

'Yesterday.'

'Hm . . .' The Chief looked agitated. Possibly he wished to console me, but this was such a foreign feeling for him that he just cleared his throat. Well, a discerning person might have considered this as a sign of sympathy.

'And yours?' I asked, trying to be polite. 'Is he okay?'

'He's good.' He came to life again. 'Tomorrow I'll think about taking him home. He seems to have overcome his loneliness.'

'How lucky!'

The Chief nodded.

'Wait.' His professional suspicion was suddenly aroused. 'After its disappearance, did you notice any traces of violence? Were there fingerprints? A thief? A break in? A maniac?'

'No. It ran off. Through the window. Anyway, who would steal it? It's just an ordinary cat.'

The Chief shrugged; the situation was hopeless. Though he was willing to help, there was nothing he could do about it.

'Ask Atali to bring some brandy. Not too much. The funeral is at two.'

Brandy was always the best solution when there was nowhere to go.

Through the yellow door to the other world, silky rose petals will fly and swim, carried on the back of the wind . . .

'One more,' I said to Atali.

Atali hesitated.

'I need one more wind-borne petal. One more!'

Atali looked at me carefully; the Chief must have mentioned Yin Yang disappearing. She poured me a small glass and then locked the bar decisively.

I sighed. It was in this way that, painlessly but cruelly, bones could be broken – crunch, and that was it, swim wherever you wish.

'No need to get so upset,' Atali said, critically. 'Anyway, there are too many cats in the world.'

'People too,' I snapped back. 'That's the reason I'm upset.'

'Pointless. You had better get some lunch.'

It was always a good idea to listen to Atali, if only because I had never seen her drink brandy from the station bar. I tend to believe that she was the same at nights, when everybody had left; her moral imperative wouldn't allow her, and we all know that any imperative is good.

Swaying tansies, tansies, balsamita, your blossoms are like yellow bones. Along the edge of the cemetery the woods shiver, covered with honey bees.

Oh damask rose, your petals, transparent in the midday sun, drop on my pale skin, al-Ghazali wrote. Do you not think about your dreams as if they were something constant and unchanging? When sleeping, do you ever doubt them?

Oh, river of Iran, winding through the mountains, great Orphian snake, do you have anything left of the lower tier of life, a poisonous sting? *People sleep, and when they die, they will awake!*

But it was not al-Ghazali or Averroes that walked through the town that Spring, spreading their wisdom; God's soldiers were singing hymns in the parks and the young rushed to them, especially the women, mistaking them for joyful, returning birds. I would have rushed, too, but I couldn't. Beside me was the flower of Iran, a relative of Ibn Rushd, a dark eyed Persian from Lyon, a participant of the Vilnius university theatre festival 1992. My poor French couldn't compete with the birds' song.

'*Est-ce que tu voudrais coucher avec moi?*'

Dear God, how was I supposed to reply to that?

Let it be one of the cries of spring, nature's wild tactlessness. In nature anything tactless becomes natural.

Saying goodbye to the Persian, I received a packet of disposable tissues – something you never saw in those times. If I said I placed those tissues into my copy of *The Rubaiyat of Omar Khayyam* and would open it only when seized by a feeling of religious ecstasy, I would offend religion as well as common sense. And one of the rules of common sense tells us that by using things for the wrong purpose a person loses the possibility of communicating with others. Magde, when she used my mother's faïence vase as her night pot, acquired the features of a cow, and even mooed at times. As I was afraid of cows, I talked to her in human language.

Forgive me, damask rose with the trembling pearl in your fragrant cup, I am *mandragora*, my scream cannot be heard among the *bromus, absinthium* and *wormwood*. Only the yellow skull of a gnome glimmers in the dark. Seeds with the transparent wings of a dragonfly fly by rustling drily. It's not the wind whispering, nor the bees buzzing, but you can hear teeth grinding.

What luck that I listened to Atali and had some lunch. Near the cemetery a localised tornado caught me and nearly carried me into the spiky bushes on the corner. I grabbed hold of the gates and held on, waiting until it passed, raising, as it did, dust and gravel and leaves, clinking empty bottles as it moved on its way. I stepped carefully through the old cemetery, keeping close to the mossy crosses; I might not survive a second tornado. In the shady, empty corners of the cemetery there were sometimes the remains of snacks. Usually it was smoked sausage and some muddy onion heads. You could hardly blame the dead for that; but was it a crime?

In the new part of the cemetery everything was modern, including the fashion in headstones. The best example was the grave of the local gangster who had been killed by competitors a couple of years before. It featured a human-sized figure holding a mobile phone in his hand and gazing wistfully into the distance. At his feet, looking rather like a hyena, lay a stone Pit Bull Terrier. I didn't doubt that they all were buried there – the dog, the gangster and the phone. The collective conscience is a painful thing. The only things the gangster lacked in order to be fully happy was a wife and a car. He could drive the highways in the other world, his wife looking in the mirror moaning that even there time was spoiling her beauty.

At the fence, behind a big heap of sand, a priest sang a hymn slowly. He was almost fully hidden, with only his aspergillum visible, swinging in all four directions. A drop of holy water splashed on the Chief's nose; he reddened, like his tie, and sneezed loudly, making everybody jump.

'He must be possessed by the Devil,' an old woman with a trembling head hissed.

'You're mad,' her friend snapped back. 'He's the chief of police!'

The old woman's head trembled more intensely.

'But he isn't God!' She snapped back.

The Chief sneezed once more, an ear-splitting sound. The trembling woman laughed malevolently and nudged her friend in the side.

'I would like to make a speech.' The owner of the furniture factory stepped forward. Respectfully, everyone stepped aside to let him pass.

Fat, short, with a round inexpressive face, he looked lovingly at the coffin tied with white ribbon and sighed.

'We are gathered here today to say good bye to an innocent soul, to a lily that was cut short by ruthless fate. We came here with our hearts full of noble sadness . . .'

'Nothing of the kind,' mumbled the shaky old woman. 'I came to count the wreaths.'

Her friend nudged her, but the woman, her head trembling, kept on.

'Not that many. Two wreaths, three baskets. The flowers are artificial; nobody's going to steal them.'

The noble furniture maker, after a couple of thoughtful minutes eyes cast down, continued.

'Just look at these fragile hands, her forehead, her eyes closed in eternal sleep.'

Everybody looked at the closed coffin; even the priest lifted his heels.

'Pitiless death, you severed the thick thread of life. This girl could have done a lot. Death, you have no consideration! The poet was right, saying, "How many Einsteins and Galileos sleep in the ground.'"

'One Einstein is more than enough,' the old woman croaked, her head shaking violently, moths scattering from her hat in all directions. 'And Galileo was burnt at the stake; what was so good about that?'

The furniture maker fell silent, as if he had heard this. But his sky-blue eyes were saying something else; he was simply waiting for a meaningful thought to mature.

'Rest in peace, dear child!' His voice trembled. 'Remember, there are people who will hold on to your memory in the presence of cruel forgetfulness. People . . .' He strained himself, casting a look at those around him, 'People who understand their civic duty, the importance of sympathy and who love their homeland not just with words. Dear voters . . .' the trader shouted, excited, 'life is ungrateful and hard, but I assure you I will look after you at all times! Like a father, citizens, like . . .' He was suddenly speechless, overwhelmed.

'What is he on about? Neither this nor that!' The old woman's friend was confused.

The old woman grinned merrily.

'Oh, he's a candidate for the council, my dove . . . If we elect him, he'll ensure we all have a coffin. For free.'

The furniture trader took a handful of sand and threw it into the hole. That was the signal to the grave diggers. The clods bumped angrily on the coffin lid. I felt suddenly dizzy and collapsed onto a wooden bench meant for meditation. The black shadows of old people tiptoed past, with chapel-cold breath. I just managed to note one harpy's nails clasping the handle of a mouldy handbag.

They had probably come to visit their peers, resting in the nineteenth century graves in the old cemetery.

Everybody dispersed. Even Atali disappeared into the depths of the cemetery. I hoped some rusty orthodox cross didn't grab her by her plait.

The furniture trader was the last to leave the side of the grave. It was not just that he had to pay the grave diggers, he probably wished to believe his recent declaration of love for citizenship and his homeland. But everybody had left, and there was nobody to see him. The trader squirmed as if ants had crawled into his collar. He stamped his foot and strolled elephant-heavy towards his Mercedes.

From somewhere in the deep darkness, a harpy screeched. Perhaps it was pleased with the victim that had ended in its claws, and the new cemetery – wide and green as a golf course – cowered uncomfortably. For a moment a cloud shaded the gangster's face. Neatly weeded clover bristled. It's not true that all are equal in the cemetery! The latest technologies haven't left the dead behind – just look at how backwards the dead are in the old cemetery, compared with the recently deceased! Even in the grave the old seem unimpressed by the fresh spirit of liberalism, while the newly buried shake their bones free of Social Democratic ideals – even in the other world they seem impossibly idealistic.

A gust of wind blew, the ribbons on the wreaths rustled. Then there was a quiet mewling sound.

Yin Yang was sitting next to the victim's grave, watching as wind ruffled the black ribbons on the wreaths.

I took the cat in my arms, warming its cold little feet in my palms. Where have you been, my little homeless one? Her ears pricked up like antennae, though her yellow eyes didn't look at me at all.

'Did you think that it was me that got buried here?' I pointed to the grave with my chin.

The cat tensed; its weight increased so that it felt like I was holding a boulder and I struggled to hold her. I ran, stumbling, through the gravestones and mossy hillocks. The cat jumped from my arms with a piercing meow.

'Are you possessed?' I bent to pick her up.

Yin Yang glanced at me, cold and unfriendly.

'Do you have depression, like Omar? They're not going to allow two cats in the station. *Quod licet Iovi, non licet bovi.*'

Yin Yang didn't care for Latin sayings. She lay indifferently in my arms, as if I was a stranger.

'Fine, I'll take you to the station,' I said to Yin Yang. 'Hopefully the Chief won't be there. And if he's there, he won't be able to resist feminine charms. Not mine, of course, yours.'

I tucked the cat under my coat so that my breasts looked exactly like Magde's, starting at the throat and ending at the waistline. The surprised eyes of the policeman on duty followed me as I tumbled through my office door. I placed the cat on the window sill and listened carefully.

The only sound was the monotonous chatter of the fax machine in Atali's room. There was no sound of detainees swearing, no screeching of tires, no gun shots, no phones ringing. The station floated in the twilight, blocking any signals from the outside world.

26.04.2003

The red-haired woman, as improbable as it might seem, had official connections. A small group of specialists arrived to investigate the case of the demon-builder. The group was headed by the Government Expert for the Investigation of Spiritual and Astral Phenomena. I had never heard of such a position in my life. He presented his powers of attorney to investigate the woman's complaint. He explained to the astonished station that his position was fairly new and had been created due to recent circumstances. The circumstances were such that the rational brain was no longer enough to solve the complicated problems of our times; absolute faith was also required. Both for the highest and for the lowest social classes. For the intellectuals as well as for the marginalised.

He proved his point, without doubt.

But the investigation did not proceed successfully. The builder had gone on a drinking spree; he was chasing his own demons and had no interest in those of others. Especially sexual ones. 'The one who is born to drink wouldn't . . .!' he roared in Russian at the gathered experts, throwing an empty bottle at them. As the lead investigator had no telekinetic powers, he was not able to stop the bottle mid-flight and had to address an egg size bump left on his head.

'This case has a bad aura,' he said, knocking back a brandy, while the woman wailed and replaced compresses for him.

We attempted to suggest simpler ways of solving the conflict. For instance, they could commit the builder to the regional psychiatric hospital as a danger to society. Both were offended. 'These aren't domestic issues!' the psychic medium shouted, pouring some more brandy. 'This is about clashing spirits!' He knew this, having come across it more than once in the government. Demons and spirits are clever creatures, they disguise their activities through financial machinations.

'A person must take responsibility for his actions,' I interrupted. The psychic smiled contemptuously.

'Dear lady,' he said, gazing forlornly at the empty bottle, 'Your words are a cry from the depths of prehistoric times. These days nobody takes responsibility for anything. Now the blame is either on fate, or the president, or an unlucky lottery ticket.'

'Where do demons and spirits come into it?' I asked.

'Demons and spirits, my dear lady, appear as a justification for powerlessness – so that a person is not scared among other people.'

'Aha . . . But still, I'm curious about what kind of investigation you're going to conduct. Will you need the laboratory? To use the services of the forensics expert? The card library? The files for the case?'

'You provincial criminologists will never understand our methods of investigation,' explained the lead government expert for the investigation of spiritual and astral phenomena. 'Furthermore, I'm not obliged to disclose professional secrets.' He stroked the bump on his head.

'Okay . . . Then will you use a divining rod? A crystal ball?'

The governmental connoisseur of spirits frowned in disgust. I could see in his eyes that he considered me a complete idiot. I probably am, as they left three days later, having dug through the archives and drunk half a dozen bottles of brandy and left the woman to pay the bar bill.

That bar bill was evidence, most probably, of their mysterious ways of working.

The builder had to be sent to the hospital, though not a psychiatric one. He toppled out of a first floor window, having thought he was going to the bathroom, and broke his leg.

When the woman visited him in the hospital and asked if it had been Sirens that had tricked him from the window, punishing him for having seduced a woman. The builder, sober and angry as a wasp, snapped that he had been at home not at a fire station and he had simply been going for a piss. Sometimes doors and windows swap places and that was normal. It wasn't the first time it had happened to him and he couldn't see anything supernatural about it.

My God, sometimes the stubborn stupidity of a person can be so disappointing!

*   *   *

The station felt eerie as the fax machine spluttered in the deafening silence. Everybody had left except for the policeman on duty, who had already blended into the interior. I was not sure I would be able to decode the notes sent from the institutions of the other world. Especially as the cat, who should have been lying calmly on the desk reducing my tension and stress as animal lovers claim they did, had escaped into the corridor.

The Chief's office door was locked; the key hole breathed an official cold. Atali was nowhere to be seen either, her door stood open a fraction and paper rustled in the darkness. On her desk, back to back, both cats were sitting – Yin Yang and Omar Khayyam.

A long fax roll draped onto the floor, winding around like a mummy's bandage, marked with Egyptian writing. Only the yellow cats' eyes knew what was written there.

Man is *terra incognita* to a cat, like the ancient gods to man; you never knew if he was going to adore you, to mummify you and sprinkle you with holy herbs, or to hang you for serving witches, as happened in the Middle Ages. A cat's nature likewise was double-sided. Company both for Eros and Thanatos; the herald of passion and the death instinct.

I tucked the cat under my jacket and left. The policeman on duty was dozing and didn't notice how my breasts raged and growled unhappily.

The next day was Saturday; in the afternoon I would go to the lake. I would buy a bottle of Merlot on the way. To be honest, a small bottle of brandy might have been more suitable for a cool autumnal evening. The summer had long gone. I would bid farewell to the migrating birds and to the Merlot.

On the way home I met two drunks, with a white-haired child in tow; in two years somebody would be able to take him without a problem, offering cigarettes instead of a sweet.

I carried the wild cat home only for my peace of mind; she scratched me so badly I would gladly have thrown her into a bush. At home I dropped her on the floor and left her to sit, hostile, next to the radiator.

An enemy is sometimes more eager to know what's on your mind than a friend is.

I was woken in the night by the sound of the rain. It rustled in the high trees, dripping onto soft moss that subdued the sound, ran off the angel's stiff wings, fell onto sand, leaked sadly through soil, through wood. Seeped into my nose and mouth. Somewhere beneath my ear, untroubled by the dampness, the wheels of a clock were ticking.

I closed my eyes, trying to tuck my hands into the damp sleeves of my shroud to warm them, but the rosary was in the way, binding my hands tighter than handcuffs. Something slid down my chest – perhaps the holy image had fallen out. I wanted to see what was on it, the Virgin Mary or a white sheep, but my eyes were covered by cold five cent coins. People are terrified by the eyes of a dead man, but he's simply interested in innocently looking around.

Where was I sailing in this flood? Who would open the door so that I could get warm and dry these strange clothes? Who would lend me a mirror so I could check if they suited me? Only the one who loved me.

Do you love me? Will you take me in, all wet through? Will you whisper that it's just ordinary rain, after which the earth will steam and puddles form in the pavement cracks, not some sign telling us that we will part forever.

An ordinary rain which knocks on the window pane and which a sleepy somnambulist's hand tries to wipe away.

VII

The upper layers of water were clear and warm, veiled by silver oxygen bubbles that prevented breathing. Falling face first. Then a thickening shroud closed above the head. Hands grasped at the slanting, broken rays of the sun, but they were too fragile for the black nails that stuck from hairy pink paw cushions. In the deeper layers of the water, where the sunlight was dimly blue, the nails transformed slowly into the feathers of a bird. It became more and more difficult to discern their colour. Only a creature used to the depths, whose vision had been replaced by intuition, could do so.

And when intuition dissolved too, having flashed for the last time with a black lightning and shaken off its scaly, amphibian body, I, like a blind shell, sank to the bottom and it was no longer important what kind of touch it was going to be.

I woke up to the phone ringing.

Somebody was breathing heavily into the receiver. Was it that under-aged Pocius again? Was he after telephone sex again?

'I am too old for such things,' I said sternly. 'Do you know how old I am? Thirty-three. Call your classmates instead.'

'Is that the boiler house?' The phone wheezed. 'Peter? Where?'

Then he swore and put down the receiver.

It was probably a good thing that it wasn't a secret admirer, just an alcoholic looking for Peter. At seven in the morning, it's terrible to look in the mirror; the face has the pallor of Brie and instead of eyes, two pitiless slashes.

The cat dozed near the radiator. She lifted her head and looked at me with hostility.

I put down some cat food and began to think. Could it be that she had started hating me because of this constant diet of Friskies with ersatz beef? Should I cook her some real beef? Dear God, what was beef? What did it look like?

I locked the door.

Red hawthorn berries were scattered across the grey pavement. There were black leaves from the ash trees in the gutter. And fresh dog shit. It would have been so good to lean upon summer's golden chest and breathe into its perfect ear.

It was the third summer when I finally met the owners of the farm.

Halfway through July a Merlot-red Toyota pulled up. I was in a tree picking apples and nearly fell out, blinded by the redness. I had, I imagined, just glimpsed a vision of the Antichrist.

I would have rather stayed quietly there, but the woman, seemingly used to being served within a second, and failing to see me, began calling.

'I'm here!' I shouted. 'In the apple tree!'

The woman's white, poodle head turned upwards and her purple lips twisted into a polite grimace of surprise. Then, perhaps bored, she turned away, slapping a twig against the heels of her sandals, not waiting for me to get down.

Only the last branch remained, one foot was nearly touching the ground when strong hands enclosed my waist and lifted me onto the grass. It gave me such a fright that I hid behind the trunk of the apple tree.

But the owner seemed patient, slapping a twig against his shoe (was it some kind of family tradition?), and waited for me to show myself.

'Are you able to look after a horse?' he asked immediately.

I flinched. Had he mentioned a cow, I would have replied no. But . . . Hmm . . .

'You aren't,' he stated. 'No worries, I'll teach you. Margo!' He shouted towards the bottom of the garden. 'Are you coming to the village to see the horse?'

Margo appeared from behind a raspberry bush, looking unhappy. Perhaps she had nettled herself.

'No,' she snapped, inspecting her heel. 'I'll go to town instead. I hate the countryside; nature makes me paranoid. Look, there's some dirt stuck to my heel. It must be shit, but whose?' She fixed her eyes on me suspiciously.

I blushed. Margo considered me wild, though she herself looked like an uncultivated necrophiliac. She even wasn't an artist; she knew as much about art as a pig did about clouds. The Van Gogh, tortured by insomnia, and the easel in the attic served only to liven up the interior – nothing, according to Margo, better suited the wilds of nature than art. But as she couldn't stand the wilds of art for long, she announced she was going to leave the next day. She had an appointment with her pedicurist and the editor of the magazine, 'Woman's World'. She didn't look at me once. I was as insignificant to her as the shit in the nettles. I was only glad that she didn't say to her husband, 'Take care, dear, not to touch the girl, in case you get dirty and smell.'

She even failed to enquire how her niece, Irma, was doing. I wasn't surprised; she had such an over-scheduled imagination!

The proprietor didn't find his wife's leaving difficult; he wished her a good journey and told her to come back in a week. Then he went to the village to check how Richelieu was doing, hoping he didn't limp and that the scoundrel Garsva had given him the right amount of oats and trained him daily.

And so he left, whistling carelessly, slapping a twig against his shoe having disrupted the happiness of my quiet days. How would I live with these strangers? And that Margo, for God's sake, going away, leaving her husband alone. That was, with me. What was she thinking? Nothing probably. She had no time for such thoughts; her time was consumed by periodicals and merciless pedicures.

I woke in the night in a cold sweat. I had dreamt that Margo stood at the foot of my bed, her long red nails stretching towards me, like a predator who had just extracted a sliver of live meat.

I pricked up my ears for the sad dying scream.

Nothing. Only the sound of midnight slithering through the garden, its dry scales rustling. When I got up and discovered two wide tracks in the wet grass in the direction of 'Woman's World', I immediately felt better.

Maybe they had both left?

While I was brewing tea, I heard a loud neigh from the yard. I ran out onto the steps to see a grey horse fly like a bird over the low hedge and touch the ground like in a good western film.

'That bastard Garsva,' the owner said, jumping down off the horse. 'He gave it some oats, but the vitamins meant for Richelieu went to his cows. "Horses," he said, "don't give milk, no need for vitamins then!"'

'How do you know?' I asked nervously.

'The neighbour told me, out of jealousy. He thought the horse belonged to Garsva. Thank God he didn't hurt his legs.'

'Whose? Garsva's?'

'The horse's. The horse's!' The proprietor said sternly. 'Garsva's legs are of no importance. Who would be interested in them, crooked as they are?'

Having stroked the skittish Richelieu's mane, he added, 'I'm lucky he didn't use Richelieu for ploughing his vegetable garden. I could tell from his eyes that he'd considered it. Next time I won't leave Richelieu in the village. I'll take him to a private-stables near Vilnius.'

Richelieu neighed in agreement.

I stepped backwards, frightened by his soft, shining mane, the colour of molten steel. The proprietor must have been joking when he said that Richelieu was as calm and peaceful as a lamb, only St George could tame such a monster. I didn't believe that the reason he flew across the fields like an uncastrated four-wheel drive, foam dribbling from his mouth, was because he had stayed in the stable for too long.

*   *   *

Three days later, when I had learnt how to comb Richelieu satisfactorily and could clean his coat using the several brushes (I was too scared, though, to clean his rear hooves), the owner was taken by a whim to teach me to ride.

'Back straight! No hunching! Heels up!' he shouted, holding Richelieu by a long rope. The horse trotted peacefully in a circle, stopping occasionally to smell a mole hill. 'Don't take your feet out of the stirrups.'

'Ready steady, go, with a song!' From deep in my subconscious rose the voice of the military training teacher. 'Cavalry advance!'

'A hundred young soldiers from the Budyonov brigade
Jumped in the fields on reconnaissance.'

Richelieu, scared by a frog leaping from beneath a hump, broke into a gallop; the bumpy trot was replaced by a pleasant and stomach wrenching bouncing, so joyful that I let go of the reins and slowly – even slower than in a slow motion film – I flew into the blooming buttercups. When I opened my eyes, the sky seemed to be gazing down at me – the blue, worried eyes of the proprietor.

Don't worry, dear Proprietor, nothing happened to me and nothing ever will. How could anything bad happen when a cowboy carries a woman in his arms and promises to tend to all her wounds, including her hard-beating heart. Tequila and lemon was fantastic for that. And, as he was a medical-equipment salesman, he had some knowledge of medicine. He assured me that nothing was broken or dislocated, except, well, maybe my interest in riding. No, I whispered, enchanted, breathless from the lemon I had swallowed. I'll ride, I will ride . . . And fall as many times as is needed, I was about to add.

But that was almost like saying, I love you, so it was better to leave that declaration, with its slow-acting, metallic-tasting poison, probably arsenic, for midnight, whose phosphorous eyes peered through the leaves in the garden. And perhaps I should leave it for Richelieu too, snorting in the moonlight, having been transformed from grey cardinal to silver knight. He put his head upon my shoulder and attempted to graze on my hair. Don't, my lovely horse of St George, you might get poisoned; arsenic stays in the hair the longest, as has been proven by legal experts as far back as the nineteenth century.

In a week's time I would be riding fairly well and the proprietor's eyes would not just flash good naturedly, but with the dark blue lamps of passion. But the long-nailed Margo would come and take him away, leaving Richelieu behind to console me. But not for long. A week later a truck would arrive to take the horse to a private-stable where the farmer's apathetic cows would not be able to eat his vitamins.

Westerns are a totally uninteresting genre, and not just because in them women get less attention than horses do. There is no alternative to their one-directional linear time-lines, to the red aesthetic of sand and iron. Men as well as women are equally, eternally enslaved to it.

Why couldn't the lunatic send me a rose, a blood-red rose, darker than the Persian's eyes, cut from its roots by an invisible guillotine? Obviously he couldn't, as on the desk there was a simple foxglove with dangling violet petals, a wintery white moonlight shining from inside them.

Atali claimed she hadn't seen anybody. The policeman on duty hadn't let any suspicious people in (God forbid!), while Arnold thought that it was the cleaner who had brought it. The cleaner cried so much that the make-up ran from her eye lashes. 'What flowers?' She would rather die than interfere with the investigator's work!

I was angry. I stuffed the foxglove roughly and mechanically into the drawer. When would he, this slave of poisonous plants, finally step through the entrance and stride into my office, astonishing us all with his boldness? When would we look each other in the eye? And when would this anxiety that tortured me finally dissipate? Why me? Why not Atali? Why not the sixty-year-old cleaner, who rejuvenated herself with bright red lipstick and loved nature? In autumn she would decorate the whole station with twigs and bundles of rowan. She didn't even forget the detention cells; she would hang the leaf of a maple tree on the door handle.

Finally, in these times of anything goes, why not the Chief?

He probably didn't even know himself, my strange, silent admirer.

As it was Saturday, there was little point in him showing up; the only people in the station were Atali and the duty policeman. Saturdays were marked by the gentle hum of boredom, which is why they were so lifelike and so real. It was nothing like those scenes with frantic officers working night and day, not even stopping at the weekend or bank holiday, with something new always turning up. That all belonged to the world of cinema, not real life. Life is inert, but that's no good for producers; they want to grab you with their incredible story lines. You wouldn't want to sit and watch people dying, strangled slowly by inertia.

Somebody knocked politely on the door.

Oh God, might it be him?

'God bless you.' The town priest stepped through the doorway. He wore a grey suit, a raincoat and checked hat that reminded me of Doctor Watson; only the rye-coloured moustache was missing.

'Good afternoon,' I said.

The priest took off his hat and looked like he was about to say something. He blinked, his eyes red from reading (if not reading, then what?). But then his innocent eyes caught sight of the poster of the Mr Olympia 1985 on the wall (in bathing trunks, the size of a fig leaf), and his hand pulled the hat back on.

His head was level with my shoulder, which made him uncomfortable.

'Would you mind,' he asked politely, 'if I sat in your chair?'

'Please do.' I didn't mind.

Being used to the confessional, he was probably suffering from agoraphobia.

The priest settled in the chair, placing his hat on a pile of case-files. He even half smiled.

'So, what has happened, Citizen Priest?'

The priest looked down at me in admonition from the heights of his chair. Perhaps he considered the question rude.

I attempted to rectify the mistake.

'Forgive me, Holy Father, how can I, a poor sheep, be of service to you?'

The priest looked at me, surely moved, and then looked at his hat.

'You see, my daughter . . .' He was about to start, but composed himself, cleared his throat and frowned solemnly.

Atali placed two cups of coffee on the table and fluttered silently out through the door. Only the corner of her grey cardigan fluttered.

The priest's eyebrows evened out again.

He clearly couldn't decide how to behave – as strict confessor or an ordinary citizen.

'You see, Citizen Investigator . . .' He began, after a sip of coffee. 'I came here on an important matter concerning the moral health of our society . . .'

I nodded.

'Yes, Holy Father, I understand. You really can't find a case unrelated to moral health.'

The priest looked up surprised, but said nothing. He drank his coffee in silence. When he had finished, he pushed away the cup.

'God is almighty, but sometimes, daughter . . . Citizen, His power is not enough. Unfortunately we no longer have inquisitions, and that's why I have to approach the police. I want you to punish a witch.'

'A witch?'

'The red-haired witch from the suburbs,' repeated the priest. 'Not only does she invite people into her bear pit for 'healings', but she also proclaims herself a Catholic. She comes to church, comments on my sermons, distorting them unforgivably. The sacristan told me that the witch was explaining to people in a stage whisper that the world is ruled by astral bodies, that Jesus and Christ were two different persons, one human and the other some Aeon.'

'The witch knows about the early Gnostics,' I said, not without respect.

The priest looked at me, puzzled. Maybe he hadn't read any of the Gnostics.

'The oblate told me,' he muttered sadly, 'that the witch spat into the holy water to 'load it with positive energy' so that it could heal properly and chase away evil spirits. It's the darkness of Moloch, the unruliness of Baal!'

He stopped.

A shout came from the street. Somebody cursed expressively. A dark gust of wind breathed past. The servants of Beelzebub creaking across the thin ice, avoiding puddles, carrying people's souls off to hell.

'So, based on two unconfirmed incidents, heresy and spitting into holy water, you would like the woman to be arrested and . . .' I paused, looking for the right words, but failed to find them.

The priest's red, dove-like eyes blinked. He, too, it seemed, was not sure how to proceed. The most reliable means, tested by inquisition, did not, unfortunately, work in this immoral age.

'I have to disappoint you; the police are helpless in this case.'

With a sigh, the priest climbed from the chair. Upon leaving, he turned.

'What a pity. Other state institutions, not only the church, should listen to the confession of sins and grant forgiveness. The church alone is not capable of doing so . . .'

He closed the door without a sound.

'But not the police!' I shouted. 'The police station isn't church! Detectives aren't psychics, for goodness sake!'

Fortunately, at our police station nobody had created the position of medium. They would crawl in their thousands to take up the position. But who, I ask you, would be able to verify their competence?

The priest probably could, with the help of God's Army; they loathed sorcerers and did not tolerate witches. If, when they performed an exorcism, the witch didn't fall flat on the ground when touched by the sergeant's hand (God healed and punished through that hand), the exorcist would trip her. The heretic had no choice but to fall flat in the mud.

But priests want nothing to do with sects, which is a shame. They could learn from one another.

The Church today, by renouncing mystical powers, has handed them over to witches and sorcerers, and the latter have abused people's blissful ignorance.

I used to like God's Army's cosy, conspiratorial meetings which took place in peoples' apartments; the meetings were held on Tuesdays, after my criminal law lecture. I would still be burning from the articles of the Criminal Code and the punishments applied through different ages: death, torture, penal labour, whipping, public repentance, exile, hanging, cutting out of the tongue, chopping off of the hand, the breaking of bones on the wheel, being burnt alive, being hung, drawn and quartered. I would climb up to the fifth-floor apartment suffocating with horror. Unfortunately, God's Army didn't promise an easier life for sinners: they would burn in the lake of sulphur, be given over to demons to be torn to pieces. I would tumble down weakly on a bean bag. The head of the group would bring me some hot tea and ask, sympathetically, if I was ill; possibly I needed a session of exorcism. They could instantly chase from my body the spirit of the flu, as I reclined there cosily.

Then it would be time for our testimonies.

A freckly sixteen-year-old said she had bravely told her zoology teacher that Darwin had been inspired by the devil, which had helped him formulate his theory of evolution. He couldn't have done it by himself. The zoology teacher took her to the head teacher, who then called in her parents. The parents called in a psychiatrist and it all ended with the grinding of the teeth, tears and her being grounded from the God's Army meetings. But the brave critic of Darwin had no intention of obeying that.

Auntie Salomeja, a pensioner with nothing much to do to kill her time, declared in a heated fashion that she had saved a cursed bus. On All Saints Day she had been about to go to the village, but the busses were so packed that the Vilnius-Birzai bus had not been able to take on a woman dressed in black, with a bunch of white chrysanthemums in her hand. The woman had become so angry that she cursed the driver, the conductor and, of course, the passengers too. 'I wish that you should crash!' she screamed, stamping her foot, holding the chrysanthemums carefully. 'I wish that you be so chopped up into pieces and badly mixed together that your relatives will not be able to sort you out!' Salomeja, who didn't get on the bus either, was so horrified she shouted, 'Silence, you evil spirit! Let these people travel happily and not get chopped up!'

She had listened to the news for three days in a row, but heard nothing about any bus crashes.

Everybody rustled their support and the head of the group hugged Salomeja lovingly. That was quite a significant sign of acceptance.

I didn't seem to have done anything worthy of sharing. Possibly God, having seen into my heart, where guilt reigned, for thefts as well as for miracles, didn't think me worthy of such an opportunity. But I was full of desire to convert somebody; it wasn't important to which religion, only that the convert should believe unconditionally for their whole life, while I, their spiritual mother, would lose my faith a month or so after.

30.05.2002

Klepavicius, the vet, filed a complaint that somebody had ruined his tulips. When he had got up that morning, only their naked stems had been sticking up from the earth. The flowers had probably been chopped off with a sickle (the trajectory of the cut was wide) and a sharp one at that, because the stick with a label planted among them identifying the type of tulip he had planted, had been cut so neatly that not a speck of sawdust could be seen. The detective joked that it must have been the work of the Grim Reaper. Klepavicius merely groaned at that. He had his suspicions about P.R. who had been unhappy with the vet's services; his neutered cat had died mysteriously following the operation, instead of living a life of happy tranquillity.

The fact was that the vet, who stank of intestines and had a secret passion to get his nails into proper medicine, had most probably cut the tulips himself so that he would have the excuse to accuse somebody else. Or, anyway, that's what P.R said during questioning. He had a cast-iron alibi; on the day of the crime he had stayed at the pub until late and only went out for a piss and even then he had not been on his own (for some reason he blushed saying that). The forensics expert, familiar with all types of death, identified that the tulips had been cut at about 10pm.

Klepavicius called that perverse. His heart would burst if he raised his hand against a tulip, such a beautiful wonder of nature.

There was no sickle to be found in his shed and his garden knives were so clean they shone.

As P.R. had an alibi (it was confirmed by his drinking partners, as well as by the man who went out with him to have a piss), Klepavicius suggested a couple more suspects. But at that point the Chief intervened and roared that the investigation of the killing of tulips was ridiculous and that there were more serious jobs to do. Klepavicius bristled at this, replying that the ravaging of his flower garden was as bad as murder. He wasn't prepared to leave it, he would go higher! The Chief laughed. He knew well those higher institutions.

Serves you right, Doctor of Moerae, you remind me of my frozen feet in childhood and the stupid doctor's assistant who had advised salt solutions as a cure. He was a flower-fanatic too, though geraniums were his thing, not tulips. He was crazy about them. Women couldn't understand it and quietly gossiped about him, calling him a paedophile. A lonely crank, expending his sexual energy in a blooming greenhouse! How sad he must have felt in the winter.

How transparent you are, oh Saturday afternoon! You are an old yellow net. You flutter like an opera overture performed on violins, with the occasional clink of plates followed by the sound of the tuba, like a distant, despairing moan.

I didn't want to go home. Nor did I want to take the hat from the bust of Pushkin even though it was cool. I would drop in at Sarkiene's and then would head to the lake. Without a hat, my head naked, the ghosts from the war cemetery would not recognise me. Sarkiene would be surprised too; she would draw a fat brown line towards her ear while applying her lipstick. I would ask not for Merlot as usual, but for brandy.

'Has something happened, Commissar?' she would ask, worried. 'No? Then it probably will.'

Of course it will happen. Something always happens in the world. Especially when a person's habits change.

'It will happen, it will,' the ghosts in the cemetery whispered, following me on the gusts of wind. I could almost hear the clank of a dented travel pot among the metaphysical whispering, so cosy and familiar. I heard several Russian expletives.

I put up my collar and started to run. The whispering wind could not catch me. Even the curses were no longer audible. The only sound was the gurgle of brandy in my handbag.

The lake opened by my feet, black as glass, a piece of terrible evidence, touched by people and ghosts; the fingerprints of the latter shone with hellish blue phosphorus.

I opened the brandy with my teeth, spat out the cap and drank straight from the bottle. Its neck was as fragile as a new-born baby's, frozen in deadly palsy. A couple of careless knocks with my fangs and the sharp teeth of the fragile neck would stick in my throat.

By the end of the third year of my studies, a happy event awaited me; God's Army were to award me the official status of a member and give me a certificate with my photo on it.

The night before, Nutcracker knocked on my door and, with the wink of a conspirator, reported that he had some interesting material, which would one day be certain to be included in the criminal process (criminal processes haunted him constantly, exceeding anything Kafka could imagine). He had two invitations to an illegal club and as he couldn't find another suitable candidate, he was inviting me.

'And in what way have I pleased you then?' I asked, surprised.

Nutcracker grew pensive.

'It's difficult to say,' he mumbled at last. 'You see, I like watching your facial expression during the criminal law seminars. When we were examining bullets, it looked as if you would be happy to shoot anybody who couldn't tell the difference between a Brenneke bullet and a Shirinsk-Shachmatov.'

I was a little puzzled. As far as I could recall, I had been thinking about whether I would have enough money for lunch, as having been caught by a charitable impulse, I had donated several not-so-small banknotes to God's Army. I had been tempted by their saying, 'Give and you will receive a hundredfold.'

Damn my greediness!

'It might be a good idea for you to dress up as extravagantly as you can,' Nutcracker said, a little deranged. 'And make-up . . . Don't forget make up.'

'I never forget it.'

'But this time – make a special effort.' Nutcracker wouldn't leave me alone. He was a nuisance!

'And remember, one hundred per cent confidentiality!' he hissed, nearly stepping on my heels as we crept under a narrow arch in the Old Town. 'We can't give ourselves away.'

I said nothing. Nutcracker had watched too many old movies.

At the door we were stopped by a broad fellow with a mean facial expression. Having checked our invitations, he let us in, his malevolent gaze following us. He softened slightly having glanced at the mini-skirt I had borrowed from Lucy, a sex-bomb on the eighth-floor. The skirt was too wide for me and swung round my hips like a drunk.

We ended up in a smoky hall with an enormous screen upon which black and white objects flashed, accompanied by a monotonous moaning. I was scared. I remembered the first videos I had watched back in the village: the dead rising up, dragging their feet, intent upon eating the living (I understand now why they used to put food in ancient burial places!).

I looked round, but Nutcracker, instead of looking after me, had already disappeared. I looked at the screen again and realised suddenly that that gasping hole which I had thought was a toothless mouth, was not a mouth at all. My powdered cheeks blushed. A bottom. A man's bottom! And that sausage he was about to swallow. I was going to kill Nutcracker!

Wading through the smoke, accompanied by the shame-less sound of swallowing coming from the screen, I at last managed to reach the bar and ordered some vodka, which I knocked straight back.

I didn't dare look at the screen, or, worse, at the hall, though I did hear somebody mention Nietzsche. When a strange girl winked at me crudely, I closed my eyes.

'You don't like it here?' Somebody touched my elbow.

I opened my eyes.

A brown-haired man in a red shirt. A necklace and bronze chest hair were visible through the open shirt. He was hold-ing a glass of wine in his hand and smiled pleasantly.

'I understand.' He nodded, took me by the elbow and steered me to a table in a niche. A wall blocked my sight of the screen and the hall.

'First time here?'

I remembered Nutcracker's orders and shook my head.

But the brown-haired man wasn't stupid. He smiled, leant back, sipped his wine and seemed to suddenly grow sad.

'Tell me, what should I do if I am not like other men? God doesn't need my soul and as far as nature is concerned, I'm a dry branch.'

I shrugged. True, two perverts on an uninhabited island – what could be sadder?

'Have some.' He pushed the wine towards me. 'Really, have some. You'll understand me.'

I had some.

'You know. I'm nervous of men. They're so aggressive and rough and I long for gentle and playful love. Usually women are gentle and playful, but . . .'

He stopped, pushed the wine towards me again.

'You're not attracted to women,' I finished. I felt sorry for the fragile and unhappy man.

'Do you like Vermeer?' he suddenly asked. His eyes lit up and his hands, holding the wine glass, trembled with excitement. 'The light in his pictures, the light!'

He had hit a soft spot. I hiccupped in agreement.

'And Bruegel?' he hissed, leaning close to me. 'The space of dreams . . . Cold and distant like blue glass on the snow!'

To stop myself crying, I swigged straight from the bottle.

'And Caravaggio?' He seemed determined to finish me off. 'Just look at his Sleeping Cupid! What unknown horrors lurk in the sleeping body!'

I looked at the ceiling. Something blue was floating there, lazily, odd, with a dangling penis, looking like a seed pod.

'You also need to see the terrible light in Goya, which seems to drown the forlorn dog's head in blood!'

I closed my eyes. I didn't need a dog. I was drowning myself – in wine and in art.

He grabbed me by my hand.

'Listen,' he said, determined. 'I'm bored here. Everybody is kissing and groping each other, and I have to suffer. If I can't give myself to love, at least I can give myself to art. Let's go to my place. I live only one building down from here. I have some good slides; I'll show you the Impressionists. We haven't spoken about them yet. Would you like to?'

Of course, I wanted to.

In his apartment he locked the door and turned on one dim standard lamp; pale light shone on an orange bedspread. So it was here that he longed for the soft touch of a lover. The poor thing.

'Lie down,' he muttered roughly.

'Why?' I was surprised, struggling to stay on my feet. 'I'd rather sit down.'

Without a word, he undid his trousers, threw the belt aside and jumped on me like a grizzly bear.

I remembered my karate training and attempted a kick, but it's hard from a prostrate position, especially when you're pressed down by eighty kilos of flesh and a similar amount of unpleasantness. In addition, Lucy's skirt slid down happily. The bastard; I would never borrow it again.

Flakes of bronze fell from his chest hair onto my face. I closed my eyes, waiting for the moment when I would become a sad monument to the victims of criminal violence. The Impressionists, who we had not even managed to discuss, fluttered in the twilight like orange fish, their tails reminiscent of brushes from which miraculous paint dripped. It poured between my thighs. There would be no paint left for the freshly stretched canvas! No masterpiece was going to be painted.

Naughty Nutcracker defended himself by saying that he had been in the toilet and hadn't noticed what had happened to me. He didn't add, though, whether he would have been able to do anything about it, even if he had seen us. Well, that's what you get from a lover of legal processes. He might just as well crack nuts instead.

As the bright summer sun set over roofs of the Old Town, I sat in a cafe opposite St Nicholas church and gazed through the glass at its shining onion domes. In front of me lay the certification of my God's Army membership. I had become one of their soldiers, but it brought me no happiness as it didn't allow me to shoot my enemies or take hostages.

It was better to be a witch and stab him through his wax chest with a sharp pin.

With a trembling hand, I wiped my nose and corked the brandy bottle with a ball of tissue paper.

Across the dark surface of the lake, barely touching the reflections of the town lights, the lonely silhouette of the child moved away.

The gods are not able to walk on water, without becoming entangled among millions of disembodied children. Dark depths, full of terrifying creatures, replaced their warm dream-waters.

Oh, how hard my heart was beating! How the blossom trembled, brimming with moonlight, as I roughly picked it, bending over the black water.

VIII

At the end of the spring term of the third year of my course, my source of income was supposed to dry up. The teacher had no further intention of supporting me.

I dragged my feet to the central post office, weighed down by a feeling of doom. It was the day I received my money. The spring sky was gradually clouding over, threatening rain. The early July leaves were covered with a pungent dust and rustled menacingly like brittle banknotes stored in safes before a black financial crash.

I unlocked the post office box. Next to the traditional white envelope, fatter than usual, I noticed a bundle tied with a red ribbon.

I ran to the former Cerniachovskis Square and sat on a lonely bench. The sky grew increasingly dark and there was, in the air, the feeling of water suspended. It smelled like sludge in a dried up ditch. A coiled, cold metal spring ready to flash.

I stuffed the envelope into my bag, untied the bundle with trembling fingers and threw the ribbon into a flower pot shaped rubbish bin.

A Paloma 717 revolver landed on my lap, perfect from the front sights to the cylinder, the barrel and ivory handle and with a graceful curving hammer reminiscent of the bridge between life and death. With it was a typed note on a grey sheet of paper, in which the letter 'n' was in Russian; the typewriter font didn't seem to have been fully Lithuanised. 'The sum is three times bigger as it is the final one. The Paloma is a present for you, for the start of your independent life. I am no longer in any way responsible for you. Good luck in your new life, which is of no interest to me.'

Lightning flashed silently; a bloated seam in the sky ripped and water came forth. A thunderous sigh of relief shook the park. I imagined that the stone Cerniachovskis was coming to reclaim his place on his pedestal, breaking the wet branches that stood in his way.

I squeezed myself under the plastic roof of a trolleybus stop, pressing my handbag to my chest. Almost nothing could be seen through the grey curtain of water, except for the white, electric flashes. Through my bag I felt a heart throbbing and I was not sure whose, mine or Paloma's.

The sea floor embraced the closed shell passionately and gently, squeezing it sensually, releasing a naked, flaccid body, no longer vulnerable to shame, or condemnation; it opened up, giving itself to the stars.

I knew, now, that the nucleus of the galaxy was made up of dead people's souls, that the cold nebulas between the stars was their frozen breath and that the Milky Way was the broken path home that in irregular orbits slowly approached the bright, sparkling quasar in the depths of the universe and that the latter was moving away from them at the same speed.

The speed of a dream is different to that of light, the direction and purpose of its journey are unclear, it penetrates the depths of another universe, consciousness, and the distance between the balls of light are terrifyingly enormous.

The silence woke me.

My alarm clock had stopped at two thirty. Grey morning light flooded the room like badly pressed oil.

My mouth was dry. My tongue felt like cod battered in stale flour; if you tried to fry it in that unrefined oil dribbling from the curtains, the whole house would start to stink of dead meat. The neighbours would call the environmental health department and, having chewed down both my nails and my fingers, I would end my days in a flat buried under a thick layer of sorbent.

I poured myself half a glass of tomato juice and half of mineral water. Drinking it, I climbed back to bed. I hoped I wouldn't throw up.

The cat sat on a chair and inspected me with her yellow-eyed gaze. For some reason I felt embarrassed.

'Get out of here!' I shouted.

If Yin Yang had been able to shrug her shoulders she would have done so. As it was, she only lifted her eyes to inspect the ceiling, attracted by a cobweb fluttering in the corner.

I shouldn't drink with spirits. I covered my head with the quilt. It didn't console me that expletives sounded different on the lips of spirits. Spirits are so insubstantial, it's hard to believe they used to be people made of body and blood. They forget everything. They pretend to be God knows who, then try and teach you and guide you! Who then, for pity's sake, needs an after world?

It was Sunday and my admirer wouldn't be bringing me a poisonous plant, which was a relief. He obviously preferred the official, working me; Olympus tossing in bed wouldn't even get a miserable toadstool from him.

Irmute announced the sad news; the proprietor was selling the farm. Margo could no longer bear either the secluded location or the dying screams in the night. Or the shit in her favourite corners of the garden. I could carry on living there for a while if I wished, the proprietor said, but only until the fifteenth of August. The new owner should not see any of sign of me being there. If she was anything like Margo, I thought, it was a shame I wasn't some kind of leper so that my touch would leave a fatal infection on the door handles and the furniture.

From the train station, the road through the woods was a good distance, so when I reached the farm it was getting dark. A slice of sun pierced the black forest wall like the heated blade of a knife. In the field of uncut grass, a mysterious force moved the massive buds of goutweed and the yellow tansies. I stopped, scared that I might never return to this.

The proprietor had already moved some of the furniture out, but I still found Van Gogh and last year's herbs dangling from the ceiling. In my room was the old bed with clean bed linen. In addition, I noticed a bunch of purple forest lilies, cuckoo's tears, placed in a litre jug on the window sill. The flowers looked like they had just been picked. By the wall nestled a cardboard box; I opened it and took out canned food, dried bread, vacuum packed sausages, chocolate, packets of tea, coffee. There were even paper tissues and toilet paper. And not just any! Zewa, the touch of which was pleasure for your bottom.

The roll was blindingly white. It made me so sad, that I opened it and wiped my eyes. What a perverse, rotten world where such softness had been created just to wipe your bottom. The disposable tissues were much rougher, obviously, as they were only used to wipe noses. Snot – that's what all our tears turn into.

Half waking, I couldn't work out from where the distant cry of an oriole was coming, from the depths of the garden or from my dream that was already sinking into oblivion. A dust path sparkled in the pale sunlight; invisible dream-creatures had walked it but a second before. The dust glistened still as it slowly drifted to the wooden floor.

A voice of the golden bird sounded again from the garden, sharp and clear, like a thin blade melting in the heat.

It was probably not an oriole. It didn't look like it would rain; the sun, though pale as a lemon, had pushed away almost all of the clouds, only a few crept still across the sky, spreading like ripped thread.

I wended my way down towards the river, clinging to the knobbly roots of unknown trees which stuck from the sandy loam.

The wind, travelling down with me, overtook me, flying on towards the cherry trees and the pinkish-white limestone, or possibly the gravel hillock, ruffling its ridge and returning, its breath stinking of carcass.

A cloud of bluebottles rose from the gravel hillock, disturbed by the wind, and separated into single bullets. Their loud buzz foretold a rapid death.

The wind moved over the hillock again, ruffling its ridge, fluttering the fair mane of a horse.

I stood back. One of the blue bullets was approaching.

Grabbing at the roots of the tree, I clambered back up, the bullet, ignoring the laws of motion and trajectory, followed after me, leaving the click of the trigger, the smell of gunpowder, the soot and empty barrel on another plane.

A lonely person's best friend, apart from their pet, is the TV. Though you can't argue with it, it's good that you can switch it off during an argument; it's practically impossible to do this with people.

Now, for instance, I switched it on and out it poured, carrying on without pause, which I didn't mind, as pauses remind you of the eternal silence. In that eternal silence, TV, like anything else is doomed to loneliness and lovelessness. And I don't necessarily mean the grave; a human soul stretches out like a wasteland, like salty soil.

Leaning back on the pillow, I drank some hot broth and flicked through the channels. I'm not fond of nature programmes as they show a world where humans had to walk on all-fours. They were happy then though. When Christian Hour came on, I usually switched it off; it made me feel impure and corrupt, because I hadn't been able to learn how to do miracles or do missionary work. But what was that? A familiar face flashed on the screen and then disappeared, swallowed by a view of a misty lake accompanied by some music by Ravel. Then he reappeared. In an instant he had changed totally; he had a double chin, swollen cheeks where once there had been soulful cheekbones and in place of the long fluttering hair there was a shabby crew-cut.

And then the mist and the lake again. It was a small town where I had never set foot and whose name I did not know (I knew, though, that there was an old sanatorium there, in the hall of which hung the body of a communist party secretary who had hung himself two decades before, his dry bones chiming like Eastern bells). Music again. Torches. Poems.

The figure with the crew-cut read the poems too, as the mist swirled; his trembling voice was the only thing about him that hadn't changed.

We were two leaves of the same tea bush.

The screen was filled by the dreamy face of a young woman and a white, moonlit sail and the music of Beethoven. 'That was the last day of that poetic autumn in the town of N,' a coarse voice said. The mist disappeared and the music stopped and I felt as if I had been tossed onto the concrete floor of the next TV programme, *Hardship Market*. I changed the channel quickly.

When the monstrous buzzing of Formula 1 had calmed me a little, I glanced at the window, expecting to see a fly dozing in the warm blanket of autumnal sun. Instead, the glass was cut by lopsided zigzags of rain. The poetry was over, along with the summer and the wet lines that winter wrote upon the glass had no artistic value at all.

I never went down to the river bank again. The corpse of the horse was a sufficiently eloquent sign that my happiness was coming to an end. I would soon be losing this home, entirely and for ever.

At night clusters of stars leaned over the farm, dripping cold glass beads into the grass. The earlier I got up, the more I felt the spiky prickling of the slivers of glass.

I dismantled the little cabin in the garden and put the planks neatly in the wood shed. I confess I left the nails in them, making the planks look like implements of torture from the Middle Ages. I was nearly finished when, accidently, I leant against the rotten wall and it broke. A flood of tiny mice poured through the gap, rolling around my feet with such a dreadful screeching, as if I was peeling their skins from them.

I leapt from the shed screaming and dashed to the house.

When I gathered the courage to look in there again, the mice were gone, probably back through the cracks, or perhaps their mother had gathered them. Only one was left in the saw dust, lying all stiff, with its legs tucked up like a maggot, having clearly died of horror.

With two fingers I took it by its suede ear. The mouse stared at me with its black polished eye balls. Perhaps it was only pretending to be dead?

I put it into an empty biscuit box and grabbed a spade. I chose a shady spot by the fence; from the other side, the branches of ash and lime drooped into the garden. From the dark woods flooded the wild, drunken scent of nature, pungent devil broom and the acid, rotting mud of the swamps, wet pine needles left to decay for years.

Pressed by the spade, the thick layer of last year's leaves bent like a soft back. A thin, fragile vertebra cracked. No, that wouldn't do. I lifted the spade and forced it down with all my strength.

The high scream of a baby electrified my hand; white sparks crackled and shot upwards, the leaves of the wild apple tree flamed and through the fire the sky flashed, sun-heated. Through the layers of leaves, red fingers sprouted quicker than bamboo, thin as thread and of varying lengths, webbing the blade of the spade. I was unable to keep hold of it.

I dropped the blood-splattered spade. It bumped dully against the trunk of the apple tree. I scratched among the leaves, unable to stop the terrible thought of a tiny fair-haired baby, injured by the iron spade's blade, curved in pain like a tiny mouse. Only its beady eye beads were not glass, they sparkled, they sparkled still, crying, 'Why? What for?' My fingers dug into the sticky porridge. I pulled it out with difficulty, then crawled aside on my knees and began retching involuntarily.

A large toad, cut in half by the spade, helplessly twitched its limbs, attempting to get as far from me as possible, the child-like scream slowly freezing in its throat.

28.06.2002

Klepavicius, disappointed by the course the case was taking, admitted to having cut the tulips himself. He showed us where he had buried them and pulled out the weapon he had used in the crime, a lopsided Turkish scimitar called a yatagan. An old friend from Armenia had sent it him; they had served in the army together. He insisted that we examine the marks of the plants on the blade, which would confirm his testimony. When the Chief shouted that everything was clear anyway, that Klepavicius was an idiot and that his reputation was damaged (who would allow the creature that had mowed down his own tulips to treat their pets?), the old man stopped talking and looked miserable. When the forensics expert announced that it was no problem for him to take samples from the buried tulips and from the yatagan, and that to examine them under a microscope was no big deal, the Chief snorted.

'Don't shock the world with your investigations,' he roared.

'What was the motive, Citizen Klepavicius, for this behaviour? You said you could never raise your hand against the miracle of nature, but you did.'

Klepavicius' chin began to quiver.

'Have you never thought of killing the person you love?' he muttered, rubbing his eyes with a dirty handkerchief, red marks clearly visible on it. He must have used it during one of his operations. 'Has no one made you mad with their arrogance, showing that they know more than you and have seen more in life, and that you were just a naïve fool in love? And what heart can survive unfaithfulness, tell me, what heart? A heart made of stone. How can you watch as the gentlest creature of all gives themselves no longer to you, but to the secret passions of the night and they fly off somewhere into the spring night, their silky petals rustling and the silvery laugh of the elves pierces your stiffened chest painfully!'

'He's a fool,' the Chief said after the vet had left. 'And he wants to cure humans! Hearing some silvery laughter he would take a swipe with his yatagan and you, my friend, could say goodbye to the world. Make sure he doesn't stick his nose in here ever again. If he wanders in, put him under arrest.'

'But we can't do that, Chief! We live in a free society.'

'In a free society you can always think of a reason,' the Chief snapped back with dignity. As he left, he announced proudly that he had had Omar Khayyam neutered by another, more competent and likeable local vet. If the poor cat had been neutered by Klepavicius, the Chief intimated, it would have felt very uncomfortable indeed; it would have been as if his beloved pet had been raped by a monstrous zoophile.

The Chief was not fond of zoophiles. Despite the sensitive advice of Montesquieu and Beccaria, and even the all-powerful Criminal Code, he would have given them, without exception, the harshest punishment: the death penalty. Humans have to have it beaten into their brains that no one is allowed to rape either humans or animals and especially the latter, as people might feel fonder for them than it was possible to imagine.

The Chief was biased.

I dragged my cat to the vet in a beach bag, separated from the world by a zip. I cut some holes in the bag too, so that Yin Yang wouldn't suffocate. I didn't use the bag anyway; a colony of mould was spreading up one side of it. Besides, it had been given to me by an unpleasant neighbour with a screw loose. The bag had probably got mould on it when he gave it me and not seeing it, I had accepted it. Not that I needed it, simply out of pity for him.

'Good afternoon.'

Klepavicius was writing intensely and didn't lift his eyes from the desk.

'I . . . I'm here for the sterilisation.'

Klepavicius raised his eyes slightly.

'You want a sterilisation . . . For yourself?' he asked, interested. His eyes glittered unhealthily.

I took a step backwards.

'Sit!' He jumped up and grabbed a stool. It seemed like he was going to hit me on the head with it.

'No!' I shouted.

Klepavicius placed the stool on the floor and shrugged.

'So don't, if you don't want to. One ovary to be taken out or both?' He bent down in order to examine me better.

I pushed the bag forward. Yin Yang, sensing danger, growled angrily.

Klepavicius straightened up. He looked disappointed. Without a word he beckoned me to come closer, brought a cage and let the cat into it. He gave me a permission sheet to sign for the operation and, mumbling, filled in the cat's passport.

'Mongrel . . . Six months old, black and white, named Gangrene. It's not Gangrene, you say? Gang . . . Bang . . . For God's sake, you should have named it Magde and you wouldn't have these problems then.'

'My cat isn't a cow.'

Klepavicius glanced at me longingly.

Perhaps large cattle reminded him of something pleasant. He had probably spent his youth on a collective farm.

Chances are he met a Magde there, munching on silage.

I collected the cat in the evening, with its stomach shaven, thickly painted with iodine which looked like dried blood.

And instead of taking Klepavicius to court for this, I paid him eighty *litas*.

Which is how all loud and honourable protests end – with either a fine or a bribe.

The fourteenth of August arrived foggy and quiet. While drinking coffee on the porch, I glanced at the clouds, checking for a sign that the next day this home would be taken up into heaven and would never return.

Long clouds sailed across the sky, looking like over-washed towels. The smell of fermenting sludge and swamp gas which blew from the woods overpowered the scent of the apple and cherry trees. A week had passed without any desolate cries from the dark lime trees down by the riverside – the bullets must have all found their targets and the rusty-brown horse of death must have galloped away, leaving heavy hoof marks in the ground.

There was not much time for me there either – my train was leaving in the afternoon.

I would once more wade through the frozen zone. The wind wouldn't move the white spear-like umbrellas, stuck in the ground by their tips, because this place greeted only those who were arriving. It was indifferent to those who left.

When I got back to town, I would buy a bottle of vodka.

Perhaps in the very last moment before the sun disappeared behind the walls of the town and the vodka turned to blood, for a brief moment a familiar porch would flicker in the sky, with a dirty coffee cup on the bench and I would feel calm and happy. This home definitely deserved its place in the heavenly kingdom.

Then I would curl up on the narrow hostel bed and dream of time gnawing the large empty building and of how the scruffy, tiny balconies crumbled and the heavy plaster fell into the darkness, never hitting the ground.

I hid Paloma deep in the wardrobe. I said nothing of it either to Irma or to Nutcracker; they wouldn't believe somebody had given it to me as a present and would grow suspicious. Later, during training, when I asked the teacher, an expert on guns and ballistics, if such a brand of pistol existed, he merely shrugged and remarked, unpleasantly, that my imagination was too vivid. He had noticed that quite a while before, had even thought that I had chosen the wrong profession.

'But, dear teacher,' I disagreed. 'Imagination and intuition play an important role in criminal life. The role of aesthetics, as you know . . .'

'I know.' The teacher interrupted my tirade. 'Now, look at the parts of that revolver and name them.'

'The forward sights, barrel, frame, trigger shoulder . . .'

'No!' He interrupted again. 'Trigger guard. '

'Slide spring . . .'

'No . . . Slide stop.'

Nutcracker, sitting on the back row, tried not to look at me, which was his usual means of expressing sympathy.

November flung wet snow against the windows. The lecturer's glasses shone deadly in the electric light and I was pierced suddenly by a deep and painful presentiment that I was in a ruthlessly complex algebra class and the door was about to open and the music teacher would appear and save me; he would take me away, saying he had the headteacher's permission, as the celebrations were around the corner and the main piece for the concert had not been rehearsed enough. And I would run out after that straight back that looked so right in a uniform.

'You got a fail,' Nutcracker said when I sat next to him.

'How do you know? You can't see much from the back where you sit.'

'From the way his hand moved and the lines of the wrinkles on his forehead,' Nutcracker replied, drawing something in his exercise book, probably the schematic plan of the location, feverishly drawing in the legend.

'You had no time to complete it at home?'

'Of course I did!' mumbled Nutcracker, agitated. 'It's just that the first plan seems somehow . . . Somehow . . . Unreal.'

He went quiet, looked at the second plan and grew sourer.

'This one isn't perfect either,' he said in a worried voice.

'Don't let your pedantic nature drive you mad. This is only the schematic plan of the crime scene. And there are no perfect murders.'

'Do you really think so?' Nutcracker murmured thankfully and turned his eyes away.

It's not that hard to lie, though professional ethics forbids it. When Nutcracker tearfully invited me for a coffee, it wasn't a problem to go and listen to his stories about a childhood spent being an ugly duckling which, it seemed, wasn't about to end any time soon, and to have a drink of the throat-scraping *Green Lake* . . . When a rough, badly-carved hand ended up under my skirt. I pushed away the coffee and shook off the scared Nutcracker and went out into the

November sleet. The cold snow glued up my eyes as I sang the *Internationale*.

I slammed the door.

It was evening. The grey drizzle tossed by the wind was like an invisible drill screwing into the thick, fat clouds, their plaster crumbling, revealing a bright, shining, uncomfortable under-belly, like a bone opened to the eroding elements.

Thankfully I had buried my head in a hat, otherwise halfway to the lake I would have had a perfectly polished skull.

I stopped outside Sarkiene's bar.

Should I drop in for the sake of my health? A glass of brandy and a cup of coffee would do the job. Well, okay, not a full glass, a small glass. Even a half, perhaps . . .

I stood looking at the window which glinted merrily. My suffering meant nothing to it.

At least some hot coffee, I decided, pressing down the door handle.

Sarkiene glistened just like her window, though for some reason she was frowning. From the wrinkles on her forehead, I decided she was probably thinking intensely. She was at the coffee machine. Two teenagers sat at a corner table, looking, at a glance, like twins, wearing horrible wide trousers. Sat with them was a severe-looking woman, who looked like a teacher. She could have been their mother.

'Oh, miss . . . Miss Lawyer!' Sarkiene awoke from her thoughts and smiled widely. Her teeth were smeared with red lipstick. 'Some coffee and some brandy?'

'Some coffee and . . .' I stopped. 'Just coffee.'

Sarkiene pretended to be sorry.

'Well, then, just a coffee,' she said, her tone suggesting she was doing me a huge favour.

'And also some brandy.' I said, defeated ignominiously. 'But only fifty grams.'

'Here you are!' Sarkiene lit up and reached for the brandy bottle.

'Not that one!' I shouted. The stern woman at the table gave me a withering look. 'I don't want that liquid rust!'

Sarkiene pulled her hand away from the *Gloria* and poured some *Metaxa* in silence.

'Thank you,' I murmured, and went to hide in a dark corner.

When I left, it was already dark outside, only the diagonal lines of bones shone white, high up in the sky. When the street lights turned on, the bones shone blue, as if they were being eaten by a deadly virus.

It had been a good idea to have the brandy. I felt warmer and not so unhappy. I wouldn't have had more than the fifty grams. If I had, it would have been after another drink, but still, not more than fifty grams. My will power was strong.

Somebody was sitting on the bench next to the lake. I slowed down.

An old man wearing a fur cap and a brown fastened up coat, next to him a birch plank.

I stopped.

I should have had a hundred grams.

The old man turned his head; I heard the crack of neck vertebrae. Slanted eyes, beneath low eyebrows looked through me as if I was glass, a long, empty gaze down in the direction of the war cemetery and the new region of Brezhnev era apartment blocks.

'There is nothing here,' he said in Russian to the plank. 'All the world is empty.'

He scratched his stubbly chin.

'I cannot find my way home,' he complained. 'I walk in circles, and I walk. Good, a little time has passed, I'll definitely find my way home before lunch. And as for Nastya, I won't leave her any pork, only cabbage. The woman will gobble you up!'

He groaned standing up from the bench, took his plank and tucked it under his arm.

'The French fool.' He cleared his throat and spat. 'She'll get the plank on her head . . .'

He spat once again without having finished his sentence and moved towards the new town as slowly as a sideboard eaten by woodworm.

I bent down to inspect the bench. Not a single worm in sight, though on the very edge there was a large moth, softer than Persian silk, sitting with its brownish wings spread wide which the Master of Miniatures' feather had subtly outlined.

I had to go back and drink that one hundred grams.

The hall of the House of Culture was empty and the doors firmly closed. The November wind cut my hair in uneven clusters screeching like scissors grown rusty from dampness. An icy thumb pressed against my forehead, a deadly cold forcing its way in. I couldn't sing. I shivered. The teacher noticed and closed the lid of the piano and put his palm to my forehead.

'You have a fever.' He looked at me with warm, summer eyes. 'Do you have any medicine at home?'

'In the hostel? No,' I mumbled, my teeth chattering. 'I had a bottle of cough medicine . . . But we drank it. As a liqueur.'

The teacher waved with his archangel wing, which meant come with me. And I went, carefully lifting my feet so as not to tangle myself in the teeth of the wild blackberries that had arranged themselves like mouse traps. I came back to my senses in bed. I could hear the dentist's drill in the distance and the howling of a patient; the sounds made me feel happy and calm. The teacher poured a glass of water and made me swallow a bitter pill. His voice wandered somewhere, saying that I was excused from lessons; I just had to lie down, to lie down . . . Magde pushed a bottle of moonshine towards me. I fought her off with hands and feet, then she clasped my hands with her one paw and with a powerful bovine sigh pressed down my feet, opened my mouth and my father, giggling merrily, poured the stinking liquid into my mouth.

Dust fell from above into my eyes. Who was walking in the attic, making the ceiling sway heavily? My grandmother must have climbed up to take down the dry bed linen; she would iron it and put it under my cheek; a pillow smelling of the wind.

But it wasn't my grandmother. It was my teacher; the uniform suited him perfectly. The shoulder boards shone severely as did the peak of his cap. Instead of medals though, he had fastened some blood-red berries to his chest and the holster of his pistol shone a cold blood-like colour.

I closed my eyes, unable to stand the brightness. I could smell only berries ripened by the sun and my thighs parted as if they were at a crossroads and red raspberry blood ran down, cooled, became sticky and again the November wind blew, having shorn my hair, leaving me open to public mockery, its hungry scissor blades still chopped, attempting to cut, perhaps, the silky veins of my body.

I woke up in hospital. I learnt that I had flu with complications (a woman on the ward had asked to be moved somewhere else – she couldn't stand any more of my erotic nonsense). I also learnt that the October concert had had to make do without the main piece of music and that somebody had sent me some oranges. The nurse had eaten one, she hoped I wouldn't judge her.

I didn't judge her. I asked her if they had brought me from the run-down farm. No, from the hostel, according to the ambulance driver, the nurse had replied, eyeing the oranges greedily.

I would have given them all to her if only she had been able to say it was the teacher that had taken me to the hospital worried that he had not able to take care of me well enough and was worried for my life. Anyway, I was close to believing I was in heaven and would always hear that blissful humming of the dentist's drill.

The Cheka , the Stasi, the CIA . . . Gusts of winter wind, the rustle of frozen leaves, the piercing, smothering frost and the thick layer of snow which covered it all like a conspiracy.

I stole a packet of sweets from a shop; nobody would have noticed it if hadn't been for a hole in my pocket. The bag fell out right next to the door, ripping so that the sweets scattered across the dirty tiles. *Gentleness*, in pink wrappers with an aromatic white filling.

They took me to the store's security guard. I had to listen to a telling off and escaped by a whisker from being entered on the young offenders' register (I was saved by my active extracurricular and social activities and the fact that I had won the second place in the Russian language competition – the policeman was a Lithuanian born Russian). But I did find a place on *The Spike*, the satirical corner of the school's noticeboard.

I was only glad that the music teacher never stopped to look at the noticeboard, however juicy and provocative their headlines were. '*The USSR – the honour and conscience of the epoch*', '*Pioneers – heroes*', '*Uzbekistan – our sister*'. And so on. He probably sensed that Uzbekistan couldn't possibly have been our sister, the connection seemed artificial. He sensed it, though couldn't be fully sure. You see, the key to all secrets, including genetic secrets, was kept by the great alchemist who gazed sternly from the wall display, a frown creasing his bushy eye brows.

There was probably no winter in Uzbekistan. The dismal wind from the steppes twirled greedy clouds of sand and whistled the names of the secret services. Those names were the only real connection between the make-believe sisters.

From a corner of the dark corridor white blobs stirred and swam slowly towards me, curling around my leg, ignoring the sharp scream.

It was I that had screamed, having mistaken the cat for a blood-thirsty goblin.

Yin Yang was interested not in affection, but in the smells I had brought in from outside. Her whiskers stirred and she moved away – she had probably smelled the old man.

The first thing I was going to do was have a bath. I would wash off the weird smells: the raspberry juice, the mark of the icy thumb, the sweat of the illness and the black ink on my fingers – you see, it was I who had drawn the caricature and written the text for *The Spike*, the school's satirical noticeboard, hoping to incinerate the sin of theft in the fires of social realist art.

With my head on the side of the bath, I felt like singing the song of the Great October Revolution. The lapping of the water and the humming of the pipes reminded me of that concert many years before in which I hadn't performed.

IX

The sunlight shone golden beneath the heavy, still, greenish water, unruffled by rough caress. My mother's face seemed precious and old, though she was not more than thirty-five. The touch of her fingers was so cool and light as she stroked my short hair that I immediately understood I was dreaming. There was not much point in reproaching the figure in the dream and it made no sense to complain, to say, 'Why didn't you let me have plaits? Why did you cut my hair boyishly short? Why didn't you protect me from a brutal pubescence?' The figure in the dream would have answered only with a furtive sparkle of greenish-gold. It wouldn't say the name of the dimpled, childish face with the fluff of a first moustache; I realised it was my father only by when the light changed. When the cloud covered the sun the shadow of molten iron reflected briefly in his large eyes.

Everything was warm and clean. For once, having come home for the holidays I wouldn't have to scrub the floor and the pots. The light of the dream washed them, renewed them and filled them up. I only needed to lift the lid of the frying pan to see bright yellow meat balls, lying side-by-side, like eggs in a nest – they wouldn't have a scent – gold doesn't smell. On the undersheet in the bedroom there was no sign of blood, or sweat, or discharge from sexual organs. Only on the corner of the pillow, hissing quietly, a grey spot of poison steamed – diluted spirits or possibly perfume, mixed with the saliva of an unsettled sleep.

It seemed that my secret admirer could see the colours of my dreams. That morning I found on my desk a grass the yellow of my dream, with large leaves in the shape of an ellipse. The botanical guide explained that it was a white hellebore. It was on the Red List.

He was nothing but a bastard, that admirer of mine; he didn't even spare rare plants.

Or could it be that the hellebore was from a different time zone?

And perhaps my admirer was too! From a different time, where there were no words for 'endangered' and 'prohibited'? Didn't such inhuman abundance scare him? Obviously it did, as the plants were miniature bridges across which he wanted to come to me.

The thief we had been investigating at that moment, on the other hand, had most probably never known times of abundance. He had spent his childhood tied to a table leg and had learnt to crawl rather than walk. That had stayed with him for twenty years. At the crime scene there were not only the black prints of ragged soles, but also palm prints located so regularly you could see that the person had walked on all fours. He had probably opened the drawers and cupboard doors with his teeth – we discovered something resembling teeth indentations on the handles of the drawers. He probably only walked on two feet when other people were around; a *homo sapiens* on all fours would attract too much attention.

Why hadn't Atali brought me some coffee?

There was a sound in the corridor. It must be the tray with the coffee cups, I thought. I opened the door for Atali, but it wasn't the secretary who swam in. Rather, it was an untidy looking woman with a net bag full of empty beer bottles. She stopped, like a ship lost in fog, and froze with her mouth open.

I recognised her. It was the best friend and companion of the woman whose child had been snatched by aliens and gigantic monkeys.

The tall woman's clothes were steaming strangely, emitting the smell of sea sludge. A dry, shuddering whistle came from her chest and it looked like St Elmo's fire would start to twinkle in her hair at any moment.

'B . . . bottles. Will you take them?' she mumbled, thrusting the bag forward.

'No!' I snapped.

The tall woman looked surprised.

'W . . . why not?' she groaned. 'No containers?'

I stuck my head out into the corridor. A policeman was leaning on the wooden barrier of the booth, casually chatting to the officer on duty.

'Officer!' I shouted. 'Could you please show this person the direction towards the bottle collection point?'

The lost ship was turned around and directed on a different route, though she continued to stare at me for a long while, surprised that I wouldn't accept the bottles.

I had just managed to chase out the smell, wafting the case files, when Atali appeared with the coffee.

'Today, at 3pm, at the cultural centre, there's a meeting with the parliamentary candidate for our region,' she announced.

I waved my hand.

'No . . . I get headaches from long talks.'

Atali smiled politely, though her eyes showed no shadow of sympathy.

'The Chief would like you to go,' she said in her silky voice. She smiled and ruthlessly tightened the loop around my neck.

'You never know when you might have to do business with somebody from the government.'

The door closed without a sound, just the click of the handle, sounding like the wood-stiff tongue of a hangman.

Atali was probably right – people, especially those in power, were unpredictable. I would like to stick him in the interrogation room and uncover his guilt! But what if the opposite happened?

I was overwhelmed by a tremor of horror.

What terrible thing had I done that those in power might condemn me for without feeling a jot of remorse?

I would. I would definitely go to the meeting. Then at least I would know what I might be condemned for.

My God, how was it possible to forget the most fundamental thing you were guilty of – that of being a *homo sapiens*! All your deeds are sinful, even your love poisoned the environment, causing irreparable harm to nature! The last feeble thread connecting me to the teacher had snapped. I felt like a discarded button.

Nutcracker had no problem persuading me to go out with him again. There wouldn't be any perverts this time, he informed me in a jovial manner, just poets and intellectuals. There was no chance of being raped.

Perhaps it would have been better if there was.

How those conceited egocentrics' conversation and quotations differed from having your arm twisted behind your back and a rag shoved in your mouth, I don't know. I moaned, squirmed and attempted to say something, but my intellectual drinking companions galloped ahead, sparks rising from their horseshoes, trampling over the gentle seedlings of a woman's thoughts.

The only honourable way out was to shoot myself. Let them take me out feet first. A metaphor.

Nutcracker, who felt right at home among the intellectuals, as if they were his relatives, didn't attempt to run after me; he had probably only needed me to distract the attention for a while, so that he could infiltrate the group unnoticed and then calmly collect material on criminal process.

Do it, collect it, my dear. It was only a pity that 16th century punishments had been abolished; they would have been so fitting for writers abandoned by their muses.

I sat down on a bench in the municipal park, cursing the arts and calling Pegasus an ass. I stopped when something in the bush snickered and two hooves covered my mouth. The creature of the night was like a real demon; it wasn't just my handbag it was after. Breathing sulphur from his nose, he forced my head against his hairy belly and told me to suck his poisonous teat. It was trying to confuse me so that I would renounce my soul.

I grabbed his *teat* with one hand and used the other to pull out the Paloma (I had tucked it in the back of my knickers when I was considering whether I would shock the cultured elite by shooting myself or one of the famous intellectuals). Now there was no considering. I shot right into the dark belly of Moloch, easily and with joy.

When I got back to the hostel I counted the bullets. Five were missing, so it was highly probable that I had hit him. It was a good job there was nothing written in the Criminal Code about killing the Devil. I hadn't dropped anything in the park and the only witnesses were the trees and the tulip-shaped rubbish bins. Nobody would be able to identify the Paloma bullets, the firearms expert had said that type of pistol didn't exist.

I had probably only given the Devil a scare: there was nothing on the news about a male corpse being found.

He had probably recovered and crawled to some witch to moan and lick his wounds. God forbid that, driven by a lust for revenge, he might try to attack me again!

How prescient of my dear teacher to give me a pistol rather than a necklace! An expensive instrument tuned by passionate fingers that I could use to defend my body.

Amnesia is a popular device used in Mexican soap operas; it usually happens when the protagonist has to behave in a way contrary to common sense and the laws of logic. A bolt of electricity which illuminates how all things change.

Somebody was sat on the side of the sand pit, playing the guitar and singing:

'A Russian girl has two plaits
But an Uzbek has twenty-five'

I looked at him, toy spade in my hand, while the sand beneath me grew wet. I didn't dare abandon the fateful song and leave, especially not to go to the toilet!

It was only when lighting flashed from the dark clouds like a forked tongue and when I saw my mother running towards me, fluttering like a pale angel of death, the sheets from the washing line around her shoulders, that I began to cry loudly. My legs were numb. I felt as if I couldn't stand up from the wet sand, into which fate had planted me like a fence post.

My mother scooped me up, enclosing me within her white wings and then the sky ripped with a bang. The cloth wings stuck to my face.

When I opened my eyes, I realised I was lying on the narrow hostel bed. Beside me Odete was moaning, homework on the table not yet done, a music textbook open on a page about Franz Liszt; his picture reminded me, for some reason, of my teacher.

What was it that I had temporarily lost – my memory or consciousness? Or simply time?

But can you lose time? You turn the hourglass upside down and the sand spills into the other bulb and that's all there was to it.

I argued with Odete. I insisted that the headteacher was a coward. In order to prove it, I took one of the hostel under-sheets and made a ghost costume, with black lines drawn around the eye holes. Just before midnight I hid in the woods, through which the head used to pass after spending the evening with the biology teacher, a lonely atheist. As he wheezed by, I moaned like a ghost. When he jumped and looked round, I appeared for a moment and then quickly hid again.

The headteacher began to walk faster, then started to run.

Odete was annoyed; now she would have to do my homework for me and all because of her gullibility. The headteacher, who taught us about the mechanisation of farms and tractors and how to harvest, had, she said, turned into an old machine himself and rusted away from the inside.

'It probably wasn't you he was afraid of. He probably thought it was a thief.'

'Thieves don't moan,' I said.

'Or maybe a murderer.'

'Murderers laugh,' I snapped.

Odete shook her head.

It was easier to understand the behaviour of ghosts than of people.

I was told off for damaging the undersheet, but not seriously. The resident tutor at the hostel was fond of songs from Russian films and my teacher, sensing how to reach the hearts of lonely women, had chosen a sad one for me, which we performed for International Women's Day to great acclaim. The good woman couldn't turn her tongue to telling me off properly. She simply caressed my head and told me that the undersheets were the property of society. Then she sighed heavily and shuffled downstairs, the worn steps creaking under her feet.

What if I had tried to scare my dear teacher? I was

terrified at the idea of seeing his fearless eyes piercing right through me, pitilessly! Because it was his responsibility not to be afraid of anything.

The forensics expert rang. The prints left by the thief had been made by leather gloves. The results of the analysis of the teeth marks: the thief had an irregular bite; one tooth, the canine, was false; the gap between the front teeth was half a centimetre. He had identified the blood type from the saliva sample and noted that the intruder didn't have good hygiene routines; he didn't clean his teeth before going out to rob people's houses as evidenced by the unpleasant remains of food on the drawer handles.

'Thank you, enough detail,' I interrupted. 'Just put it down in writing. Just think well before you write.'

The expert muttered that there was nothing to think about; how could he not tell the difference between rotten and healthy teeth? Teeth were his passion. He had even thought about opening a dental clinic.

I put down the phone.

Enough already. Two Klepaviciuses were definitely too many for one town.

Somebody kicked the bottom of the door.

I jumped up angrily.

The door swung open and a woman with greasy hair and a greasy face stepped in; the mother of the kidnapped girl. Her trousers were so hideously bright that I instantly developed a headache.

'Hi,' she said, informally, and slumped into a chair and took out a cigarette.

I looked at her, then at the open door. I was going to have to call the policeman on duty again.

'Don't even try.' The intruder winked at me, brazenly, and lit up the cigarette. 'You kicked out the tall one, but you won't get rid of me that easily.'

'What do you want?' I shuddered with fury. I hated, loathed, that style of trousers! It was enough to justify murdering somebody.

'Me? Nothing. I thought I should invite you to visit me. You've stopped dropping in altogether. You don't say hello in the street. We were best friends just a year ago.'

'What?' I shouted so loudly that my voice echoed in the corridor. 'Friends? Have you lost your mind?' I glanced at her orange trousers; they made me nauseous. 'What have you come here for? To get a refund on some empty bottles? I don't have recycling bin, or money. I have nothing! Please leave! Now!'

'When they assigned you here, you looked so unhappy.' The woman scratched her flat chest. 'You had no relatives or friends . . . Not even a boyfriend. I gave you shelter. I introduced you to the gang. We used to have a good drink and a good time.'

'We didn't have a good time!'

'You did, you did,' the woman said. 'You used to sit on the Chief's knee and sing nationalist White Army songs. *There, beyond the river . . .*'

'I have never sat on the Chief's knee!' I cried, horrified.

'You did, you did. But then the Chief got a stomach ulcer. He stopped drinking vodka, bought a cat, turned his nose up. You got all posh too. You didn't recognise me in the street, you wouldn't drop in. You even gave me ten cents once. At the kiosk. And with such a self-righteous expression on your face that I nearly threw up. I got friendly with a girl who was a thief, but it wasn't fun like it used to be with you. She was only interested in getting drunk. Strangers were a delicate matter to her.'

The woman stopped.

I looked at her, choking on angry vapours and a strange intuition; something familiar shone in that pale, freckled face which I could not ignore. A burning name. A name in the dark.

'Do you remember how you tried to pinch my Richard?' There was terrible gap between her teeth. 'And he, the idiot, chose the tall one. The longer the legs the better, he thought. I wanted to kill him – hit him with that metal bear on the bookcase.'

I grabbed a file from the desk and threw it at the giggling ghost. The pages rose to the ceiling and then started to descend, turning in circles, white and cool. When the last one reached the floor, the gap-toothed woman was no longer in my office. Even the pungent smoke had followed her like a faithful drinking-partner.

To sit on the Chief's knee! Jesus, could anything be more horrible than that?

I buried my head in my hands.

Could it be that there were moments in my life that I was incapable of remembering? Your memory guards everything, doesn't it? It's dangerous to lose your memory, even for a short time – anybody could convince you that you had done something wrong and that you just didn't remember.

Something stung deep in my belly; it must have been indigestion. But possibly it was the voice of my conscience, reminding me that spiritual processes were closely related to physiological ones. Anyone saying otherwise is devoid of a conscience.

30.02.2001

The forensic examination on the corpse found in the sewerage drain was carried out by the local lab. The idea that it was old Burdiugin was rejected immediately; the bones were young, strong and not yet thinned by osteoporosis. They had belonged to a tall and bulky forty-year-old. True, one bone (to be more exact, a group of bone segments) confused the expert. The head of the department was hysterical; he couldn't bear the idea that his competency in the field of forensics was inadequate. There was a dry note in the report; they had found a strange bony growth, starting at the end of the spine, an atavistic anomaly that occurred so rarely that on practical level it was nonsense. Two pictures of the reconstructed remains were attached. The photofit of the victim, to be exact. With the anomaly and without it.

Our forensics expert, having glanced at it, just shook his head. Nobody could convince him that in such a well-used area where the sewerage drain was, you could find prehistoric bones. That was not atavism; it was theft. The bones must have been stolen from a museum.

'But no museum has complained about a missing display!' I argued.

The eyes of the forensics expert, who was in a sour mood as it was, flashed as sharply as scalpels, slicing the layer of fat under my skin. He muttered that the findings had been established on sandy foundations. Then he slammed the door and locked himself in his lab to develop the photos of the crime scene.

The rejected photofits remained on the table, lit by a piercing, red, autumnal sun; one of them with a long, thirty vertebra segment of tail which might well have been interesting to the field of science, as well as to society in general. And to the media too. What cruel blow of fate had cut the thread of life of this specimen without him having become the object of global interest? And how did it happen that for forty years we hadn't known about such a marvel?

Fame could have changed his life; maybe he wouldn't have died in a ditch, but instead, perhaps, from a cocaine overdose.

That's something, at least . . .

Anastasia was a pale and fragile senior lecturer. She looked like the ghost of the Tsar's daughter, weighed down by heavy horn-rimmed glasses rather than a tiara. She was our literature lecturer, one of our extracurricular subjects, of course, and, of course, only focusing on the texts where crime and punishment were dominant themes. In essence, as Anastasia used to say, holding her glasses in place with her small fingers, it was practically impossible to find a piece of literature without some trace of crime. If not with the actual killing or crippling of the protagonist, then at least as a part of the narrative or as a stylistic device. This law was as sound as Newton's laws of physics. Besides, Anastasia had noticed one more thing, no less fascinating and strange: no matter how terrible the suffering of the protagonist or style were, or how torturous their death, for some reason the author always remained alive, and what's more, was not held responsible for his actions.

'Maybe he has immunity?' Nutcracker's voice trembled in the auditorium.

Several head turned towards him.

Anastasia grinned; she liked Nutcracker, probably because of his big head. Without answering, she began talking about Raskolnikov, about the negative effect the small, coffin-sized room had on him, which could be compared with the chest of a moneylender. It's not as simple as you might think to live in a chest full of money. Raskolnikov was not just the victim of claustrophobia, not at all. The chest had limited his actions and desires. You would grab an axe too, if you were prevented from taking part in the reality show, or could get drunk for free.

'Isn't that right?' she addressed the few left in the audience. Nobody replied. Nutcracker jumped up and held a piece of paper towards her.

'What's this?' Anastasia lifted her glasses.

'It's the map of the crime scene,' Nutcracker explained helpfully. 'The corpse of the moneylender, the trajectory of the blow, the acceleration of the spray of the blood. A metre and a half away – the chest . . .'

Anastasia slowly pushed her glasses back up her nose and said nothing for a long time. She didn't dismiss them – it helped her to remain balanced.

Nutcracker, his forehead furrowed, gazed intensely at the teacher. In his soul, too, a drama was probably raging; with all his might he was trying to understand the importance of literature to crime.

The light of the street lamps sank in the wet tiles of the yard; the wind rushed through the arch, rustling the dry, blackened leaves, wrinkled by fire, unreadable, hiding in their capillaries the very precise nature of the crime – the time, the place, the reason.

Atali was in a bad mood.

She snapped that there were no coffee beans left and told me to get my coffee from the nearest bar. As she communicated all this without opening her mouth, using gestures and her eyes, I decided she had tooth ache.

I would do without coffee. It ruins the skin on your face. And as for Atali . . . Perhaps she should visit the forensics expert? It would cheer him up to have a client. He would probably get so worked up he would tear out all her teeth except the aching one.

A small crowd of women had gathered outside the House of Culture which had been built at a time when art belonged to the masses and the masses had no idea what to do with it. They glanced at the dark windows of the hall with respect and worry. Their silence seemed sombre and fatalistic; any of the women would have given away a month's pension in order to hear again through the rusty windows a fresh child-ish soprano: *The Homeland hears, The Homeland knows*!

A grey Mercedes pulled up right by the steps; it was only by a miracle that it didn't crush the large flowerbed from which a clove bush stuck out in all directions. The furniture salesman, wearing a grey suit, jumped out hurriedly and headed inside. The women were huddled like nervous quails blocking his way, but that didn't deflect the businessman from his trajectory. He ducked right through the thick of them, like wind, and appeared a moment later at the top of the stairs. His striped tie hadn't budged an inch.

Having pushed myself through the rowdy crowd, I saw him slumped on the front row, on the chair to either side lay a folder, like bodyguards, tense and unhappy. All three of them stared at the stage, where a pot of withered asters sat on the table.

I sat by the door so that I could sneak out when needed. Ever since I had been a child, performances by great artists had excited me so much that I had to flee full halls and hide in the toilet. When the band Nerija performed in town, I threw up from the excitement. Odete didn't understand at all, she shouted at me, thinking I had vomited on purpose. She couldn't get her head around the fact that true art turns not just your worldview upside down but the stomach too.

I clenched my fists so hard, my nails dug into flesh. God, I had already begun trembling! Fortunately, I hadn't had lunch.

When the candidate climbed up onto the stage, accompanied by the director of the House of Culture and the representative from the local government, his features blurred before my eyes. I struggled to calm myself – don't worry, it couldn't be worse than death. But when I managed to see his face properly, disappointment cooled my ardour; the candidate looked washed out, somehow, and faded. That's what it's like when you get used to photo-shopped electoral images – the moustache of Clarke Gable, a military cap and sinister Mexican eyebrows!

Perhaps it was better that way. At least the poor man wouldn't make me throw up.

The director opened the meeting. He expressed his joy about the rejuvenation of the town and the changing winds. Somebody from the audience shouted out that unemployment benefits were too low. 'Fuck the winds, they can blow up your arse.'

The candidate promised to sort everything out; if they elected him he would immediately propose an amendment in the law increasing benefits for job seekers. He spoke in such a rich and strong baritone that women loosened the knots of the scarfs under their chins; their throats became sore, swollen from excitement. The furniture salesman bent forward, eager to hear every single word. The more the candidate spoke – richly, truthfully, tearfully – the more the salesman leant forward. I grew concerned that he was about to kiss the floor. But instead of a kiss, he leapt up and fired a sudden shot; the candidate was splashing around with unmeasurable promises, he was the pushover of the party, higher political forces pushed him around.

The secretary, in a mustard suit, jumped towards the furniture salesman, officiously handing him some water with lemon and explained to the curious audience that the Candidate had no reason to worry; the businessman was a candidate for the local council and was not in competition with him.

The salesman grew as red as a turkey. He slumped into his seat, leant backwards and listened no more.

A handsome brown-haired man climbed onto the stage, nodded politely to the audience and introduced himself as the candidate's deputy and invited the people to join them for a beer after the meeting. For free, of course.

He shouldn't have said it; the audience exploded in a commotion, heads turning towards the door. Only the stern voice of the brown-haired deputy managed to save the meeting.

'The beer will be brought in an hour.'

The audience calmed down. Only somebody by the wall continued to swear, joyfully. In an attempt to see the brown-haired deputy better, I leaned forward.

Where had I heard that commanding voice?

While I was trying to remember, two teenagers, possibly amateur artists, brought in the state flag and spread it out behind the candidate. Music, reminiscent of a *pasodoble*, came from somewhere and the candidate swore a loud and solemn oath that he was ready for anything for the sake of the homeland.

I felt a hot and bitter lump travel up my throat. When the brown-haired deputy, lit by the flag's red strip, pushed his chest forward, looking like Alexander Matrosov, I rushed for the exit bumping into the door frame on the way out and vomited green saliva into the toilet bowl. Fortunately, nobody saw me; rumours would have spread, each one nastier than the next one. Like that the investigator was pregnant, or that she had been drinking cheap spirits again, or had got worms from her cat. Nobody vomits because of excitement these days.

Ah, Matrosov's chest, with those golden hairs!

Political figures are definitely ruled by higher powers than we imagine.

But, are there no other figures in life, just political ones?

'Wait! Wait!' somebody shouted, running after me.

Jesus! Now they would order me to lie down in the middle of the road and surrender to the Homeland.

No chance! I didn't turn. I picked up speed.

'If you don't stop, you'll be disciplined!'

I stopped. There was only one person who would say something like that.

'I didn't realise it was you,' I said to the Chief, who was breathless.

Sweaty and angry, the Chief cast a glance at me, collapsed onto the bench and spoke with difficulty.

'It's a work disc . . . each.'

A breach of work discipline?

'But hold on, Chief!' I said, concerned.

The Chief cast another sharp glance at me.

'I'm waiting,' he said sarcastically. 'I'm not rushing around like mad. As you see – I'm waiting!'

The candidate's talk must have made him feel insecure too.

'While all of you here,' the Chief accentuated the plural, formal *you*, though his comment was probably directed at me personally. 'You keep running. You don't know how to work slowly. When I need to – I can't catch up with you! That's what you get – the world today!'

'What are you talking about, Chief?' I said. 'Not only does *the world today!* not run, it's actually stuck in one place. Just look at those drunkards who hang around at the beer kiosk . . .'

The Chief looked, though not at the beer kiosk, but rather in the direction of the House of Culture. He mumbled something. It sounded like he was making a mental shopping list. He stood up then and, without rushing, began to float like a heavy barge back towards the station.

'Did you want to say something?' I shouted. The question froze in the air. The Chief didn't reply; only the sides of his raincoat fluttered.

Aha, neither of us can hide behind rhetorical questions, Chief. I know it's been painful to run the station for fifteen years with no higher responsibilities because of the displeasure of the forces above. It has a dreadful effect on the nerves and even the purr of a cat doesn't help. What's the use of *The Rubiyat of Omar Khayyam*, when for a breach of work discipline you can't sentence somebody to death or hard labour, or at least prescribe corporal punishment to be executed in the market square and the confiscation of all possessions?

And you, damask roses in the garden, have your sleepy, black-red petals, the colour of blood, ever dreamed of such poetry breathed from dry, chipped passionate lips? They are not the words of a wise man, nor those of the poet who used to walk along the paths of the garden, but the dark shadow of the twelfth angel.

I went home and took down the poster of the candidate, rolled it up, fastened it with a string and put it into the wardrobe, at the very top where old jumpers went mouldy and moths multiplied without being disturbed. I didn't dare throw it away; you never knew if the torn pieces of the monster might come back to life and crawl over to you in the night, smothering you, whispering his party's programme in your ear. You wouldn't be able to shift the creature perched upon your chest until you had finished listening to the whole programme, starting with the rise in the job-seekers allowance and finishing with the introduction of torture for thieves who stole from cars. And the glitter of his green eyes (how was it I hadn't noticed before) guaranteed that he would win and then a metaphysical punishment would descend upon me, for having thrown the poster out. Professional paranoia, for example.

I hit Yin Yang for having chewed the corners of the poster. It had obviously never occurred to her that the wellbeing of cats was also dependent upon keeping a strong party line. When a state descends into anarchy, then cats lose all their privileges too and are forced to catch mice.

Anyway, what did Fate mean by singing, '*A Russian girl has two plaits*'? Was it that the republic was being threatened by pro-Russian state powers? And what did it have to do with the Uzbek Republic? Nothing. It just confirmed that Fate was eternally meaningless.

My mother carried me through the rain, covering my face with the wing of the undersheet, hiding from me how Fate disintegrated, like a melting snowman, the patched clothes, soft body tissue and tiny finger bones slowly falling from it. Cracking like rotten joists. It headed towards the woods to die, to turn back into what it had always been – a gust of rain, a dissipating smell, a gap in the clouds.

But I didn't see that, the cloth wing covered my face.

Mother, mummy, don't take your white wing from my face. I don't want to look Fate in the eye. Its blood-stained corpse lay on the moss like a badly tuned piano. The wind fastened strands of its long hair on the low branches of the birch trees, where they swung like mistletoe, shining darkly in the sun.

Don't let the child near the corpse, a militia man shouted, holding in his hand a polished high heeled shoe. Women, attracted like hyenas to the crime scene, surrounded me, cackling, ready to lay eggs – eager to comfort the poor orphan. Think: is it fun to see your mother having been savaged by dogs? My father was not there to comfort me; he sat drunk under the juniper tree eating blueberries mechanically. 'What?' he shouted when the militia man asked why he didn't look for his wife and didn't alert the station even after the berry-pickers had found the remains? 'She had gone to the forest in her heels, the bitch!'

He said no more, only swore.

Mother, mummy . . . Your transparent wings lay crushed beneath your back. You didn't make it as far as the blossoming whore's grass. I would have wrapped you in your wings and carried you there, it was so close, only some five metres, but the women didn't let me. They dragged me further and further away. I will hate that kindness for the rest of my life which denied you those last few pleasant minutes. You would have sensed with each and every one of your separated fibres the sweet joy of infidelity.

The erotic was hidden away from the world's eye, deep in the grave, like a dream you would never wake from.

X

The corridors were like cool, dark arteries, the blood in them had turned into dry air. On the wall greenish, sharp, dust sparkled gold, mysterious dream-bearers.

To find the right door here was as difficult as in reality and there was no-one to ask where room 235 was apart from myself. And then, suddenly, there he was in front of my eyes, like a ghost in uniform, but before I was able to open my mouth he had gone.

If they hadn't had names plates with job descriptions on the doors, I would never have been able to find either the chief prosecutor or the barrister. It occurred to me that there was no reason to distinguish between them, they were like Siamese-twins, they just needed to be found. But I couldn't find what I was looking for. Precipitator of Processes. Open until lunch. Meditating Prosecutor. Manager of Procedures. What procedures? It wasn't a clinic, was it? Doctor, please don't try to separate the Siamese twins! It's too much of a risk, especially if the brain is shared. One twin prosecutes and the other defends, so the punishment depends upon the defendant himself. If the defendant is not a total idiot, he would choose the most severe.

That wasn't a dream. That's how they speak in the real life.

An old man in a uniform who looked like a railway worker with eyes like red traffic lights shouted that I was a complete fool. His words were cut short by the rattle of an approaching train. Somebody got off and came closer and closer, his shoes stomping heavily and then, when he was just about to appear, burning with the anger, like an offended official, I suddenly woke up.

Clump, clump, clump, my dream stomped away down the street, cursing as he disappeared.

I tore open my eyes; in the pale strip of light the hands of the clock showed four-thirty. I closed my eyes again.

I saw him, face down, arms spread wide in the round swimming pool. Green ripples, tinkling like barely audible notes, intermingled with matted strands of hair and, from afar, where there is no water or life, came the sound of Nutcracker's music accompanied by the whistling sound of a flute – the king of mice was about to put in an appearance. However, it wasn't the three-headed mouse that approached the pool, the figure that swam slowly closer was the one who had so shamefully, so unexpectedly and carelessly severed the most important cord, slowly being covered by single-cell algae, that is used to indicate the amount of time a body has been underwater.

You are like a drowned ancient civilisation, your interior is closed for ever and the current takes me, a microscopic grain of time, past large, stony eyes. I am moving away from you so slowly that your Greek profile and your torso, eaten by erosion, will stay in my sight for a long time.

A cuttlefish, like a swollen eye lash, bumped against my half-closed eye lid; it touched my ear with a black sucker.

I screamed. The cat jumped, frightened and looked at me angrily with its yellow Martian eyes.

The sun-lit Martian landscape spilled a harsh, dry, yellow light across the floor and the bed linen. If I had looked out of the window at that moment, I would have seen deep craters and a fast thinning atmosphere – dissolving into patches and, with a blue flash, gone. No longer stopped by the atmosphere's protective layer, the harmful rays of the cosmos would jab downwards wildly like spears.

The phone was so hot I couldn't touch it; it sizzled as if it was being fried.

I wrapped my hand in the cloth of the dressing gown and lifted the receiver.

Atali was so agitated that she gobbled like a goose.

'You overslept!' she shouted, horrified.

I glanced at the clock. It was nine. Hell, I had forgotten to set the alarm the previous night.

'Don't worry.' I calmed Atali down. 'I'll dress quickly, have a coffee and come to work. It's not the first time. The Chief told me that just because you rush, it doesn't mean you work well.'

'But!' Atali didn't seem ready to calm down quite so easily. 'There's somebody in your office from . . . sitting . . .'

She swallowed the name of the institution together with the exclamation mark.

I quailed.

What did the person from . . . need? To rummage through my unsolved cases?

With trembling fingers, I buttoned my coat, ran my fingers through my hair. In the mirror a pale ghost in civvies gazed at me.

If I knew that the person from . . . had come with good intentions, I would have put on something nicer and maybe a little lipstick. But now – no. There was no point. Nobody from there came with good intentions. If they did they would inform you about it in advance, six months in advance, so that everybody had enough time to get to their heads around it. But there was no getting your head around the bad stuff.

And I would have a coffee as well. I had no intention of dying without my usual dose of caffeine.

A receipt from the shoe repair shop fell from the shelf into the coffee grinder. I realised only after I had ground it with the coffee.

I ran down the street feeling a rubber weight in my stomach. A yellow October flooded the town on all sides, and from not far away, on an island not yet drowned by flood water, came the lonely tap of a cobbler's hammer.

I didn't meet a single soul on the way in to my office. The thought flashed through my head that they had all been wiped out by some kind of plague. It would be awaiting me in my office, in human form. Probably wearing a tie.

He was indeed waiting for me, leafing through my papers. His eyes were half closed so that the deadly rays didn't emit so strongly. When he lifted his head and looked at me, I felt I was about to die; my red blood cells were turning into white ones, my ribs were smouldering and the plague rose up my oesophagus, choking me.

'You're not feeling well?' he asked politely.

Had he not recognised me?

'I'm okay,' I whispered. 'Thank you,' I added, for no reason.

'You're welcome. Take a seat.' He indicated the chair. 'We're going to have a chat about your competency and your working methods.'

I swallowed the sour lump. About my competency? My working methods? Why not about Franz Liszt, showered with wild garden petals? By the time of the next blossoming only the hard, cellophane wrapped covers would be left from the textbook. The pictures and the biographies would have been devoured by the pink sodium chloride of the apple trees.

From the corner of my eye I noticed that on my desk there was a twig of bittersweet nightshade with ripe red berries. Franz paid no attention to it, and I nearly cried. So it was not him; the secret admirer was not him! It wasn't possible that the worshipper wouldn't recognise his goddess. And now the goddess would gladly poison herself with the bittersweet nightshade berries.

Yin Yang was becoming very mysterious. I had slowly got used to her sitting on the philosophy books when I came home, right on the page where Origen talks about an animals' souls, their imagination and brain. Another time I found the TV on and on the table a glass of evaporated brandy and a sheet of squared paper covered with lopsided numbers and colons. It looked like a set of football results. The cat, unfazed, was licking her paw. She was not drunk. And when Razanauskas scored a goal that even Oliver Kahn himself couldn't stop, she didn't howl wildly, or fall upon my chest and hug me or bite my nose off.

I'm more or less convinced her behaviour is a display of vanity. She can't accept being equal to an average human. She thinks she is a genius.

No, the sterilisation hadn't been good for her.

It wasn't the silver-haired jackdaw but Yin Yang who was stroking me – with damp, cold fingers, sharp nails tapping each vertebra. When I woke I saw a black and white fur hung upon the wall, it had been electrified by the blue moonlight and its hair stood out like the sparkling nails of a cobbler.

No, that was impossible; Yin Yang was not able to experience some kind of fairy tale metamorphosis, not least because of her gender. For the same reason I couldn't enjoy the experience of metamorphosis: what would I do with an enchanted princess? Two strange women, like two female cats could only put up with each other for the sake of politeness, though politeness isn't a virtue and doesn't last long.

Thank God, it was just the moonlight.

The real Yin Yang was in the wardrobe; she had settled herself in a drawer from which a pair of tights was dangling. Two emerald dots flashed in the black depths. Slowly, slower than time, their rays travelled through the blind darkness as far as the weightless, cold field of moonlight.

The ray's journey was long, slowed by a multitude of other light sources. It flew like a javelin aimed not to pierce but to glance off, touching the artery of sleep with a feather's tip.

Imaginary guns are so easy to use! They don't let you down when you run into improbable creatures. The old

Kalashnikov, bruised by constant assembling, was a different matter though; there were no holes in the target, but the walls and ceilings were ploughed by bullets.

The school firing range, built away, behind the teachers' vegetable garden and separated from it by a brick wall (probably to prevent us from shooting the much-hated chemistry teacher while he was weeding his bean plants; and even if we were firing blanks, taking a shot itself was satisfying). It was a good place to think about the meaning of war and lost bullets. Mine probably even missed the walls. Where they went, God only knew; the firing range instructor certainly didn't.

Usually, he just shook his head and put a minus next to my name. What God noted down next to my name, I'm not aware; probably the number eight lying on its side to signify infinite stupidity.

One evening, having nothing better to do, Odete and I sneaked into an almost empty church. There were several women dressed in black dozing on the benches. The candles crackled and in front of the altar there was, on a catafalque, a coffin covered with a black baldachin. Jesus looked down at me sternly, his radioactively shining heart laid bare by some unknown anatomical pathologist.

Without waiting for the women to raise their heads from the benches and look at us with their deep, tunnel-like eyes, or for Jesus to say that it was I that had shot at his heart with my blank cartridges, we rushed out, though Odete was adamant that she needed to take a look at the dead man. She even took a mirror from her pocket, putting it to the dead lips; if it misted slightly, it would mean that the person was still alive, just in a deep sleep.

'Stop, Odete. Nobody can survive an autopsy. If your mirror mists up, it's only the breath of Death.'

My teacher, the spirit of the bubonic plague, having closed one file, reached for another. It seemed that Atali had brought all the unsolved cases in. She, herself, had her nose pressed against the door; I saw an eye, round from horror, not its normal pink, but pale as heated aluminium, without pupil or iris. Like Miss Koko, she seemed to have been shrivelled by marasmus – deep to the bone, like a smoked mackerel.

He shut the file with a loud slam. The eye disappeared.

'Don't you think that such procedures would be better suited to the nineteenth century?'

'W . . . what procedures?'

'Your work ones.' He pushed away the papers, with obvious disgust. 'Your work ones!'

'Well all methods are good, if they help to uncover a fraction of truth . . .'

The teacher raised his eyebrows.

In the door way, reflecting the sunlight, a round aluminium dot flashed again.

'Never mind. I didn't come here to argue with you.' He glanced at the watch on his wrist; the strap shone hard gold, like his sleek hair. 'And it's not the crumbs of your truth that I'm interested in.'

He spoke looking above my head, addressing the crumbling plaster wall.

'Why is The Copper Foot case still open? Didn't your Chief get the instructions?'

'I . . .' I mumbled, surprised. 'We . . . closed it ourselves.'

'You?' The teacher looked at me with the same charming indifference the poster had. 'Very good. Then who re-opened it? Why did the ministry receive an odd query that sought to discredit not only me but also the governmental service?'

'I don't know . . . I don't know . . . You're not the killer!'

The teacher fell silent. His golden eyelids lowered slowly – probably so that his deadly gaze didn't finish me off at once.

'I'm giving you twenty-four hours. Find out who it is in your station that is behaving in this amateurish fashion and what their motives for this behaviour are.'

He said nothing more, but it was clear that the amateur's head would roll. Good. Did he not understand that the painting of the professional was 'Saturn, Devouring his Son'.

The teacher looked at his watch again.

The surgically sharp hands of the watch were driven around its face by the energy of an incarcerated teenager. The barely audible ticking was identical to the sound of rodents' teeth crunching into a body. And when moonlight flooded the bath – that miniature pond of death – a Beethoven's sonata began to play, the rhythm stumbling and dissonant; the pianist must either have been drunk or struck by the weight of cinematographic amnesia.

The door pushed open so suddenly that it would have hit the teacher's head, but, as if expecting it, he stopped it with his tough, golden hand.

Atali stood in the doorway, as white as the porcelain cups, with a tray in her hands and attempted a smile.

'Some coffee, perhaps?'

The teacher looked over her head.

'No, I'm short of time. Has the Chief arrived yet?'

Atali's hands shook. The spoons clinked melodically and the sugar bowl leant to one side, like the tower of Pisa.

'He's in his office.' Some coffee spilled from a tilted cup on to Atali's wrist; it hissed angrily and a white steam rose from it.

'Thank you,' the teacher said coldly. He closed the door politely and walked off noiselessly. He flew rather than walked, spreading wide his cemetery-shroud wings, which shone like greedy, satanic potassium nitrate.

I grabbed the tray from Atali's hands and placed it on the desk. Steam still rose from the secretary's pale skin.

'Don't look so worried, Atali. Ministerial ghosts are short lived, here today, gone tomorrow. What can they do to us? We're real people, Atali!'

The secretary looked at me, her eyes brimming with tears. She grabbed a cup and drank the coffee in a couple of gulps. She opened her mouth – I thought steam would come from it – and then turned slowly paler and paler. An autumnal grimness slowly began to rise from the hollow at the base of her throat, flooding her cheeks, her forehead and hair line. Atali was calming down.

Nobody saw hell's messenger leave the Chief's office, which, in principle, was understandable. When I knocked on his door half an hour later, the response was a hostile silence; there was nobody inside. I felt numb. What if the Chief had been dragged alive down to that bewildering basement corridor with the innumerable name plates on the doors? History is full of examples of mysterious events. And besides, people don't like to walk anywhere; they would prefer to be taken in a carriage, even on that last journey to heaven.

Oh my God . . . Only a drop of brandy could save me. If Atali hadn't drunk it all. She had good reason to. Agents of the Ministry weren't conducive to sobriety.

Just look in your mirror, Odete, at the thick mist spreading from the grey amalgam, coiling, pungent with the smell of devil's broom and hay and how funny that we squatted in the blueberry bushes, slapping our sides and cursing the mosquitoes with Russian obscenities. Just look, Odete, we hid there safe from the breath of the corpse, safe, even from the radioactive heart of God. We were just like the corpse under the black sheet, embroidered with crossed bones, nobody could force him to stand up, not surprise, nor love nor galvanisation.

Oh, Odete, Odete, how alive the language of our bodies was that night! Could you ever have believed that we would run away from a church, death's tidy home! The more a body lives, the less space there is for death. Isn't it wonderful that *La Perla* underwear made us want to make love, not die?

I felt like dying when the children from the hostel were driven to the clinic and had to undress down to their underwear, which were old and faded and badly patched. The contempt of the world was reflected in the nurses' smiles. It was my dream to lie in bed ill with some terrible, noble disease – cholera, for example. Then I wouldn't be forced to have that horrible health check; they checked only the healthy and the dead. I wouldn't die of course, people usually recovered from noble diseases.

Later, in year eight, I started stealing washing from gardens, along with the pegs. Once I even took the washing line along with the dry branch it was tied to. I would throw away the bras, you could easily fit a melon into the shrunken cups and I had no interest in the men's pants either (one pair was made from the same cloth as the hostel curtains; I couldn't look at the curtains for a long time after that).

I grew more and more afraid of those ruthless medical check-ups; the scrutiny of the nurses cut more painfully than the knife used to kill pigs, slicing off anything that even slightly covered the trembling body. Even the stolen pink knickers with a yacht on the appendix side didn't help.

Oh Odete, Odete, the apple trees were sunk in such a heavy fog that I could barely find the washing line. The tiny pink yacht struggled to find its way home. I was trembling when I got under the duvet, pressing the damp clothes to my chest, while you slept. Your cotton tights drooped peacefully from the end of the bed, and when the first rays of the sun, having penetrated the fog, turned their stripes golden, I thought that they would attack me to protect you in your innocent sleep.

Why didn't I stop him and tell him that it was me who used to run along the wild nettle path, their poisonous silk closing behind my back? I could have leant upon his shiny wrist – after all, gold isn't steel, it's softer. You would have held me like the hands, melting like wax in the sun-bright operating theatre, held the unborn son, who whispered, '*No gentle breast touched my lips and no milk ran down my throat.'* The furnace door slammed and it rained white ash. *'Don't worry, mamma, the time will come when I won't leave your arms. You will never be alone. We will burn in the same fire.'*

And what would he have said?

And to whom? To me or the all-seeing wall plaster?

I feel so old; I've lived the lives of two seventeen-year-olds almost, while the teacher, walking in the Caliph's rose garden, caresses only the opening buds with his warm finger tips . . . Oh, heavy damask roses, aren't you all equal in the eyes of God?

Frail fingers placed the poisonous bittersweet nightshade berries into my mouth, cold unpolished gemstones; I will die like that, with my mouth full, having not yet tasted them . . .

'Another brandy.'

Sarkiene looked at me, worried. I had never had three brandies during working hours and then asked for a fourth.

But what was so unusual? A drunk police officer – is that something strange? The higher the position, the more natural it looks. If I were a prosecutor I would drink the whole bottle.

'You see, Sarkiene . . . Listen, for God's sake, what's your name?'

'Isolde.' Sarkiene's hands trembled as she held a bowl of jelly.

'Well, well, well,' I expressed my surprise. 'Isolde! Why then in the records does it say it's Antanina?'

Sarkiene placed the jelly on the table and turned her whole body towards me.

'I'm a new person, now,' she said, determined. 'I crossed out my old life and I don't want my old name.'

'What about the surname?' I said sadly. 'Your surname's the old one?'

Sarkiene switched on the coffee machine. Steam rose with a hiss; it seemed about to start moving, like Lenin's armoured vehicle.

'I'm going to get a new surname too!' Sarkiene shouted through the steam.

When the machine quietened down, Isolde-Antanina placed a fourth glass of brandy before me and whispered:

'Kidman.'

'What? I jumped, and looked around nervously.

'I'm going to be Isolde Kidman!' Sarkiene smiled widely, and, horrified, I noticed that her teeth were also new, as white as a porcelain toilet. Her perfume smelled like Ambi Pur.

'But, Isolde,' I said growing melancholic, 'What was wrong with your old life that you want to change everything?'

Sarkiene was dealing with her hair, gazing at her reflection in the window, and didn't hear my question.

Some man must have been to blame, I decided. It was usually because of them that you felt the need to change your life. God, how lucky snails were not to have gender! They just crawled through life, leaving their mark, a glistening trail.

Watson, the priest, entered the café wearing a raincoat and checked hat.

Why weren't priests allowed to grow a moustache? Was it some decision made by the Synod of Bishops? No, the truth was hidden elsewhere: priests wanted to resemble angels, and angels don't have moustaches.

The priest would look more human with a moustache, or, better still, he would look like the protagonist of a novel. Whenever you saw him, you would be waiting for the other one to turn up, the important one. He would enter with a pipe in his mouth and scan the crime scene with his sharp gaze, the tension swelling.

Sarkiene applied some more lipstick. She turned to the priest looking like a satisfied vampire, hiccupped, surprised, and attempted a smile. Her canines were red; she must have been grinning when she put the lipstick on.

'Glory to Jesus Christ,' Watson whispered.

Sarkiene let out a strange noise, like the whistle of a deflated ball. That must have been the response.

'I would like tea with rum . . . No, rum with tea,' the priest said in an even quieter voice, sitting down at the corner table. He nodded to me and froze, his eye fixed on a glass out of which paper napkins stuck, cut into small pieces – so small you would need tweezers to take them out. Isolde, while changing her life had, unfortunately, failed to consider such important detail as napkins.

The door slammed. The red-haired woman came in, sat at the central table and shouted, 'Bacardi Breezer!' She tilted her head back proudly. A burning bush, waiting for Moses to come and humbly listen to her.

'Mr Pries . . . Prie . . .' choked Isolde, her neck stretched towards Watson. 'Would sir like a Bacardi Breezer too?'

'No,' the priest snapped back. 'Havana club.'

It seemed that tonight we, the lonely ones, would be tied

by the strings of strong drink, which were often stronger than human bonds.

My dear, lovely teacher, with your cool dry wine, you are a total stranger to us! What a pity! I would force myself through the darkness, clasping that human bond, until finally I bumped into you like a vine tree and you would fill me from top to bottom with young and fragrant Beaujolais!

The woman cast the priest a sly look.

'I don't understand,' she said, addressing the carafe of rum, as the sun broke through the ribbed glass and fell flaming onto her hair, 'Why we need an institution if it is totally ineffective!'

The carafe didn't reply. Neither did the priest.

The woman glanced at me.

'If we had more faith in paranormal forces,' she said, 'the facts of the crime wouldn't have sunk into the darkness.'

I shook my head. The brandy, like suede needles, stuck into my clammy, poisonously glistening skin which began to grow numb.

'What are you talking about? The police or the church?' I tried to sound as serious as I could.

The woman was not put off.

'I was talking in the abstract,' she said, not blinking.

'You can't be talking in the abstract. There are no abstract crimes.'

'Nor sins,' the priest rustled, quieter than a midsummer breeze.

The woman took a sip, sighed, and shook her head.

'My dears, everything is abstract in this world. The only concrete thing is the soul's connection to man.'

The priest said nothing. It was impossibly difficult for him to comprehend what, for the woman, was banal.

I recalled the church in town. The air there felt the same in winter and in summer. The temperature was similar to that of the body of a corpse; dead electrons and protons filtered through a black deathly sieve, no longer forming structures reminiscent of bouquets of flowers. Slowly and awkwardly they turned on their axis, carrying a crushing weight. The soul had no connection with the dead, they are as far from each other as dead stars.

'The case, for example,' the woman said to the carafe, 'of the girl in the bath. I'm sure it was the revenge of a dead soul.'

'There are no dead souls,' the priest objected.

'Oh, but there most definitely are,' the woman snapped. 'If you had asked me,' she glanced at me crossly, 'I would have found evidence of it.'

It amused me to picture us trying to push a dead soul into the detention cell as it screamed and demanded a lawyer.

The woman fixed her eyes upon me.

'I would have given her absolution and told her to rest in peace,' she said sternly. 'No need for lawyers, or people being arrested.'

The priest sighed feebly. I doubted that he understood a thing. He was a serene and soft provincial priest, grinding out Latin quotes to the local female parishioners and the drunks. (They thought that the sorrowful *veni, spiritus* was the magical name for heaven). Secretly, he missed the old days, which could no longer be called the good days, when pagan customs mixed benignly with Christian ones and even party ideology served to nourish the Godly cult. How annoying that so many flocked to witches and clairvoyants; never mind, that was the law. Spiritual experts were needed by both the simple and the leaders of the nation; that was probably the most important link connecting the select ones with the ordinary people.

The priest did understand that, so he sat with his head bent sadly over his cup of tea and didn't have the courage to curse the red witch. 'All the sorcerers are doomed for the second death!' A sorcerer was a sorcerer, that was fine, but how was it possible to imagine the Minister of Internal Affairs flying with his personal clairvoyant straight into hell fire and sulphur? Everything seemed so simple until you were confronted with real people. So, the problem was not what is real *per se*, the priest thought, sipping his tea and nearly choking, but real people.

The woman had probably asked a spirit to make shorthand notes of his thoughts – she simply sneered at the priest, stood up, stumbled, adjusted her dress which was slipping up her thighs and, with a wiggle of her bottom, which was as round as a paddle, made her way towards the toilet.

'And it's worst when that real person is a woman,' the priest thought and then grew upset. He recalled a brown-haired neighbour called Jolka from his childhood who had kept hitting him around the head with a toy spade, spitting at him and who had even showed him her bottom (which was, thank God, not naked). She had been a witch. And yet, somehow, he didn't want Jolka to burn in the fiery lake. Secretly, the priest believed in reincarnation and hoped his terrible sand pit friend would come back as a different, more peaceful creature rather than a woman. A tiger lily perhaps. And he would bark joyfully and cock up his leg.

Then an unexpected idea shot into the priest's head and he grew pale. What if the woman was Jolka? It was a small world, wasn't it?

He attempted to make his escape unnoticed, but the woman blocked his way with her massive chest.

'The world is horrible not because it's so small,' she said, reading his thoughts, 'but because one by one all the animal species are gradually disappearing.'

The priest looked at the madam's *décolleté* fearfully.

'And what's the consequence of this?' The witch wouldn't let go. 'It's this that you, Sir, will have less and less choice. When all the animals are extinct there will be nowhere to reincarnate yourself.'

'A man is not an animal!' the priest shouted, attempting to get past.

'An animal has a soul too,' the woman disagreed. 'Otherwise you wouldn't want to be reincarnated as a dog.'

The priest closed his eyes. The depth of the *décolleté* must have made him dizzy.

'Police!' he shouted in a weak voice.

The woman chortled.

'The police won't help you; they're the weakest link in the chain.'

I should have contradicted her. At least for the sake of decency. If witches started besmirching the police's reputation, then whatever next?

As I was thinking what I should say, the priest rushed towards the door like a wounded bat. Momentarily, he regained control of himself, then hit his head on the door-frame and with a moan disappeared out into the thick and intense darkness.

The woman returned to her seat and adjusted her dress.

'A shame I didn't have my toy spade with me,' she muttered.

When I awoke from my sleep, the brandy I had drunk had formed a warm and protective skin around me; seven swords could stab it and they would only sever fat, poison-ous veins and rust up. Like those keys Sarkiene was clinking when she was about to lock up the bar. I had probably managed to leave before that. The wave of heat had carried me out like a salamander. I was glowing as I flew through the dark wastes, seeing with my third eye how the ghosts gath-ered around a table in the bar. Nice that they were so friendly and that they didn't give a toss about what uniform you wore.

I would really like to know what there is in place of alco-hol in the world-to-come. You can't tell me that you have to exist for all eternity sober.

15.06.2002

The case of the corpse with the relic tail acquired new intrigu-ing detail some time later (after the case had been closed, of course, the Chief was right – time cleared up everything). The pathologist discovered that his silver cigarette case had gone missing (he kept his condoms there) and decided he had left it at the crime scene. Crawling through the waste pipes he found not only his cigarette case but behind a pipe he discovered a false hand, the artfully ripped shreds of a sleeve, an American beer can and an invoice written in English. It turned out that about a year and a half before an American cinema production company had filmed there, charmed by the 'authenticity' of the location (the lopsided sheds, the outside toilets and inhabitants who didn't understand Lithuanian). The production company, Madam Vanda explained sternly, *pro jakich to gadov*, had said the film was about mutant anacondas. The producer must have felt that the untidy sheds seemed the most suitable place for mutants to multiply. And there was some truth in that. My grandmother, having found some apple cores and dirty socks under my bed, used to say crossly, '*Sutre tu, sutre!* Snakes will soon start breeding under your bed!'

I wouldn't have been surprised to discover that the corpse with a tail had been a prop for the film. Nobody had missed him or the false hand and the beer cans. Cinematography has little value for human life.

Dark eyed June, its eyes sparkling like a Persian cat's, gazed lovingly at the glistening green sewerage drains, from where came the dull rustle of a reptile.

XI

It should have been morning, but mysterious signs seemed to indicate that night had just fallen.

Silence, for example, crept by with the tread of a smiling schizophrenic; if you didn't fall safely asleep on time, it would draw dangerously close to you.

And when I nodded off, and the night's silence had stepped carefully over me and walked away, I dreamt of Orangerie. Despite her name, her windows were covered not by yucca plants or dracaenas but by simple curtains as dirty as the ones in the school hostel. Orangerie sat at the kitchen table, smoking and talking about the sadistic behaviour of her parents (darling, no need for detail, your name says it all). Her step-father used to beat her with the cable to the iron, while her mother would shout that the cable was broken as it was, the insulation was worn out and he should look for something else to use. I felt sorry for Orangerie, in the same way that I felt sorry for myself; my father had never beaten me, which only demonstrated his lack of love and attention to me. I told Orangerie that I felt like a stranger in the town, it was my first year working there, the Chief didn't understand me, his secretary didn't make coffee for me and the cases I had been assigned were no good.

'Have a drink,' Orangerie convinced me. That was the way she always consoled me.

It wasn't only I that found this attractive, but her constantly changing partners too. Though Orangerie had graduated from the Institute of Florists, she worked in a second-hand shop and it seemed that she sold her partners along with the old clothes. A new sweetheart would appear together with a new clothes delivery. Sometimes several of them at the same time.

'Would you like me to find one for you as well?' she offered on a number of occasions. I shook my head. No. No, thank you. And Orangerie would secretly think I had a superior attitude and was a snob.

How long did I remain that way, sneering at the gentle floristry mistress and the narcissi she selected? Was it true that one stuffy night in July I woke up next to a withered blossom, breathing acrid Prima cigarette smoke into my face? It didn't rain for a whole month. Gin evaporated from bottles, leaving intricate oriental patterns on the ceiling. I sat on the Chief's knee and sang White Army songs, and then I cried and requested that the Chief discipline me. The Chief said he would do anything for me.

There is nothing worse than memory, but it's reassuring at the same time. I know for sure that the Chief has never smoked Prima cigarettes and he has never disciplined me. He probably forgot. If a person, instead of doing everything he can, neglects to exert his power, without exception or rule – that is the definition of happiness.

You walked off into the distance, oh riding-hag of the night. The clink of dry finger bones is heard no more. You are probably paddling across the rag-shop floor and the pink ribbons of the dress become tangled between your squeaking calves. You carry my memory, spread wide in the wind, its edges eaten by chemicals, like injured petals.

The Chief sat on my bed, looking like a wardrobe dressed in a white dressing gown, behind him was Atali looking as sad and pale as a young moon. An orange grapefruit shone on the sideboard.

The door slammed and the doctor came in, looking like a gipsy. I grew tense. I don't trust people with eyes like anthracite.

'You see, she's more or less all right now.' He addressed the Chief rather than me.

The Chief leaned over me; I closed my eyes and put my fists out to stop the wardrobe from squashing me. But nothing fell upon me, breaking my bones. He carefully opened my fist and took something from it.

'Here,' said the doctor.

I opened my eyes and saw a piece of pink material held between his two fingers. 'The cramps are over now. We can throw this away, it's unhygienic.'

As the Chief and Atali were out of uniform, the doctor obviously thought they were my relatives. He addressed the Chief, tapping his fingers on the cupboard.

'Your . . . Your wife . . .'

The Chief flinched.

'Employee!' Atali hissed.

The doctor raised his eyebrows.

'Employee,' he said, deep in thought. 'There you go! A traditional balance of genders. And probably most healthy.

When both are the boss, there's nobody to follow the instructions. Anyway, in short, your employee has nothing wrong with her. We can't call short-term memory loss an illness, it's such a fleeting condition, it's nothing to take seriously. The sunlight takes longer to change and the clouds to move and the lightning travels much longer than your wife's memory . . . Sorry, your employee's! There's no need to roar at me. I'll discharge her today, I can see you can't sit still – so eager to give her instructions!'

It was true that the Chief couldn't sit still. He ran out of the room, a tsunami carrying Atali with him. The doctor's fingers froze in the air like a pianist's, but he was no sandalwood god, just simple alder. He might catch a pulsing vein of a lightning, but he would never be able to make the heavy, black tropical night talk and would not stop the pink dress from moving away, wouldn't seize it in such a way that the bones scattered and the slippery material ripped.

What did I do that made me renounce you, Orangerie? Who made me drink that medieval elixir, mixed from brandy and gin and with the muddy Lethe's waters?

The nurse upon entering the waiting room, looked at me like I was some kind of artichoke.

'Where is the child's father?' She looked around.

I looked around too.

'Not here,' I said.

'Not here?' The nurse turned angrily towards me. 'Is he not known?'

'Well, not exactly . . . Not that he is not known. I would say he was *supposed*. That is *they* are supposed.'

'And how many of them are supposed?' The nurse noted something down.

I considered for a moment.

'Four. No doubt about it,' I said with resolution.

A strange expression crossed her face, like that of a were-wolf at full moon, ready to bite. She slammed the door and then came a horrible dying howl, which shook the whole post-natal ward.

I blocked my ears and held my hands to them, not moving them even when the rich, greedy scream of the new-born was heard. The nurse gave me a piece of paper to sign (probably to confirm that Orangerie was not mad, as she had bitten the midwife's hand when the latter was about to give her a friendly pat on the cheek). The four fathers were now a four-kilo baby richer, she said. A kilogram for each.

They unfolded Orangerie's legs, took her under the armpits and dumped her on a stretcher, covered her with a sheet and wheeled her out of the birthing theatre like one of Chikatilo's victims. The midwife slammed the door with a white nozzle; I just managed to see how the loose leg stirrups flashed and the blood glistened in the metal basin under the table.

'How did you manage to get in?' a nurse as strict as a soldier's timetable, without papers or questions, shouted. 'You'll bring in an infection!' She pushed me out of the door. 'Only men are to be present at the birth' she added. 'There's no business for women being there.'

'But in Belgium and in Holland . . .' I opened my mouth, but the nurse wasn't listening. She locked the door with Prussian principle. I could see her lips moving through the glass which was as green as a toenail with a fungal infection. This isn't Belgium or Holland! I guessed she was saying. There's no place for miserable liberalism here. *Jawohl, kaput* and *hande hoch*.

Was it time to wake up? No, not yet. The night's silence was returning and approaching the bed with tired, heavy steps. Wet soil and yesterday's butterflies must have stuck to its skeletal soles. I would wait for it to step over my child-like body and go, its shiny rib bones clinking.

Animals are gifted with a subtle spiritual intuition; humans often forget they have it too, which is why clairvoyants always seem so wonderful. My father could ask a wild animal or a dog where to build his house so as to avoid building it in a place where the tread of an unsettled ghost would shake it at night.

But perhaps it wasn't a ghost. Perhaps it was time approaching, strolling noisily through the empty rooms. But who then was it, with eyes like a sphinx, that peeped through the windows, preventing sleep, pressing heavily upon the chest, ruthlessly reminding me that it was not my home?

Things are so lawless in the world of my dreams. I couldn't just close the door and draw the curtains. Maybe somebody was holding them open – after all, the dream didn't belong just to me.

I sat up in bed. It felt like I had wet myself and my mother was pulling the sheet towards her silently, her eyes shining in the darkness like Bubastes. The sheet was endless, a viscous mummy's bandage.

I switched on the light and examined the sheet. It was dry, clean, unsoiled. Thank God. Horror films today assign so many mystical powers to common objects that you start being afraid of a coffee grinder, while it's too frightening to even to think about the mysterious qualities of a toaster! I should buy a radio set to make my toast with.

I looked around. The TV, the Wi Fi, the ironing board leaning against the wall – they were all swollen with an angry, threatening silence. I shuffled to the kitchen, but it was no better there. There was not a single friendly face. The cat was sleeping under the radiator, having seemingly accepted the hostile environment.

Only the brandy bottle emitted any human warmth. It was a shame it wasn't Sunday the next day.

But so what if it wasn't Sunday? A small drop wouldn't do any harm. I would tell the Chief about how hard it was to live in this material world and if he didn't agree, it could only be because he didn't have the bare basics of electrical equipment. Or to put it another way, the bare basics. Losing a coffee grinder or a TV for no good reason was as painful as losing your virginity these days.

I found some cheese in the fridge. Cheese is excellent value; you can keep it as long as you wish – the mouldier it gets, the better it is. If the Chief didn't show any sympathy, I'd tell him I got poisoned by mould and had the brandy for medicinal purposes.

He, remembering those oriental nights when the gin had drawn patterns upon the ceiling like the ghosts of the Ottoman Empire, wouldn't be too hard on me. At least his intuition . . . What was I talking about? The Chief had no intuition. I hastily poured myself a second glass. Then we were left with logic, but logic is ruthless and it told me that he would definitely kill me. He would only possibly take pity on me if there was nobody from the ministry present.

There was only one solution – I wouldn't go to work. I would call Atali and tell her that I had been attacked. Somebody had leapt out from the cemetery, jumped on my back, dug his lopsided teeth into my artery . . . What? What else? The flu, of course. No, maybe a hooligan was better. He beat me badly. All my interior organs. It wasn't visible, but it hurt a lot.

I lay down and covered my head with a quilt. There was the smell of Nile sludge. Through the rough holes in the net, blue cheese crystals sparkled and electric stingrays shone, horrible creatures that used their electrical energy for God knows what and didn't even get billed for it. I wondered whether they ever needed to replace their bulbs and how they dealt with electricians?

Electricians are full of negative energy which usually forces itself out as soon as they open their mouths, hissing like a bottle of sparkling water being opened. They don't call sockets plug holes, it sounds indecent to them (electricians have their code of honour too). And they don't electrocute you from a distance, though they could. How stupid people are, taking away the electrician's superpowers and giving them to X-Men.

The python's dark coils wrapped around the old pavilion on the edge of the park, the stuffiness squeezed the bones and muscles. Above, the clouds swelled, turning blue. Orangerie was not afraid of darkness – she laughed between the two electricians, sparkling, and the wine which she drained from the bottle, bubbled down her transparent oesophagus. You see what it means to find yourself between two desirable men! While I was stuck between a mechanic who hadn't washed his hands and had pockets full of bolts and ball bearings, and some basilisk, who was like an aged vamp. And so I didn't sparkle.

'Have a drink,' Orangerie said passionately, her voice sparkling from the high voltage.

I shook my head. I didn't want to get involved with these two unsuitable men. I retreated to the corner of the pavilion. The smell of cyanide flooded in from the park, as if the almond was in blossom, but there were only hawthorns – I had noticed.

Death was close. The python squeezed its coils. White lightning flashed and everything went dark before my eyes. Orangerie screamed like a naked electric cable. I stumbled out into the rain. The hawthorns were illuminated, as white as almonds, not from the lightning, but from the basilisk's stare. I sat down in the mud and waited meekly, not just for him but for the other too, pressing me down with the weight of his bolts and nuts. And then the shining electricians ran to me like angels and when the rain stopped, we stayed with Orangerie as the sky swiftly sobered up, dirty from head to foot and still alive.

How could I, being so wild, have taken such a responsible job? Police work required a clean past, social stability and healthy genes. And I had none of these. I'm from a bear pit, from the dwelling of angry grey gnomes. As time goes by I notice more and more of my terrible shortcomings (cellulite and dandruff don't count, they are more merits than short-comings; only an idiot could get upset about changes to the skin on their thighs. The changes that are least avoidable occur in the most remote and unfamiliar continents – the hemispheres of the brain).

The streams there are as cold as iced wells. Shadows of fish tap with wet noses against shrivelled soles.

I woke up in the kitchen. I was sat on the table, my bare feet dangling down, the cat next to me, her yellow eyes shining in the grey twilight, like two miniature golden brandy labels.

I sipped from the brandy bottle my teeth clicking against the neck of the bottle. Five in the morning is a terrible hour; the world is concrete, cement, lime and construction noises tumble around your head.

No, I was wrong, it wasn't five yet.

A pale sun, the colour of lime trees penetrated through the gap in the curtains, laying a warm path across the floor; if I was able to walk through walls, I might end up in the summer. But what did I need with summer? Orangerie had gone to a funeral (her second 'aunt' had died, the one who years before had grabbed an iron from her father's hand and hit him with it). She would be back in two days' time. It wouldn't have been decent to miss the funeral dinner. I had promised to look after the parsley-haired baby fathered by the four dads. I had nothing to do anyway; I was on holiday. She couldn't take the child with her, it was too small, it would have screamed all the time and wouldn't have given her a chance to dance!

The parsley-haired baby was sat on the floor, her nappy swollen, looking as sour as a tiny Japanese god. She looked at me dubiously. I was nervous and put her scattered clothes and toys into the cupboard, thrusting her hair-covered dummy in with them. The child waited until I had buried the dummy with rags and then started to cry.

I jumped as if I had been nettled, but she kept screaming, saliva spitting through her rabbit teeth. She demanded something in her unintelligible language and drew hiero-glyphs with her fat hands in the air. By the time I realised, finally, that she wanted her dummy, half an hour had passed of total misunderstanding and mutual dislike.

Having spat the last spoon of porridge into my lap, she fell asleep. I tiptoed away from her cot, as if from a monster. When she screamed in her sleep, I grabbed the door frame so as not to faint.

Fortunately, I had some Millers' Brandy with me.

At night, probably having a nightmare, she began to cry sadly. I jumped; the note of sadness was so familiar. I heard not the cry of the daughter-of-four-fathers', but that of a fragile, fair-haired boy. With the same tearful voice, I took the baby from the cot, laid her next to me and put my chin on the back of her head, careful not to breathe brandy fumes into her soft hair, but into the darkness, which didn't mind what it inhaled. We nodded off like two spoons, a soup spoon and a tea spoon, glistering in aluminium and gold.

Orangerie returned three days later, angry, a bruise under her eye and ripped black tights. After a glass of cranberry liqueur, she calmed down a little, began sobbing on my shoulder and said that all men were pigs, you couldn't trust them, even at a funeral.

'I bought some baby food with plums,' I said, wiping the swollen, unhappy face of the mourner.

'Then give it to her,' Orangerie snapped, sobbing non-stop.

I glanced at the toddler as they were leaving. She wobbled on tiny legs, holding to her mother's skirt and didn't bid me farewell, not with any single Chinese word. Only a golden hue sparkled in her almond eyes, so brief that I persuaded myself with little difficulty that I had just imagined it.

It was twelve o'clock and nobody had rung to enquire why I wasn't at work. Which was bad. Very bad. My co-workers had become strangers to me. Much time had probably passed, it was already spring outside, but nobody remembered me, except for my dogged admirer who left pots of henbanes on my desk; the cleaner didn't touch that pyramid of Cheops, which was good, as tomb-thieves are plagued by Pharaoh's curse.

I opened the window; the harsh October wind lifted my nightie. The man in jodhpurs rode by, again disinterested in the free erotic show; he would probably ride along the street for ever and every time he passed I would open the window, half dressed.

I slammed the window shut, rattling the glass, drew the curtains together, finished the brandy and slumped onto the bed. Yin Yang looked at me reproachfully – she must have been hungry.

I woke to a pitiful sound. It wasn't, I realised, a hungry cat or a child caught in the door. The day light had changed; it was the colour of Van Gogh's sunflower. Somebody was scratching in the kitchen, a cupboard door squeaked, a bag ripped, the cat meowed happily. The water ran; somebody was washing their hands. Or perhaps they were preparing to drown me, leaving the tap turned on. A glass clinked. A glass? A bottle? I had no problem with them flooding my apartment, but just don't touch what's left of my brandy!

I would wait until the water reached my bed. I was so thirsty. Hey! What's the matter with you? Switch off the tap!

He appeared in the doorway with a tray, handsome and as silent as a marble column. Red wine, two glasses and cheese, yellow like a waxed Lenin – it must have been parmesan. Very nice, my dear teacher, that you brought that particular cheese; I hated it. And nobody serves it with wine. They should have taught you some rules of etiquette at spy school.

'Did you walk in through the wall?' I smiled as I looked at him, realising that he had been pretending he didn't recognise me.

'No, the door was unlocked,' he said calmly, pouring some wine.

I smiled more broadly. What a liar! His pockets were probably full of skeleton keys. I put the glass to my lips and drank and my head cleared fast. I wouldn't be able to hold in the laughter long.

Pockets full of skeleton keys, nuts, tweezers, condoms, stiff handkerchiefs, silk strings useful for strangling, vials of poison and possibly dry cat food, as Yin Yang came in from the kitchen licking her lips.

'I fed your cat. I found some Friskies in the cupboard.'

The cat confirmed it with a meow.

I grew suspicious.

There were no Friskies in the cupboard, either wet or dry, if there was, the cat would have helped herself.

I didn't doubt for a moment her human abilities and her capacity to adjust. Myself, I couldn't, so I would have to die. I had just drunk a glass of poison. What would he do with my corpse? Would he cut me into pieces and put them in the fridge?

'Why have you come here?' I asked, crying. 'You won't poison me, will you?'

He drank the wine and said nothing. The darkening yellow shone through the gap in the curtains; soon the sunflower petals would spill black seeds.

'Close the case,' he said at last, wintrily, as if the case was an open door. 'I know you're still digging into it, looking for . . . You won't win.'

I leaned back on the pillow. For a moment it occurred to me that I was lying in a cold bath and looking lovingly at my death. I definitely wouldn't win. There was no chance for happiness at all.

'Why did you drown her, but didn't drown me? How am I worth less to you than her? Was I too old? At eighteen? Why are seventeen-year olds so special?'

For the first time, he looked at me directly, not above my head, not at the wall or at the chandelier. He even smiled. I trembled like a teenager in love, realising that you couldn't reach the stars with your hands.

'Who was Eliza?' I couldn't stop, shaking with a hopeless

desire. 'What did you do to her? Why aren't you answering? Answer!'

'Your questions are your answers,' he replied gnomically.

I grew angry.

'No!' I screamed, spilling wine on my chest. 'Explain everything right now, you old Lothario! At the end of the day, we're tied by the same power structures, who is bothered if you're a policeman or a KGB agent? They all defend people, or protect them or shoot them!'

The teacher raised his eyebrows. He probably doubted you could compare such things. He placed the glass on the table and went over to the window. He tucked his hands into his pockets. He was slim still and tall, he smelled of expensive perfume and no longer wore the gold chain. I closed my eyes, sweaty and ashamed, pretty sure that I would choke to death on erotic fantasies rather than poison.

'Neither numbers nor coincidences have any significance,' he said without turning round.

'What has then?'

'Fate.'

I laughed like a lunatic and grabbed the bottle and drank. Choking on a dry gulp, I fell backwards and struggled for a long moment to catch my breath; when I came to my senses, the teacher was gone. The cat's sad expression was witness to the fact that he had left and I moaned, from horror and desire.

Oh my God, why didn't he rape me or at least beat me? Why did I annoy him with my questions? To hell with the answers! You can always find answers somewhere when they're needed, no matter how unpleasant or meaningless they were!

The cat, scared by my howl, growled and hid under the bed.

My love, my darling, your hands are the golden palms of abundance, they are full of signs of affectionate love, silk strings, handkerchiefs that stop the breathing, angular, hard wrenches, poisonous Friskies and unshelled almonds. And my bullets are in the kitchen in the spice box and I can't answer you with the hot and bitter salve of love.

For you, I would close not only the case, I would close everything I could: doors, windows, chimney flues, police cells, the Chief in his office, the local newspaper and even the church, and, with a special pleasure, bars. No, I would lock myself in one. Dying is easy having tasted the pleasures of the world! No, I am not ready to die. I will simply be fired. It wouldn't mean anything to my father; he jumped from one job to another on the collective farm without a second thought. But times are different now; to lose your job is like losing your status as a human and descending back along the food chain to the category of primate. A chimpanzee has next to zero chances of getting a job.

You, my executioner, my maniac, my Cedar of Babylon, I don't care about your case. It's only in novels that a detective, if he fails to solve something, stops eating and going to the toilet. I have the opposite problem; I'm tortured by bulimia and diarrhoea caused by my nervous nature. Don't say such conditions don't exist. I could shoot the kind of annoying person who stuck their nose into all the details and drove state institutions mad in order to stop their diarrhoea.

Why do we have to close the case? It's not a door to be slammed shut by a draft. I will close your gentle eyelids and lock your lips and the evolutionary ladder will flatten out into a huge car park and instead of a haze of blue petrol smoke, God's white dove will flutter above it.

I ate all of the parmesan because of the heart ache. Piece by piece, hiccupping unpleasantly, because who can enjoy eating slices of a revolutionary leader. But such is the trait of our national character; if you can't shoot yourself or shoot somebody else, at least gorge yourself, in such a way that your terrible suicidal hunger will be partially satisfied.

The morning had been completely shuffled; among the clouds shone a light grey moon, no, not the moon – a postman's hat with Russian lettering on it and a fluttering sailor's ribbons. I opened the window and saluted him. A black cloud floated by looking like a pea coat, a patrolling policeman whistled, the man in the jodhpurs rode by and I finally understood why he didn't turn to me: his head was completely empty inside, it had just been stuck on a stick; he would have had to turn with his bike and the whole road in order to see me. And that was not possible; the negative energy powering him ran in only one direction.

Was it so important to show off my womanly beauty to the poor old man? His rotting eyeballs just about managed to light the road in front of him. He would hardly be pleased to run into another obstacle in his way. He would stop and ring his bike bell until all the telephone posts had scattered from before him.

Strange, the ring of the phone was so similar to that of the bike bell. I answered. Atali. At last.

'Stop,' she said sternly.

I felt uncomfortable. Since when had she become so informal?

'I don't want to stand in anybody's way. You can drive by. There's a spacious, empty road ahead.'

'Stop,' Atali repeated and put down the phone.

Now, really! I was sat in bed with the quilt around my ears and she tells me to stop! Should I run round the fields instead? Atali was so rude! As if she had never stood under my window consumed by dark passion!

I hate fields. The seniors in God's Army (sergeants according to their military rank) often used to explain to us, the soldiers, what hell was like. You, let's say you Astute (Astute jumped and spilled her tea on her trousers), you lie in a box (a banana box? Astute queried), it's not important, you lie in a box with holes in its sides, demons walk round you and stick their spears into you through the holes. But I haven't done anything! I even stopped masturbating! Astute cried. *Whatever for?* A sullen silence followed. The sergeant pressed his lips together, and I, for no reason, saw the collective farm before my eyes. The beetroot rows stretched away, horrifyingly long and a child with a hoe bigger than himself, like Dostoevsky's philosopher, was forced to go a quadrillion kilometres across the endless interstellar space for their failure to believe . . .

No excuses, Astute, child of an elephant God, you would have to get into that banana box as punishment for your indecent sexual behaviour. I looked around at the God's Army soldiers. They all sat with their eyes cast down, so that,

God forbid, a filthy pornographic image didn't slide beneath their eyelashes. It would have been so much better if the sergeant, rather than painting inspirational visions of hell, had lectured us on appropriate sexual behaviour. He could have taught us that the most decent way of multiplying was as it was in nature, though no butterflies should be allowed to come close; we would have to pollinate ourselves.

Astute, knowing that she was condemned anyway, asked the sergeant if he disliked the missionary position. The sergeant barked that he liked it well enough and that when he was ready, he would take that position in some African jungle and would spend the rest of his life in that position. Astute, shaking her head, mumbled that HIV was raging through Africa, wouldn't it be better somewhere in the North, where there were fewer microbes . . .

'Chastity is a fiery armour, any worldly harm burns when it touches it!' The sergeant slammed the quote against Astute's head, making her dizzy and silent, only her lips moved. She probably wanted to ask whether the armoured virgin would not himself be burned from the heat.

Later Astute stopped coming to the meetings, the sergeant kept looking for her untidy curls which looked like rusty sedge; she was probably masturbating calmly somewhere, trying not to think about the sufferings of hell.

All questions arise from a lack of faith; the faithless are doomed to be left alone in eternal beetroot fields, left to chop down with their hoe the Devil's seed which prospers and multiplies in all possible ways. Especially from that need from which you can only defend yourself in rustling, titanium armour.

21.09.2002

It's not really relevant to the case material, but I need to record this information because currently the state officials (they say, even the area prosecutor) treat spiritual matters as a serious issue. If I don't record the metaphysical aspect of the crime, I would not only be disciplined but the local spirit medium would infest my flat with cockroaches and would inflict an illness upon me, which would have all the traits of Korsakoff Syndrome; after saying something clever I would immediately forget what I had said and keep repeating the same thing over and over again until the listener threw a case file as heavy as a plank of wood at my head.

The forensics expert announced that he was going to throw away the fake hand found in the sewerage drain. As evidence it was no longer important; there was nothing to prove any more. The hand just messed about with the test tubes in his tidy laboratory and left dirty marks on the desk as it tried to open his drawers and break into the safe. He had checked. The greasy finger prints were those of the fake hand. He had even found one on the lab assistant's work overalls; the hand must have secretly slapped her bottom. The assistant denied this, saying the forensics expert had made the marks himself and should stop making up such nonsense. In return the forensics expert advised the assistant to either get some help from the mental institution or get married immediately. He could help with the first (and would even bring her some oranges when he came to visit her), but as to the other, unfortunately . . .

The police had the right to approach psychics in difficult cases, so we asked for a medium's assistance. She arrived as if

on wings, shining joyfully. She sniffed the corners of the laboratory like a dog (which didn't make any sense as she had no
sense of smell), stood for a while with her eyes closed and
nearly tripped over the fake hand. After a few minutes of
examination, she declared that the hand was an astral projec-
tion. Somebody from 'the other side' controlled it. The forensics expert bowed in front of the medium and asked how such
a modest lab and the assistant's bottom had earned such an
honour. The medium, sensing guile in his words, was offended.
She explained that the other side was also governed by laws
but that we were not powerful enough to understand them.

'And thank God for that,' the forensics expert responded.
'It would be even better if we didn't accommodate them
here, as hell knows what is going on in my lab.'

'It would be wiser for the government . . .' the medium
shouted, but at that moment I stepped in and said that I
certainly wouldn't want to find out one day that the Chief
was a zombie and the policeman on duty drank the blood
samples at night.

'Take the hand to the church,' the lab assistant suggested
and made the sign of the cross.

The medium bristled at that and ran out; the name of the
competition had shaken her composure.

We decided to bury the hand by the fence, with those
who had committed suicide and the unbaptized. Into its
cold palm we pressed an even colder coin and tied its fingers
with a rosary. Rest in peace you passionate astral bribe-taker,
a slap on the bottom would not mislead the police. The lust
for money doesn't disappear even in the other world, though
you couldn't say that about bodily lust.

The hand haunted no more. The assistant sighed for a week and then stopped. Somebody whispered as they consoled her, that if needed the corpse could be exhumed, but the assistant, having accepted the fate of the abandoned, snapped that passion was a pure feeling and had nothing to do with necrophilia.

Such honourable spiritual strength!

Across the sky rolled fat clouds of burned paper. On the street the postman walked away with his empty bag, his feet making a brittle tapping sound.

XII

The brandy was finished and time had stopped.

The light falling through the window no longer changed. The shadow of a maple branch fell on the curtains, black as a charred bone, the greedy sun didn't devour it bit by bit, nor did it sink into the sea of synthetic flowers.

And still, why did nobody call me? Why did the Chief not hurry over and kill me? Why could I see no senior policeman in the street looking reproachfully at my windows? I would wave at them cheerfully, despite the fact that I was only wearing my bra. For a real policeman the most erotic thing is a neatly pressed uniform.

Many days had passed, withered hours covered the floor and outside the window was the same October – clear, warm and incomprehensible.

I couldn't find the cat. On the floor Friskies lay scattered around in a trail from the cupboard, the small window was fully open. No, dear Klepavicius, there was no point sterilising animals, you see what happens, total anarchy, which is much worse than repressed sexuality.

I had to find out why nobody was shouting at me or threatening to discipline me. If it turned out that everything was okay (if, for instance, the Chief had been away for a couple of days because Omar had eaten another rat), then I could go and get some more brandy. To tell the truth, I could get some right away. Everything would resolve itself without my interference. Time was all that was needed.

But the stagnant morning light reminded me that there was no time.

I quickly pulled on a jumper, ran my fingers through my hair and squirted some perfume onto the base of my throat. Inspecting the spraying mechanism, I was disappointed to find that there was no neck to it and it was impossible to drink it. I was a degenerate, nothing less.

I had only just got down the stairs when a car with flashing lights whizzed by. I squatted behind a leafless bush and waited until I could no longer hear it.

Yellow-beaked birds, preparing for winter, were collecting worms and watched me vigilantly. They could have been starlings, but their feathers were too black. I once told Orangerie that nature, though it was cruel and terrible, inflicted less pain than people did; I would be sadder to see starlings disappear than, let's say recidivists, no matter how human they might be. Humanity is too heavy a burden for nature.

Silently, a bird flew right over my head, coming within a millimetre of my ear. It wasn't a bird. It was a reincarnated recidivist. He was just doing his job and I wasn't angry with him.

I met Miss Koko on the way. She walked along the pavement shaking furiously; even her hat, decorated with cherries, swayed.

'Good afternoon!' I shouted loudly.

Miss Koko looked at me with pale eyes, grabbed around for a stone, found a piece of clay and threw it at me. I managed to duck just in time.

'Shoo!' she hissed.

I turned round. Behind me a fat cat was sat staring straight into my face with cruel, blue eyes.

Miss Koko stamped her little feet. Reluctantly the cat stood up and loped away, making it clear from its posture that it would gladly eat a human for a change without a single prick of conscience.

And what if it was right to think so?

I shrank back, feeling how my tiny bones would crack and one by one the cartilages would separate. Oh, *homo sapiens*, renounce the title of missionary and victor, you are but a yellow-beaked bird, neither a starling nor a warbler, nature refuses even to name you and probably not without reason.

'Are you sick?' Somebody tapped me on my shoulder. I no longer had a tongue or throat to answer; they had slowly transformed into supermarket mince. Submissively, I allowed myself to be picked up and carried off to be kneaded with sour cream, herbs, raw egg, bread crumbs and quietly fried over a low flame.

Klepavicius placed me on a chair, drizzled some stinking brown fluid into a glass of water. Nothing serious, just Corvalol. He told me to drink the filth.

I drank it.

'Your blood pressure is too high,' he said, tapping my shoulder with his finger. 'I can see it in your eyes.'

'You can't tell somebody's blood pressure from their eyes,'

I said, annoyed. 'And, for God's sake, I don't want you treating me.'

'But I have to.' He jumped up. He was wearing a white gown rather than the dirty green one; in his pocket, next to his heart, a leaflet advertising Calcigran was sticking out. 'Your liver isn't healthy!'

'You can see that from my eyes?'

'No . . . from your nails,' he said, without batting an eye.

I looked at my nails.

Nails are just nails. So what if I hadn't had a manicure for a week. One had broken when I opened a bottle, there was a white spot on the little one, probably due to lack of calcium. I glanced at Klepavicius; he would never become a doctor, he had too rich an imagination.

'Thank you for the Corvalol.' I stood up from the chair.

Klepavicius jumped towards the door and blocked it. If he had stuck out his chest he would have almost looked like Matrosov. If he turned around, I could kick him in the bottom and leave calmly. Now . . . Somehow it didn't seem right to kick a man who was looking you in the eyes.

'You are interfering with a police officer's work,' I said coldly. 'Do you want to be arrested? Or maybe I should take away your licence?'

The last threat obviously affected Klepavicius. His brave front collapsed immediately, he tiptoed across to the desk and slumped into the chair and, with a shaky hand, took some drops of the indecently named medicine. Corvalol. Corva – Yiddish for whore.

On the other side of the door I found an old woman all wrapped up, except for her eyes, in a checked scarf.

'Is the doctor available now?' she whispered respectfully.

I said nothing. I closed the veterinary clinic door and looked round. October's yellow flags fluttered in the trees, announcing that human wellbeing was the most important thing on earth and that all the methods to achieve it would be used, even prohibited means. You didn't have to use Corvalol, that stinking whores' linctus, to improve your health. Cocaine helped too, and Temazepam, Dichlorvos, plastic bags, women's magazines, clearance sales, but none was equal to brandy. Dependency on brandy makes you noble. Brandy is golden, not duralumin, which was inferior even if they had used it to make planes. In addition to that, brandy's victims are usually killed on the ground, safely and without horror, which you couldn't say about aviation.

I turned the corner, into the main street and stopped, frozen in horror. In front of the Soviet-built restaurant, which looked like a stable and had never had a good reputation, the girl from the maize field and her mother were standing, leaning against the wall, smoking and looking crossly at each other. Booth wore tasteless make-up and bright red trousers. The mother, the representative of a more romantic generation, had a rose in her hair and looked like a real *Lollobrigida* from the market.

Between them a builder stood, looking at each in turn.

Instead of approaching them to check if the ladies had a licence and the gentleman had money, I began to run and bumped into the restaurant wall. I swear it hadn't been there before. The owner of The Copper Foot must have been doing good business and added on an extension. There was an enormous grill on the lawn; the owner herself, lips pressed hard together, was frying some pieces of meat that looked so similar to fat human thighs that I grew nauseous. I ran over to the blackberry bushes at the side of the slope and vomited at length. Recovering, I wiped my lips with a leaf and noticed the Burdiugin grandfather sitting at the bottom of the hill. He looked unhappy, though it's hard to distinguish a person's mood when the outer layer of their skin has slipped away and through the blackened tissues the occasional bone shone. Next to him lay a heavy plank which he could no longer hold in his decaying fingers, he just smeared it with a mass of black blood and rotting flesh. His murmur sounded like the bubbling of thick soup. Grandfather Burdiugin was probably upset that he had lost his last weapon and wouldn't be able to defend himself from the mad old woman. And not just from the old woman, but from the horse too that flew over his head like a silver aeroplane. As it landed it knocked off a part of his skull with its heavy hoof and thundered away, crushing the snails and worms and in addition a nest of wild wasps. The multi-coloured bullets buzzed through the woods searching out easy targets. Margo wouldn't do, she had died long ago, even if, being dead, she still smelled of *Ungaro Desnuda* and carefully plucked any hair growing in the wrong place and didn't open bottles because she cared about her nails. It was her head that Grandfather Burdiugin should have hit with his plank, not poor Miss Koko's who had only tried to preserve her Parisian charm and had about her still a quiet echo of Baudelaire's poetry.

No, I would not go into the woods. I never held Rousseau in much esteem. I had way more respect for Lombroso; he wasn't far from the truth when he said that crime was an atavistic phenomenon. Plants committed the least amount of crime. The roe deer and the moose, both herbivores, a little more. While meat-eaters (and people were no exception) were criminals from birth. A long-haired poet twinkled among the trembling poplars, but his fluttering wouldn't deceive me; poetry is a leech and a cannibal, it won't allow anybody to get close to it, except when it is hungry and needs fresh blood. A lynx on a lily – that's what poetry is.

I parted the bushes with my hands and flopped down in a flowerbed; it must have been by the library as nobody shouted at me or threatened to slam an empty bottle on my head. If it had been next to the old department store, I would have breathed my last breath by now. That was where the disgruntled citizens gathered. The police were particularly deserving of their loathing, as they didn't protect them day and night from taxes, from mothers-in-law or the shakes. Thieves could go fuck themselves, God would punish them, there was no need for the police for them.

Something stabbed me in the side. I lifted my eyes and saw an Iranian, young and shrivelled from the cold. He must have escaped from the refugee centre in Rukla. When I stood up, he had gone. Only his steaming footprints gave off an incense-like fragrance.

Oh damask rose, who cut off your frail head? Who exiled your fragile body from the gardens of Baghdad? Who tainted your unique and subtle breed? Was it Fate?

My mother covered my eyes with the cloth so that I could no longer see the creature with the guitar, only my mother's light, smooth, glowing face.

Will you give me some brandy, mama?

Offended, probably, she disappeared.

I stood up, brushed the soil from my trousers. Then jumped. Somebody was staring angrily through the glass library door. It was the owner of the furniture shop with his Brezhnev eyebrows. His chest was decorated with a 'Sofa of the Year' medal and 'Council elections. Vote for brain, energy and compassion'.

Oh Jesus, not again. Why does everybody always need to accentuate their compassion?

I knocked on the sofa manufacturer's forehead. He didn't reply, but merely raised his eyebrows threateningly and the sun hid for a moment behind a cloud.

'I'll vote for compassion if you give me some brandy,' I said quietly.

A grey Mercedes pulled up silently by the flowerbeds. A tinted window slid down and a hand poked out holding a bottle. Jesus, was that Hennessy? I tore the bottle from the fingers, nails curled like the claws of a condor, and ran. The hand didn't retract, though, but stretched out like they were on well-oiled springs, half a metre and grabbed me by my dirty flaps of my coat.

I turned back. The hand obviously wanted me to kiss it as well.

I gave it a peck on the ring, which was decorated with a turquoise stone that looked like a dark moon, then hid myself in the bush. Barely had I managed to take a first gulp when there was no scent of the Merc any more.

Only animals and criminals leave no scent; why a candidate for the council elections should behave that way was a puzzle to me.

Perhaps when you achieved a position of power, your major physiological bodily functions became redundant and slowly atrophied, while your spiritual qualities grew significantly. For instance, the area prosecutor had poor hearing, but was super sensitive to smugglers, pimps and others damaged by fate. A hysterical woman had once poured formaldehyde all over his desk because he had failed to gather evidence for the case against a citizen suspected of suspicious trading. She was a fool. The prosecutor would have nothing to do with it. He, for the best, advised that the case should be closed and the suspect left alone. All these suspicions make the police's work more difficult. The thing you needed most to solve a case was time.

He kept walking around the bush, his dry soles tapping, and I wasn't worried that he would stop, as I had only just started on the Hennessey.

It was strange that he walked not in circles but in an intricate ellipse like the furthest planet in the solar system. He probably didn't want to bump heads. Which was understandable. If you had to look at fate through a shroud, how terrible time should look.

But how can we work anything out if we don't look time in the eyes?

The curtain wasn't that clean but it fluttered so beautifully, like an angel. If it had decided to fly, however, it would have looked clumsy. But it wasn't going to fly as, from the other side of the block, down the hill, the kitchen staff were descending carrying large pots, all dressed in white gowns.

Any angel could see that there were enough heavenly creatures there without him.

The doctor's hands were too hairy for him to be an angel.
With eyes as hard as anthracite he stared intensely at the
desk.

'Doctor, I'm not going to be here for long, am I?'

The doctor tapped his pencil on the table.

'You said yourself, my memory lapses are too short to be
called an illness.'

The doctor didn't reply; he continued to tap on the desk.
He was probably ill himself.

'I hope that it won't have any significant impact on my
job?'

The doctor stopped tapping. He frowned. His absent-
minded eyes blinked.

'No,' he said to himself. 'It won't. For goodness sake, I've
treated law enforcement agents madder than you. You? Easy-
peasy. You could be a senior prosecutor. You wouldn't do too
much prosecuting. I'll write you a sick note in a moment . . .
Take the medicine, go to the procedure room and – goodbye.'

'Thank you, doctor.'

'You're welcome.'

I closed the door quietly, but left a slight gap. Through it
the doctor's mumbling reached me.

'It could be light case of psychopathy, if she didn't have a
serious neurasthenia. She would be a fully independent
personality, if not for some undefinable dependency . . .
God, oh God, did I have to study psychiatry for six years for
this?'

In the procedure room they gave me an injection and ordered me to lie on the couch. Don't kick, they told me and don't twitch, it's a totally harmless jab, your brain will soon brighten up and you'll be able to go home. See! The dark wall of the procedure room opened like a knife cutting through a cold lump of butter, not a piece crumbled, you could stroll out on the buttery, moonlit path and there was your home on the lonely summit, on a granite ledge, on lava ready to slide.

Somebody lifted a branch of the bush and stuck in a black nose. I was ready to hit it with the empty bottle, but seeing that it was only a Russian Spaniel, I calmed down. The spaniel, though, didn't enjoy the encounter. It swore and ran off.

I crawled out of the bush. It was getting dark. All around anxiety hovered, watery and harsh. A French bulldog trotted by arrogantly and glanced at me without saying a word; it must have been more refined than I was.

Now only a Pekingese looking like a ball of fluff was needed and I would feel like I was in Berlin, on the Alexanderplatz, next to the Kaufhof, where men from the Caucasus insistently offer to carry the olives you bought and suspicious looking Russians want to draw your portrait. It's a pity I have never been there.

On a bench not far away, a woman was sitting so straight it looked like she had swallowed a pole. She had black hair and wore a white dress which resembled a Kimono. I stumbled on a miserable lilac shrub and fell; everything crackled and buzzed. The woman gave me a lightening glance and in the twilight her large yellow eyes flashed menacingly. When

I stood up the woman was gone; on the bench there was only a set of dirty paw prints.

I shook my tipsy head.

If it had been Yin Yang, then I no longer liked her. I wouldn't live with her anymore. It would be a sacrilege to offer her canned cat food and I had no idea how to feed a human.

I needed a coffee. Without brandy.

I dropped in at Sarkiene's. She was pottering around behind the bar and didn't shout out, 'Oh, Mrs General Advisor.' She paid me no attention.

I raised my dirty fist. You can change your life as much as you want, but there are some things that don't change. Customers, for example.

Isolde, not even listening, turned her wide back on me and began applying makeup.

Big deal. If she was not going to give me coffee, I would serve myself.

I would make two cups of coffee and wouldn't pay – as compensation for her unfriendly service. And also as the volume of her radio clearly exceeded the permissible decibel limit.

I stood up ready to smash it, but at that moment the local *hit* ended. The radio's intestines gurgled and a rich baritone, like a red Merlot, flooded Sarkiene's small bar. I had to climb onto the chair to avoid choking.

The baritone said he would take all possible measures and probably some impossible ones too. Analysis, or may be anal, it wasn't important, just as long as it was good for the people.

I stood on the chair, light-headed, erotically electrified, waiting for the door to open and to see him coming in, the red Matrosov, carrying all his measures, anal and oral.

No, it was too much, even God couldn't do that, the baritone said. Forget about supernatural phenomena, the budget is not made out of rubber! He fell silent then, in order that we should understand that he had let down the nation once again. He screwed quickly without giving any pleasure at all. Mundanely, as if leaving any refinement for the future.

I stepped down from the chair, angry as a wolf and drank the coffee, which was already cold. It was always the same. Whenever you were ready to give yourself, not bothered that your bodily dignity would be violated by various perverse means, then they lost interest in you. Give them somebody impotent, a virgin, someone who hasn't yet experienced perversion.

I slammed the door so that even the glasses in the bar clattered. They were bastards, nothing better.

I found myself in front of a white blossoming hawthorn and was suddenly scared. I must have sat in the bar until the winter. I was about to bend close to check if the snow was real, but the hawthorn ran off, fluttering the corners of the sheet and I heard Odete's giggle and that made me seriously angry.

'You idiot!' I shouted in her direction. 'I'll fine you! It doesn't matter if you're under age!'

I chased after the hawthorn, determined to punish it. The laugh slowly grew distant as if Odete was falling into a deep well and when I caught up with it, the silence that confronted me was of the kind you only found in a morgue at dawn. The birds were silent, but in the freezer there was a gentle rustling. I touched the white cloth. Empty sleeves hugged the dog-chewed flaps, the material at the chest parted revealing bright red shining silk. I lifted my head; with eyes as deep as a mine, a scarecrow was looking at me. The Antichrist, which knew everything in advance and was, therefore, bored.

'Your . . . license, please,' I said hesitantly.

The scarecrow gazed at me silently. When I repeated my demand, adding 'driver's', it bent its head so low in order to hear me better, that the rotten pole failed to support it. The head cracked, fell off and rolled away, scattering rotten hay and mice droppings.

'That's b . . . bad . . .' I said with dignity. 'Now I won't be able to compare your face with the one in the photo.'

The scarecrow didn't reply; it sailed after its head, like a flame separated from a furnace. At my feet there only was a deep abyss. I put my ear to it, hoping to hear voices from the other world, but instead I heard a quiet, sad squeaking – not from underground but from a nearby bush.

I pushed back the branches. My father was sat by a mound of yellow fat, shaking still from a hangover. He whined quietly, all blue, bony, naked with dried-out bottom cheeks, his bald head shone green. He tried to lean upon the mound but it had grown cold a long time before and did not respond to his moans. It did not press my father between its two hills with their erect tips where the eternal heat of the bread oven lingered still. In the Venus woods, the gates to the other world, a thick salty fog slowly gathered, stinking of rotten algae.

I tried to lift my father but he, clinging to the already cold breasts, wouldn't let go. From my pocket I took a serviette I had stolen from the bar and covered my father's bony shoulders. He merely groaned; I was not sure whether in anger or happiness. He glanced at me with phosphorous eyes and let out a short yelp, which meant to leave him in peace. He didn't need anything from me. He had never needed anything. Even at the hour of his death, which was marked by the chime of the clock with yellow glass at the bottom of the lake, covered with sludge.

I closed the branches over his head. It saddened me to hear how the old women gossiped that a serviette wasn't a shroud, it was just a joke and that was all. Hush, old wives, I heard the clear, pure voice of my father. You have no idea what a true funeral is; my shroud is royal, my shroud is wonderful – an obeisance to the eternal body of Magde. You will never lay in such death-robes, you will live long after your husbands have died.

I wept, wiping away the tears with a sleeve. I sat on the pavement in front of the council building. Opposite me, illuminated by a street light, stood three wooden totems, folk art sculptures, similar to the Easter Island idols. Foreigners who occasionally stumbled into our town, thought that they were famous people of our nation.

You won't ruin their beliefs, will you? You won't say that they are simply monsters the artists' imagination gave birth to.

One of them seemed to move its hands, like a zombie, it must have wanted to get closer to me. Fortunately, the artist hadn't carved it any legs – even in the provinces you can find healthy postmodernism.

Somebody pulled me by my coat flap. I screamed like a madwoman and lifted my hands, to defend myself from attack by the sculptures.

A child, not older than four, held out a transparent hand, indicating that I should stand up and go.

God, I hope I won't crush the child, I thought, staggering towards the police station. I could already see the light in the windows. The child did not seem to be worried about being squashed, she walked with her fair-head down. She didn't lift it even when Orangerie rushed by, swearing and cursing, her hair all over the place, dragging her daughter – the Chinese goddess – in tears.

'You shit, you idiot!' a thin tenor screamed. A short man strolled slowly after Orangerie keeping his value and human dignity.

I tumbled down into a heap of leaves right by the station door. The child stood and looked at me for a moment – there was more pity than contempt in its gaze – then turned around the corner and disappeared.

'Where are you going?' I shouted, clambering up. 'It's not safe for someone as small as you to walk alone!'

The child did not answer, not even with a rustling of leaves.

I sighed and tried to nod off, hoping that nobody would try to park their car there. The heap of leaves was barely visible in the dark.

The station door slammed and the red-haired woman ran out, followed by the priest who exited in a dignified manner.

'You don't believe?' the woman said, short of breath. 'You don't believe?'

'No, I don't,' the priest said solemnly.

The woman spat to one side, then to the other, possibly hoping to see an atomic mushroom cloud appear in these places, but nothing happened. The priest looked at her with pity. He glanced around and noticed a broom in the stairwell and handed it to her helpfully.

The woman threw the broom aside, as if it had scalded her hands and began to scream that these days witches were intellectuals that read books. The ignorant could sweep the streets.

'*Dominus vobiscum.*' The priest stroked the air, rose an inch from the ground and levitated towards the church, calm, safe and happy to have been freed of from his childhood nightmares.

Had the Chief helped him then? I didn't believe it. Then perhaps Atali had? It was not likely. Or, perhaps, in my absence, they had established a position of a regional medium-therapist?

I pushed away the leaves which stuck to me sleepily and stood up.

The station was three very long – three eternally long – steps away.

09.05 2003

There is always one and the same character present in all unsolved cases, which exerts some kind of effect on the outcome. Usually he is neither the victim nor the suspect; rather he is a witness who never testifies. Not from fear or vanity – his words cannot be written down. And, what's more, the prosecutor would have no use for such evidence and the barrister would treat it as a joke. The criminal sections of the main daily papers would waft their hands – we don't write about paranormal dramas, go to the TV, if you present it properly then they might put it on, after all, The Poltergeist, though old now, is still popular, especially with peasants who believe in reincarnation. But, God forbid, no metaphors; the viewer might think you're making fun of them.

You wouldn't tell the peasant would you, that jasmine blossom closes their souls at night so they didn't look for the killer and so that their poisonous tongues didn't sting those sleeping innocently; that the telephone sex line disturbed the worms and killed the moles which blindly wandered too close to them and that its negative energy scattered the bones of the dead which when they tried to regather themselves, took no note of type or gender or age. Making your typical audience think was like trying to move a mountain; it was vaguely possible that one day they might grow uneasy about the quietly moving mountain.

I stepped into the corridor. It was so dark I had to lean against the wall. The wall was rough, cold and dark green and slowly led me towards a square frame of light. I would have fallen straight into it, if not for the words:

'*It's better to starve, than to stuff down whatever your hand can reach.*

And better to be alone than to be with just anybody.'

I leant against the dark wall. Whose voice was that?

I felt sick. No, vomiting wouldn't be a good idea at that moment. I would wait.

'*When you pick up the wine glass, do not look for one more foolish than you,*
  And don't tell anybody how much you had to drink today.'
It was the Chief's voice.

I bent over and started to vomit; long, dark, green threads of saliva, like poisonous spider webs.

'*So, I am a drunkard, an alcoholic, an old man,*
  But for another reason . . .'

'You see,' the Chief cut the voice short. 'I had good reason for neutering it.'

'Not at all,' the voice said tearfully. 'Not at all. Wine is a great pleasure, but not the only one.'

'I know,' the Chief said. 'The biggest pleasure is to give orders. It's such a great pleasure that it's not even important if anybody follows them.'

The stranger sighed, then said reproachfully:
'*It is better to choke on bones than feast at the table*
  Of scum that melt, clinging to power.'

'Don't say that,' the Chief mumbled, disappointed, or possibly even angry. 'If there is no passion for power then there is no passion at all.'

'*Let's step onto the path of love . . .*' purred the voice.

'No,' the Chief interrupted.

'*Don't race helter-skelter along the road to love,*
  By the end of the day your strength will leave you unexpectedly.'

'If you don't stop, I'll pull off your tail, even if I am so close to you.'

'*Prrrr.*' The stranger sounded agitated. 'Your heart is not the stone of Kaaba. You feel something for me. Let's go and have a drink. All truth is in the wine.'

I tumbled through the door, the Chief stepped over me and Omar Khayyam stepped on my hand; the perfumed brocade made me feel sick again. I closed my eyes. Somebody tiptoed towards me and hit me on the head with a rubber hammer. I hiccupped and *switched off*.

When I opened my eyes I saw another square, black and lined with artificial yellow thread; one of its sides was noticeably thicker. Aha! It was a gap in the door, I crawled closer and listened.

I put my ear to the door.

The dark depths of night gave birth to horror.
Before my eyes quivered Jezebel, my mother.
Dressed up and elegant like on that day death
Came close. Distress had not yet crushed her.
Her beauty was dignified, refined, sparkling,
Retouched quietly by brushes and paint
Gently hiding time's wicked footprint.
'Tremble,' she said, 'Noblest of my children!
The cruel Jewish god will curse you too.
His pitiless hand will crush us,
My daughter . . . my mother spoke her last words,
She bent, that her kiss might calm me,
I stretched my arms to embrace the shadow
And found nothing – just a mass of
Corpse flesh and bones that had been dragged through dirt with
*   ropes.*
Bloody rags and horrible body limbs
That the fighting dogs had torn and ripped apart. *

* Jean Racine, Four Greek Plays: Andromache-Iphigenia, Phaedra-Athaliah

Somebody sneaked up in the dark and hit me so hard that I fell into the office flat on the floor, my whole body twitched and I closed my eyes – waiting to be cursed. Then I would open my eyes and try to make some kind of an excuse.

Nobody cursed me. Pages rustled. I opened one eye. The worn floor boards were familiar. It seemed like my office. Then who was sitting at my desk?

I opened the other eye.

Atali was sat at the desk.

Her forehead was furrowed, and she looked gloomy with short, cropped hair and chocolate coloured lips. She wore a uniform which suited her surprisingly well.

I lifted myself onto my front legs. That is, my arms.

'W . . . What are you doing here?'

Lord, how dull and ghostly my voice sounded.

'And what are you doing here?' Atali snapped back.

I was offended.

'Since when have you started being so disrespectful?'

'You're the one getting all disrespectful!' Atali rose, came over to me, her high heels hammering on the floor. She plucked some rubbish from my hair which had turned into spikes and waved it under my nose.

'Belladonna you poor girl,' she said.

Shaking and wobbling like an old jelly, I forced myself to sit up.

'B . . . brandy.' I stretched my greenish fingers towards Atali. 'I feel very . . . very sick.'

'You're not sick because of brandy. You're poisonous! You're a gluttonous henbane. A swamp plant, yellow sludge.'

I shook my head.

Atali must have gone mad.

'No, not mad,' she read my thoughts. She laughed and said that she was healthy, that she didn't need me, that I was ruining her life. That I should disappear like smoke, not tossed back and forth by the wind.

'So! Disappear? Atali, do you understand what you're talking about? How can a state officer just disappear? That's a short cut to anarchy.' I tried righteous anger, but an unusual feeling stifled my anger, choked it, laughing noiselessly. Oh, that laugh, creeping in from the dark, holding a rubber hammer!

'No,' Atali cut in. 'I'm the official and always have been.'

I was about to open my mouth, but Atali was quicker.

'We don't have a secretary's position. Nobody wants to work for such a pittance. Anyway, you need to be competent.' She glanced at me with her pink eyes.

'Wait, wait, was it me then who kept bringing those plants from the botanical guide and putting them on my desk?'

'On mine,' Atali corrected me. 'On my desk.'

I looked at my nails.

They didn't look healthy. Klepavicius would have a field day enumerating my various health problems. They look greyish-green, as though they had been left for a long time dug into ripe cheese. And they were long, like the devil's, gnarled. Should I dig them into Atali's neck?

Atali took a pistol from her drawer. Jesus, my Paloma! And I had thought it was in the kitchen, in the spice box.

'Just try,' she said dryly.

I covered my eyes with my nails.

I felt the gentle coolness of the potted plants, the radioactive drops of dew that irritated the skin and left patches on the skin, the barley-red rashes that slowly turned to coal. The dust on the window sill was not much better, it burned the skin like concentrated potassium nitrate; it looked like Frankenstein's laboratory.

'It's not right, Atali, you can't just write people off like that'.

Atali giggled.

'People?' she said with a sly smile. 'You call yourself *people*? You even don't have a name! Tell me your name?'

'My name?'

Long arms with sharp nails held me in a hug. I saw my face in the mirror but I couldn't remember my name. I knew only that it was as nice as and long as Orangerie's.

'In the protocols . . .' I grasped at straws.

'In the protocols there is my name!' Atali snapped back. 'Black on white. Bright and clear. Indisputable. You need to look elsewhere for your name, not in the protocols.'

'Where?' I whined. Somebody kept hitting me as monotonously as a metronome on the top of my head with a hammer.

'Where, where . . .' Atali was not happy at how slow I was. 'Look to nature!'

The foxglove, the spotted hemlock. It could be neurasthenics if it wasn't psychopathy. Hug me, Atali, my faithful friend and we will be together again. On my own I feel so insignificant. I'll even have to pour my own coffee.

'No.' Atali kept the Paloma aimed at a spot between my eyes. Laughter again began to choke me, to strangle me with the slippery basilisk paws of the disgusting devils-seed, spawned not by nature but by the human imagination.

Atali lowered the pistol.

That's right, Atali, it's not possible to shoot a basilisk, even if you load the pistol with bitter peppercorns. Let's laugh instead. Is it that there's nothing funny left in life?

'No, only work exists.'

'Jesus, what nonsense. You just used to make coffee, Atali! You didn't do any work! Anything that was of any importance, I accomplished . . . I . . .'

I writhed on the floor and the laughter not only strangled me, it raped me. A double crime committed concurrently; hanging was the only acceptable punishment.

Atali opened a cupboard, took out a bottle of brandy and poured some. At last, one thing I could make sense of! Her face grew confused, there was a flicker of doubt in her eyes. A ray of hope cheered me. But Atali didn't take a drink. She put the bottle back into the cupboard along with the full glass and shook her head. I drifted away, carried on a wild wind and hit the top of my head on a soft stone in the yard. My mother screamed and our mutual father stood sadly in the evening twilight, bathed in moonlight, smoking and gazing into his empty hands which just a moment before had been holding something.

Now I understood why I didn't remember the earliest years of my life. I simply hadn't existed then.

My grandmother stroked my face with trembling hands.

Very carefully, I partly opened my eyes and the more of the new world I could see the stranger it seemed to me.

My grandmother's hands were scratched by gooseberry brambles, an unripe berry popped out of her sleeve and rolled down the sheet like a button that had come loose.

It occurred to me for the first time how heavy and vulnerable a body could be.

Jezebel was luckier then I. So what if she was torn to pieces by dogs? Just to have a body is a kind of happiness.

The last magic gesture by which Atali renounced me was to throw all the plants I had kept in the drawer out through the window. They glided through the dark, like disembodied ghosts, attempting to grab hold of something. Pity the accidental passer-by if a dry cobweb landed on him. There would be another secret case and the forensics expert would have to admit that not all the poison had been identified yet, let alone an antidote.

Despite all that, Atali also told me that she was going to continue to investigate the case of the drowned girl and nobody from the ministry was going to interfere. I felt an abyss opening and deepening between us, distancing us. Desire was far more important to me than truth; you cannot appeal the verdict of passion. And drunken light-headedness was more pleasant than health. Oh, Atali, neither beauty nor truth will save the world; passion, though, will allow it to perish more pleasantly. Let's party together, Atali. Hug me like the ghost of Jezebel. You will see how gentle body tissue can be having turned into rags … pink silk, blue lace veins, the heavy brocade of muscle fastened by yellow bone buckles.

Atali refused.

She hid the brandy in the cupboard; the click of the lock was unbearably gloomy. Crackling and snapping were the soundtrack of my life. In my skull was the sound of broken bones, Friskie biscuits crushed under foot, the sound of the lock turning in an empty flat, the crumbling head of Pushkin, the Chief opening his mezzanine, stiff memories and ideals which resembled corrugated wafers which crumbled easily if not smeared with jam.

Something crackled in the street; somebody must have been loading a gun. A soviet soldier strolled slowly along the pavement, it wasn't clear if he was dead or alive, which wasn't important to those proclaimed as immortals. Fires crackled too, devouring Salvador Dali's giraffe; I watched the flames rise from the tiny drawers and a thought flashed through my mind that I could easily hide in there.

But I am a work of life not a work of art.

One of the strings connecting me to life had snapped. Atali had left me. But why couldn't I connect to somebody else? To you, for example . . . To you, my dear readers. Will you refuse to feel the abyss behind your back? And to hear my soft voice saying that nothing will happen to you. That sharp stones won't shatter your skeleton.

What do I long for most? Unfortunately, not you, not you, my dear, peaceful reader. Forgive me, please, we're just not familiar enough. I long for my lover. What joy! I was no longer under any obligation to go through the daily routines and could go and find him. By a golden, poisonous spider's web I would land upon his open body, cover his eyes with nightshade and desire would finally conquer his brain and my lover would be free.

For me, freedom was of no value.

I'm happy to cling to somebody. To attach myself with the

tiny grey hairs of the wallflower, to wind around him like the pepper-vine's clinging tendrils, to touch him with mucousy cow lily leaves, to hobble him with the hairy branches of an elderberry and the thin white root of the *Helleborus niger*.

With a poisonous string, a shiny thread.

Feeding him through the umbilical cord of dreams.

21.07.2003

I haven't slept well recently. Dreams have begun to penetrate my rational, ordered life. Like grey dust, heavy as lead, they fall on the tiny memory-drawers which occasionally I open to look through my precious old things . . . Girls on yellowish paper, so dry that it crackles at the slightest touch. They were all only seventeen. I killed them all. No man, no ignoramus lacking a perfect ear, will be able to untune their fragile strings . . . They are all now beneath the lavender flowers, beneath the poisonous silk handkerchief. Nobody missed them, nobody needed them anyway. Why would I have let one live, an outcast and unhappy? No, no . . . What for? So that later she would blackmail me? God forbid, I might even have had to marry her . . . Absurd. At seventeen the lovely little wild animals turn into matrons and I don't like mature women. They remind me of banjos; you can't play Beethoven on a banjo. For that you need a violin whose strings have not yet been touched by a musician. Especially an amateur's. I hate amateurs.

I didn't leave anything in my past that might interfere with the forgetting. Women are easy to forget. I owe them nothing. I'm not a charity, there is no evidence . . .

I wonder if these memory lapses might interfere with my political career? What did the doctor say? The doctor said that short term memory prolapses aren't dangerous. There's no need to worry.

It's a shame that embarking on political career means that I will have to abandon music. That sensual pre-concert excitement. The surface of the instrument all alive and its hair-raising sigh.

The personal life of a politician shouldn't intrude into his public activities. What's that all about? Shouldn't an amendment be passed separating these two and strictly punishing anybody (especially journalists) for sticking their noses into another's affairs? How useful it would be to revive being hung, drawn and quartered and hard labour! I don't think the other members of parliament would put up too much opposition; anybody who has suffered attacks on their wealth or their privacy becomes ruthless, they just don't let it show and behave as though they were kind-hearted. They act all liberal! A politician's humanity would never be revealed if it was not for their vices.

A phone was ringing. Some grey mouse calling. A provincial investigator. What? A drowned girl? What bath? Do you take me for an idiot? What is the name of your Chief? You'll be glad if this doesn't end with just a reprimand; if you disturb me again to ask about this nonsense, I'll see that you're fired. You will be looking after corpses in the morgue. From the homeless. From animals.

That's what it means to be powerful – you get random lunatics stalking you. I'll have to start carrying a gun or I'll end up getting hit on my head with a brick in a dark alley. Or on the library steps. Readers these days are cruel. Perhaps it was true, perhaps somebody was after me? Sometimes I get such a strange feeling . . . Could it be . . . schizophrenia?

Well, if it was, it wasn't a problem. Psychiatrists have discovered that some type of schizophrenics work well in positions of power and can do a lot of good for the state.

I fancy some coffee. Where has that new secretary got to? The door is open, the fax is on . . . On her desk there's a thick book. It looks like a reference book or a botanical guide. She must have taken a course on the natural sciences and then even after changing her qualification still can't forget about it.

I hear a woman's high heels. A teaspoon clinks. For some reason I grow agitated and look at the door with such a tense expression, as if I was about to come face to face with my destiny.

Here she is. She enters with a tray in her hands, the sugar bowl leaning over on one side like the leaning tower of Pisa. Her bright red lips smile, she even winks and for some reason I don't feel cross with her. I even feel like saying something pleasant to her, but she is quicker.

'Good morning. Here's your coffee. Would you like anything else?'

If you enjoyed this, why not try some more
Lithuanian novels

BREATHING INTO MARBLE
By Laura Sintija Cerniauskaite
Winner of the European Prize for Literature

When Isabel decides to adopt the troubled young orphan, Ilya, she has no idea of the trauma that is about to be unleashed upon her family. Taking him back home to their cottage in the country, his dark presence unsettles the family and resurrects the ghosts of Isabel's past.

Breathing into Marble is a dark and poetic story of love, family, deception and death.

'Černiauskaitė could be a major talent of this generation; her prose puts some of our intellectual writers to shame.' World Literature Today

THE EASIEST
By Rasa Askinyte

Blanca works at Café France. If she actually exists. There she meets the characters of the novel, Alex and Not-Alex, Greek, the owner of the café and Anastasia her best friend. It is a story of love, of not loving and of an apartment reached only by a ladder and birds that come crashing down onto table tops.

Askinyte's novel is lightly and lyrically told, but beneath the surface bubbles a dark and disturbing world.

SHTETL LOVE SONG
By Grigory Kanovich

'I had intended for quite a long time to write about my mother with that joyous enthusiasm and abundant detail with which it is fitting to recall one's parents, the people closest and dearest to you.'

In 'Shtetl Love Song' Grigory Kanovich writes about his mother, and in so doing peels back the surface of the rich Yiddish community that lived in pre-war Lithuania.

It is a requiem for the pre-war Jewish shtetl, for a people and a way of life that was destroyed in the maelstrom of war.

Visit us at

www.noirpress.co.uk

Follow us

@PressNoir